About the Author

John Conlon lives in Milford, County Armagh with his wife and two daughters. He was born in Edgware, Middlesex and lived in north-west London until 2005. A qualified librarian, John previously worked at British Library Newspapers in Colindale and he now works for Libraries NI. Literature and writing have always been close to John's heart, and *Author of His Own Misfortune* is his first published novel.

Author of His Own Misfortune

John Conlon

Author of His Own Misfortune

Olympia Publishers
London

www.olympiapublishers.com

OLYMPIA PAPERBACK EDITION

Copyright © John Conlon 2021

The right of John Conlon to be identified as author of
this work has been asserted in accordance with sections 77 and 78
of the Copyright, Designs and Patents Act 1988.

A CIP catalogue record for this title is
available from the British Library.

ISBN: 978-1-80074-051-8

This is a work of fiction.
Names, characters, places and incidents originate from the writer's
imagination. Any resemblance to actual persons, living or dead, is
purely coincidental.

First Published in 2021

Olympia Publishers
Tallis House
2 Tallis Street
London
EC4Y 0AB

Printed in Great Britain

Dedication

For my mum, without whose love, I would be nothing.

Acknowledgements

It would be remiss of me not to, first of all, thank my wife, Louise and my daughters, Ella and Cait, who have somehow managed to put up with me over the years!

I would also like to thank Olympia Publishers and in particular James Houghton, Kristina Smith, and my proofreader, Katie Major, who have guided me through the publishing process in a most professional and considerate manner during these strange times.

I must next give a special mention to my wonderful niece, Charlotte Walsh, and my colleague and good friend, Moya O'Neill, who each took the time to read my unfinished novel, and whose frank appraisals have helped me iron out any creases.

But my biggest vote of thanks must go to another colleague and good friend, Lorraine Grimley, because it was Lorraine's encouragement and advice at the very outset that gave me the confidence to submit *Author of His Own Misfortune* for consideration, and if it hadn't been for Lorraine, you wouldn't be reading this.

"Judge ye not, less ye be judged"
Matthew c7v1

Prologue
January 2020

This morning, I was walking along the pier when I was overcome by a sudden and very real sense of impending doom. I was near the end of the rickety walkway when the feeling took hold, and I had to stop.

Leaning over the ornate, cast-iron barrier, I was staring at the sea below as it washed round me, hoping that the inexorable rushing of the waves would lift my mood as it sometimes does. But not today.

Perhaps it's the time of year, with the dark mornings and dark evenings, or maybe it's just because, in the depths of winter, Walton-on-the-Naze can be such a depressing place. But whatever the reason, as I looked down into the murky depths, I found myself contemplating what it would be like to take the ultimate *leap of faith*.

Over the past few years, other, more gruesome alternatives have routinely flashed through my mind: I have *seen* myself falling from a tall building, jumping in front of a speeding train, slitting my wrists and even setting myself on fire. By comparison, drowning seems more prosaic; more humane.

I recently watched a video on my phone: it was in the US, I think: a man in police custody. The officer was sitting the suspect down in a chair and reading him his rights. It appeared to be something minor. The man was middle-aged — a few years older than me, I guess — and once they'd filled out the paperwork, the officer asked him if he wanted a cup of tea. The man nodded and the officer disappeared out the door, closing it behind him. Then, cool as you like, the man pulls a gun from a leg-holster and blows his brains all over the whitewashed wall.

The officer was back through the door in an instant, and understandably, he freaked. The suspect, however, never looked anything but calm: resigned to his fate, at one with himself, at peace. They do say, once you've *decided*, a certain serenity pervades; but to me it seemed so pointless.

Maybe there were unimaginable horrors which were about to be disclosed — this man might have been another Jeffrey Epstein or another Jimmy Saville — but even then, if I was in his shoes, if the worst of my crimes were about to be revealed, *fear of the other side* would hold me back.

Suffice to say then, this morning, I did not jump.

Instead, as day broke over the horizon, I stared out into the distance, gazing at the freight ships moving in and out of port, thinking about my life, asking myself how it had ended up here — *"in a seaside town that they forgot to close down"* — and as I continued to pick off bits of flaking paint from the rusted, metal railing, watching each fragment float down to the briny drink, that morbid part of me was again beginning to wonder what it might be like to join them.

Then suddenly, I was woken from my depressing reverie by a hand on my shoulder and a voice from behind uttering my name — *my real name* — and as the bile started to rise in my stomach, I realised my past had finally caught up with me.

'Frank Kelly,' he repeated, and having steadied myself against the rail, I turned to face my arresting officer.

But it wasn't the long arm of the law that had me in its grip.

No.

In many ways, it was worse.

Part I
April 2013

One

At school, I was reliably informed by every English teacher I care to mention that every good story needs structure: 'it must have a beginning, a middle, and an end'!

Unlike the best fiction, however, real life is not quite so neat and tidy. It is rather a tapestry of stories, haphazardly woven together, and where there is overlap between individual threads, very often, coincidences occur. We generally only notice the remarkable ones, but life is full of them.

And so is my sorry tale.

From the outset though, I must acknowledge that, while coincidence has played its part, *I* am responsible for how the story has unfolded. In my defence, I could never have anticipated the calamitous effects of my *original sin*, but that notwithstanding, I cannot deny that I should have taken control of my actions long before I let my actions take control of me.

Truth be told, nothing extraordinary ever happened to me — not until I made it happen — and while there are others who have paid a heavy price for my arrant foolishness, let it be known that I have not entirely escaped justice as, for years now, I have had to live as an outcast in the shadows of normal society, in a prison of my own making.

By putting this down on paper, I realise I am compromising my very freedom, but it is something I feel compelled to do, so that if nothing else, when I am six feet under, my children will get the chance to read *my version* of events.

I'll do my best to stick to the facts and I'll try not to cloud the issues with conjecture and opinion, and although I am bound to forget names, times and places (and I will undoubtedly paraphrase conversations to suit myself), it's the essence of my story that is most important, not the finer detail.

And as God is my witness, not a word of this testimony is a wilful lie.

So, where do I begin?

I guess the best place would be the moment that I devised a plan to steal a valuable book from the British Library. The idea came to me in a split-second; the result of a chance sighting.

In that instant, it seemed like the perfect crime — and it so nearly was — but with the benefit of hindsight, I can see it was simply the catalyst for a trail of destruction that has been driving my life on a terminal, downward spiral.

So, I suppose it would be best to start there: from the moment I saw Liam.

Two

It was a Thursday afternoon in late April, and I was driving through Cricklewood — a suburb of north-west London whose social standing has been on the rise, ever since Thatcher encouraged its council tenants to become homeowners.

Cricklewood will never quite reach the cosmopolitan heights of Richmond or Islington, but nor will it revert to the 'town' my parents arrived into in the 1960s, when every boarding house in the district had the same infamous notice in its window: *No dogs. No blacks. No Irish.*

Back then, like most Irish tradesmen, my father would queue up every morning at the doors of The Crown, hoping to be taken on by one of the ruthless English *subbies* who, in exchange for a day's labour, invariably paid a pittance. But long hours and hard graft would eventually bear fruit for my father and his kinsmen, many of whom, through their endeavours, were able to buy their own piece of English real estate and turn Cricklewood into something of an Irish stronghold.

I was perhaps thinking about all of this as I drove past Cricklewood's most celebrated pub, but then I spotted Liam going in through the doors and my train of thought was completely *de-railed.*

And in that fateful moment, I formulated my plan: a plan which would prove fool-proof.

Well almost!

At the time, I didn't know Liam's name — I only knew him as the brother of a former neighbour. In fact, I'd only seen him on three previous occasions: the first time was on New Year's Day, when he stood outside my house chatting with my mum, the second was about a month later, when he opened Maire's front door to me, but it was the third occasion which was the trigger for my nefarious plan...

It was definitely a Tuesday or a Wednesday evening, just before Christmas, because while Brigid was upstairs putting our daughter to bed, I was in the living room watching a Champions League match on the TV.

Suddenly, there were raised voices next-door, and as the volume rose, I put my ear to the wall. I couldn't make out what was being said, but I sensed a definite edge in the tone. Then Maire let out a shriek.

'I don't see you for months,' she was raging, 'and then you have the nerve to show up at my house in a stolen car!'

There followed a protracted silence before the front door was slammed shut, and peeping out through a crack in the curtain, I watched Liam storming off and *hot wheeling* it away in a silver Golf.

At the time, I made a mental note to keep a wary eye on Maire's brother; nothing more...

But as I passed The Crown, Maire's words were ringing in my ears — because I was hoping Liam might just steal a car for me.

Of course, that would only happen *if* I could persuade Liam to buy into 'my plan', and to that end, I parked up on a nearby side-street and strolled into the pub just a couple of minutes behind him.

To my pleasant surprise, Liam was sitting all alone — at a small table close to the bar — and as I waited for the barmaid to pour my pint, I tried to come up with a plausible opening gambit.

Having paid for my drink, I picked up a discarded copy of The Mirror from the counter and took it with me across to a table close to Liam's, and as I settled down on a stool, Liam looked over. I was sure he was going to say something, but then he turned away; he mustn't have recognised me.

Just a quick glance at Liam and you would have known he was Irish — the big ears, the big nose, the big, red head, the fixed, cheesy grin, and his clothes which had a *slept-in* look — and like all good Fenians, he was right at home in The Crown.

On the Thursday afternoon in question there were only six other patrons in the pub. A moderately, boisterous group, sitting just inside the door and two pensioners posited at the far end of the bar in heated debate.

'No-one could match Bestie!' I remember one roaring — either they were talking football, or man's capacity to drink!

Speaking of which, the Stella was going down without touching the sides, and I was contemplating another, when Liam stood and made his way to the 'gents'. With the two old men still arguing, the barmaid transfixed by her phone, and a chorus of *Sunday Bloody Sunday* starting up by the door, I decided to follow.

As I opened the door to the small and squalid WC, I could hear Liam at the urinal, and from the sound resonating off the metallic latrine, I guessed this was not his first pint of the afternoon. Not needing 'to go' myself (and not wanting one of those awkward moments when one has to force out *a dribble*), I ducked into one of the cubicles and 'took a seat'. It gave me a few extra moments to rehearse what I was going to say.

When eventually Liam's torrent subsided to a trickle, I pulled the flush, came out of 'hiding' and walked casually over to the sink where *my man* was washing his hands. I followed suit and watched amusedly, as Liam admired himself in the mirror. Then, hoping that what I was about to say sounded rational, and praying that we had no unwanted interruptions, I made my opening play.

'You're Maire's brother, aren't you?'

'Do I know you?' Liam asked warily, as he looked me up and down. There was menace in the question, there was menace in his tone, and when he pushed his face right up against mine, so close that I could taste the beer on his breath, I decided that I should just say it straight.

'One time I heard Maire having a pop at you about a stolen car…' I let it hang.

'You've got me mixed up with someone else.' Liam was suddenly all smiles as he tried to push past me.

'No. I haven't,' I insisted, not letting him through.

He stared hard at me this time, trying to place me, and I held his stare.

'It wasn't your car, was it?' Liam grinned, uneasily.

I couldn't help but notice how straight and white Liam's teeth were. Liam bore an uncanny resemblance to Shane McGowan, but when he smiled, he appeared different. Handsome almost, quite unlike the eponymous Pogue. I had neither the inclination nor the time to pass on the compliment though.

'No, it wasn't *my car*!' I hissed, viciously.

'Well, what then?' Liam asked, bemused, his voice rising an octave or two.

My counterattack had caught him off guard, and I now had what I wanted: his full attention.

'I require a certain type of person,' I ventured cautiously. 'An acquaintance. No. Less than that. Someone I know nothing about. And just as important, someone who knows nothing about me.'

'You nick your own cars, *geezer*!' Liam laughed, emphasising the final word in his best Cockney accent, but I ignored the interjection.

'I *will* need a car,' I paused and gave him a knowing smile. 'But that's only part of the job.'

'Go on,' he smiled back, his interest piqued.

'Now this job's worth money — a lot of money,' I raised an eyebrow; then clarified, 'Well, a lot of money to me.'

'How much are we talking?'

I afforded myself a sly, little smile at the question: it was a sign that Liam was open to negotiation.

'Not here. Walls have ears. Go home and sober up.'

'I'm meeting people.'

'Un-meet them. You can see them tomorrow. Talk to nobody. You never met me.'

'How much money are we talking?' he asked for a second time, eagerly.

'Twenty grand…'

'Each?' It was Liam's turn to raise an eyebrow.

'Between us,' I replied, shaking my head. 'But we'll have the cash in our hands before the sun rises on tomorrow.'

'So? What next?' Liam again examined his reflection, and as he did so, his cheesy grin broadened.

'At 11.30 tonight I'll give you a call,' I told him flatly.

'You'll be needing a number then?' Liam remarked, nonchalantly.

'I will,' I smiled, watching him spend his share of the money.

I would hardly have described the tone of the conversation as relaxed, but the animosity had all but gone.

'I can't deny I'm intrigued,' he admitted, with a greedy look in his eye.

'Good,' I nodded. 'I mean, what have you got to lose — a night on the piss?'

'Listen, mister!' Liam was back on the offensive; he sounded half-cut. 'You'd better not be fucking me about!'

'I'm not,' I replied calmly, and I was wondering what I should say next when Liam reeled off his mobile number. 'Hold on a second,' I said, as I fumbled in my trouser pocket for a pen and piece of paper.

'Haven't you got a mobile?'

'I've just realised I left it in the car.'

Liam gave me a curious look as he repeated the number. I read it back to him and he gave a little nod.

'What's your name?' he asked.

'Francis.' I held out my hand.

'Liam.' He shook it. 'So how can I trust you, Francis?' His misgivings were understandable.

'You can't,' I replied, matter-of-factly. 'You'll just have to trust your instincts. You're risking nothing...'

'Not yet!' he snapped. 'But if I have to steal a car then I'll be risking a stretch inside!'

'You know the score. If you're up to the job, then take it on. If it's out of your league...'

'I don't think *someone like you* could offer me a job that is "out of *my* league",' he sneered. 'And let's get this straight: *you* came to me — someone you don't know from Adam — offering a cut of twenty large. So, I want some details...'

'We're going to steal a book,' I told him straight.

'A wee book, eh?' Liam couldn't contain a dismissive snort.

'It's a bit more complicated than that.' I could now hear the urgency in my voice.

We'd been in the toilet long enough already, somebody might have noticed, his friends might have arrived — and if Maire was amongst their number, that would certainly put paid to my plan.

'Look. I'll phone you at 11.30 tonight to explain everything and then you can make your decision. It's best if *nobody* knows we've met. Otherwise, we'll lose a real advantage. This will definitely work if we can't be linked to one another.'

'Mmm,' he grimaced, dubiously. 'Well, I expect you to be prompt with the call,' he added soberly. '11.30 tonight. And if you're fucking me about, I will make you pay.'

'I'm not,' I maintained. 'I promise you,'

Then, without anther word, Liam turned his back and was gone.

I waited another minute or two before I followed him out into the bar, and with the young men still singing tunelessly, the old men still bickering, and the barmaid still engrossed in her smartphone, I slipped out.

On the walk back to my car, I could feel myself beginning to think like a criminal — worrying about the mistakes I had already made. I had clocked the CCTV in the pub — so

27

regardless of whether anybody remembered me, images of Liam and me in the pub at the same time would exist; maybe even images of me following Liam into the gents. But before this potential problem became a real one, I had to convince Liam that the rewards from stealing a rare Charles Dickens publication, warranted the risk.

I was trusting my would-be partner-in-crime to go straight home without speaking to anybody. But alas, my trust would prove misplaced. By going on a bit of a pub crawl when he left The Crown, Liam would actually do me something of a favour. However, the phone-call he would make later that night would, one day, have me found out for my crime.

Three

Back in 2013, I was living with my wife and daughter in a terraced two-up, two-down on a moderately exclusive housing estate in Colindale — another of London's many suburbs.

Under normal circumstances, it would have been impossible for me to implement my plan, but on that particular Thursday, Brigid and Maeve were in Ireland visiting my in-laws. This provided me with an alibi of sorts — let the prosecution prove I *wasn't* home alone!

My plan was to meet with Liam in a disused lock-up about a mile from where I lived (and about half-a-mile from where the proposed robbery would take place) and to get there, I couldn't avoid crossing Colindale High Street.

Like most urban high streets, Colindale's is an unremarkable mix of bookmakers, charity shops, ethnic grocers, independent fast-food outlets and public houses, and after a twenty-minute drive from Cricklewood, I was parking up on it — outside Erin's Hope: the pub which, in my humble opinion, serves the best pint in north-west London.

Again, I contemplated another, but I wasn't in town to enjoy myself. I was there to assess the threat that would be posed to me later on by that other familiar feature of the modern high street: CCTV.

Looking up to the skies, I realised that, regardless of where I crossed the main road, an image of me was sure to be caught on camera. But if all went to plan, and the crime went undetected for a day or two, then the incriminating footage was unlikely to be linked to it.

Still, it seemed advisable for me to wear some sort of basic disguise.

Having ambled along one side of the High Street and back down the other, I decided I would take the most direct route from my home and cross at the junction with Springfield Mount on one side of the road and Woodville Avenue on the other. This would mean me passing close by two business premises, so it made sense to assess their cameras too.

On the corner of Woodville Avenue, right beside a car dealership, I bent down — *to tie my lace* — and as I did, my eyes again turned skywards. I figured that, although 'coverage' did extend beyond the forecourt, these cameras would provide the police with nothing better than the municipal cameras — at best, a fleeting image of a *man in black* — and satisfied I could negate this threat by simply keeping my head down, I crossed over to Star Wines on the corner of Springfield Mount, where I helped myself to two cans of Budweiser from the fridge.

As I queued to pay, I took the opportunity to scrutinise the off-licence's CCTV monitor which sat on the counter beside the till. Their cameras covered three angles — the first focussed on customers as they came up to the cash register, the second watched over the spirits and Champagnes at the rear of the store, and although the third did cast a beady eye over the front door, the camera was facing inwards. So, I left the premises convinced that the police would obtain nothing incriminating from this particular shopkeeper's 'videotape'.

Not that I was being complacent, because I knew there

were any number of other factors which might yet go against me; factors over which I had absolutely no control.

For one, I might be inadvertently caught out by a 'hidden' camera (designed with a completely different purpose in mind). Secondly, while I did not expect many people to be out and about at one o'clock in the morning, there was no guarantee that I *wouldn't* bump into a familiar face. Thirdly, there was a chance that a nosy neighbour might remark upon *and report*, my uncharacteristic behaviour in the early hours of Friday morning. But most troubling was the thought that a routine police patrol might just pass me by at an inopportune moment — and then I would be done for.

I had my doubts, but for once in my life, I decided to take a risk.

And, as they say, the rest is history.

Regardless of Brigid's whereabouts, Thursday night was *my* night out — nothing excessive, just a game of five-a-side followed by a few pints in Erin's — and as soon as I arrived in, I made my usual football preparations.

Having changed into my kit, I slung a towel and some clean clothes into a holdall that I left by the front door, and only then did I focus on the other preparations that I needed to make.

First: 'a disguise'.

From the hot-press I picked out an old, black, hooded, Nike jogging top and matching bottoms, an old pair of black Adidas trainers and an old pair of black socks, all of which I left in a pile on the dining table.

Next: 'tools'.

Having unlocked the back door, I disappeared out into the

shed where, from my toolbox, I retrieved a small claw-hammer, a pocket torch, a roll of Sellotape and a brass padlock I'd bought a couple of days earlier to secure the shed door. The padlock was still in its original packaging and I was now wondering if it might serve another purpose.

Next, I rooted around in a workbench drawer for an old Nokia phone that I'd picked up from a stall in Camden Market about a year earlier. It was a primitive, push-button, *pay-as-you-go* that turned out to be a complete waste of £25, because three days after I'd bought it, Brigid got a new work phone and I 'inherited' her Samsung. The 'lesser' phone had been left abandoned in the drawer — never to be used.

At least, not until now.

I switched the phone on — it was still fully charged — and then checked it for credit — £23.70 — and as I carried the phone and everything else back into the house, a crooked smiled tainted my lips.

The Nokia went into a side-pocket of my kit bag while the rest was added to the pile on the dining table, and at last, I was able to sit down.

With every conceivable eventuality for the night ahead flashing through my mind, though, I couldn't sit still, and it came as something of a relief when my brother's car-horn finally sounded outside.

For a few hours, at least, I would have football to distract me…

My performance on the pitch that night was very much below par, but the game would live long in the memory.

Pitted against a much younger side with skill and pace to burn, we found ourselves 6–0 down at half-time, and we all hung our heads as our manager ranted at us about the embarrassing score-line. But Barry's diatribe was the trigger for my brother to stir himself into action.

Tommy was thirty-seven years of age and weighed in at well over eighteen-stone. He didn't look much of a footballer, and teams often treated him with a lack of respect — but at their peril!

As strong as an ox and deceptively fast, Tommy had a rasping shot on him which, when he had his *shooting boots* on, was unerringly accurate, and I guess he must have changed footwear at half-time, because from the re-start, with the ball glued to his right foot, Tommy strode serenely through the heart of the opposition, and having brushed off a couple of heavy challenges, he thundered a shot home.

This really would be *a game of two halves*!

After that opening foray, we didn't miss a tackle, and with my big brother doing the rest, we came out of the match on level terms. Throwing away a six-goal lead must have felt like a defeat to our opponents, because for Ajax Albion, coming back from 6–0 down to earn a draw, felt better than any victory I've ever experienced.

It's for nights like that, that men like me — men who have absolutely no chance of *making it* — play football. And, as I'm sure you can imagine, the lads were in great form in Erin's later on, as we celebrated our *historic* comeback.

I cannot deny I was clucking for a pint, but I resisted temptation, absolving myself from the obligatory post-match drink with news of *a very important meeting I had first thing the next morning*. So, when 'last orders' were called, I bid my team-mates a 'good night' and headed home on foot — stone-cold sober.

From here on in, I was relying on timing… and luck.

I was never going to call Liam from home, and having walked past our estate, I entered Jubilee Park and sat on a bench where I waited for my watch to show *11.30*. At the given hour, I took out the phone and the scrap of paper on which I'd written Liam's number, and after one last breath, I dialled.

'So, what's this *big job*?' Liam asked charily, picking up from where we'd left off.

It threw me a little, and I could feel real tension in the ensuing silence.

'Erm…' I wavered. I'd had everything I wanted to say clear in my head before I'd dialled Liam's number, but for no good reason, I found myself lost for words.

'So?' Liam repeated furiously.

'As I, erm, told you earlier: we're going to steal a book…'

There was a dismissive snort on the other end of the line, but it made me focus, and suddenly, my practiced spiel came back to me.

'…Now you won't have to do anything you don't want to do. And you can back out at any stage. But the real beauty of this crime is that there is nothing to connect you to me. Nor me to you. So, at the end of the night, we can go our separate ways, and nobody will ever make the connection.'

'Go on.'

'Okay. Let's begin with a recent auction in New York where a first edition of Charles Dickens' *A Tale of Two Cities* sold for more than two thousand pounds.'

'What of it?' Liam queried, nonplussed, and I again faltered.

'Er…'

'Look, mister,' he barked, 'I might be Irish, but I'm not thick! I've checked out a few book prices on Google since we last spoke, and there isn't a Dickens' first edition on the planet that is going to make us five figures each!'

'Not ordinarily…' I countered. 'But the book we are looking to *procure* is no ordinary first edition.'

'So, what is it then?' Liam barked.

'It is, in all probability, a unique copy of Charles Dickens' first ever book — *Sketches by Boz*. And it is housed just up the road in the British Library's newspaper archive where I work.'

'Mmm?' Liam mused.

From that one sound I could *hear* scepticism. But I could also hear curiosity.

'The first *official* edition was published in 1836,' I continued assertively, 'but between 1833 and 1835, on a monthly basis, Dickens had been submitting the individual stories from the compilation to the *Morning Chronicle*, and the newspaper gave away copies of the complete set as a bound supplement with the 1835 Christmas edition.

'Anyway, two weeks ago, when researching something entirely unrelated, by total chance, I happened upon a copy of the supplement — intact and in mint condition. Naturally, like you, I went online to investigate. And from what I could see, there are no records of another copy.'

'Well, what do you need me for?' Liam snorted. 'Surely you're big enough and ugly enough to steal a wee book without my help?'

'What we have to steal is no *wee book*!' I countered. 'It is an enormous, bound volume containing six months' worth of a daily broadsheet. Our *wee book* is somewhere in the middle of that welter of paper. Therefore, I need a *helping hand* to shift it!'

'So, for ten grand, you simply need me to help you *spirit* this "volume" out of the British Library?'

'And steal a car,' I observed saliently.

'Right. Well, before we go into partnership, there are a few questions which need answering.'

Instinct was obviously telling Liam that it all sounded a little bit too easy.

'Firstly, how come nobody else at the British Library knows about this supplement?'

'Hah!' I scoffed, thinking about my place of work. 'British Library Newspapers is quite possibly the most inefficiently run governmental department in the UK — and given the incompetence that abounds throughout our public services, that's quite an achievement!

'Let's just say it is a place that tends to employ managers who can't manage: a bungling mix of long-serving bigots and wet-behind-the-ears academics, who can utilise neither people nor resources to their fullest potential.

'Let me illustrate the point:

'At one time or another, British Library Newspapers held in its possession, every edition of every comic published in this country. But it no longer does.'

'How come?'

'Because the most valuable first editions have been stolen — and almost certainly by somebody who works or worked there. And what did the Newspaper Library management team — *the guardians of the collection* — do when they finally uncovered this, the theft of their most precious assets?'

'They swept it under the carpet,' Liam answered the question for himself.

'Correct!'

'So, I'm guessing it is also a matter of management incompetence that nobody knows about this *unique and valuable* book?' The balance in Liam's tone continued to oscillate between interest and cynicism.

'The current regime cannot really be blamed for this one...' I don't know why I chose to speak up in my managers' defence, but I did. 'Maybe nobody can, because one hundred and seventy-eight years ago, when the 'supplement' was printed, nobody could have foreseen its future significance.

'Anyway, the upshot is that there is now a perfect copy of what is essentially Charles Dickens' first book, hidden inside an unremarkable volume of the *Morning Chronicle*. And nobody appears to know about it — apart from us.

'I checked the British Library catalogue and the supplement *isn't* listed. Better still, it isn't stamped which means it would be impossible for anybody to prove provenance in the future.'

'Okay.' Liam still sounded cautious. 'So, I assume you have a buyer?'

'Yeah!' I replied plainly. 'An old friend of my late father's: Marcus is a man who *collects collectables*. I contacted him as soon as I discovered the supplement and he offered me £25,000 to bring it to him.

'Unfortunately, after examining the binding, I realised it would be impossible for me to simply remove the supplement from the volume without damaging it — *irreparably* — so I went back to him to explain that it would take an expert in preservation to extract the book.

'He therefore reduced his offer to £20,000 to bring him the volume instead. And ever since, I've been trying to figure out *a safe way* to get it out of the library. To be honest, I was drawing something of a blank, but when I saw you going into the pub earlier on today, suddenly a light went on in my head.'

'So, what's the plan?' Liam was starting to sound keen.

'Well, first of all, I've moved the volume to a remote outbuilding where it is hidden in plain view amongst thousands of other similar tomes. To gain entry, we will have to break a pane of glass, but once inside, we simply take the volume from the shelf and *walk it* off the premises.'

'But before we get ahead of ourselves, we do need to discuss your *main role* in all of this... the car?'

'I have my eye on something,' Liam purred. 'A well-used run-around that's been parked up for the night in a quiet little back-street not far from where I'm stood. The passenger door has been left unlocked and I should have her going in less than a minute... So, where do you want to meet?'

My heart skipped a beat.

'You know Sheaveshill Avenue?'

'Yeah,' Liam replied casually, confirming my assumption that he knew Colindale well enough.

'Well, if you follow it down from the High Street you'll come to a mini roundabout.'

'I'm with you.'

'Go straight across the roundabout and you're into a long cul-de-sac, which leads onto the park by Colindale Station.'

'I know it.'

'Okay. Well, about fifty yards into the cul-de-sac, on your right, is a small lane.'

'Yeah! I think I know where you're on about.'

'Well, at the end of the lane are a dozen lock-up garages — six on either side — and the last one on the right is mine. It has an old, wooden, swing-door which I've left unlocked, so all you have to do is pull it open and reverse in.

'Meet me there in a couple of hours — say 1.30?'

'*Whoa cowboy!*'

I didn't really expect anything else.

'I am not stealing a car and risking a stretch inside just because some stranger tells me there's a valuable book for the taking. You need to give me a more complete picture of what we're up against before I commit. I mean, how are we going to get in and out of a public building without alerting somebody?'

Personally, I would have preferred not to elaborate — the more I told Liam, the greater the chance of him spotting a flaw in my plan — but if I didn't convince him in the next few minutes that this really could be the simplest of jobs, then the opportunity would be gone.

'Do you know British Library Newspapers?' I asked, business-like.

'No.'

'Well, it's almost directly opposite Colindale Underground Station?'

'Colindale Park is directly opposite the tube station,' he protested.

'That's why I said *almost directly opposite*!'

'Okay.'

'Well. If you come out of the station and walk through the park, the railway tracks are on your left.'

'Yeah.'

'And to your right — on the other side of the park, behind some fencing and a wall, is a huge red-brick building. Despite its size, people tend not to notice it.'

'Yeah! I know where you mean!' he chirruped. 'It looks like a bloody prison!'

'Well, it's not. It's part of the British Library… Now, for argument's sake, imagine the building as a rectangle with the main entrance looking out over Colindale Avenue.'

'Right.'

'This is where the security guards' office is situated — thus ruling it out as a point of entry.'

'Okay.'

'Now, the other three flanks are monitored by motion-sensitive CCTV… but there is a blind spot.'

'Go on.' I could hear the enthusiasm in Liam's voice cranking up a notch.

'It's at the back of the property where the library is bordered by council-run allotments. Here, one camera-post is positioned about eight feet in from the adjacent boundary wall creating *a corridor*.

'The head of security is forever making an issue of it at the monthly service meeting but dismantling the camera-post and repositioning it is not deemed cost-effective — especially as senior management don't believe that there is anything in the newspaper collection worth stealing.'

I was acutely aware that Liam had stopped speaking and could only hope that he was following my logic.

'Now, the allotments are just a two-minute walk from the lock-up. We will have to climb over a gate to get in, but then we simply follow the perimeter wall between the allotments and the library, to our point of entry.

'The wall is about ten feet high, but with trees on either side, we won't have much difficulty in getting up and over it, and then it's basically another short walk through the *blind corridor* to the outbuilding where I have hidden *our* volume.

'As I've already said, we'll have to break a pane of glass to get in. But the windows aren't alarmed. And once we've done that, I'll climb in, locate the volume and pass it out to you. Then all we have to do is retrace our steps back through...'

'*The blind corridor!*' Liam harrumphed.

'Exactly,' I replied bluntly, rising above the sarcasm. 'Anyway, the return journey will be a little trickier as we'll have our hands full. But if we take our time, we should be back to the car within, say, half-an-hour — and because nobody else knows that it exists, the supplement won't be missed.

'Marcus will return the volume to me once he's *extracted* the supplement, and I'll have it back in place long before the library's annual stock audit in September.'

'So, what about the security guards?' Liam still had questions — and I had the answers ready.

'The guards patrol the main library building every hour. But they don't patrol the outbuildings at night — not unless something is picked up on the CCTV, which means, just as long as we're careful, then they won't be bothering us.'

'And what about the mess we leave behind?'

'I'll go in first thing tomorrow morning, and I'll report the broken window as an accident. These things happen from time to time.'

'And what if the *blind corridor* is not as blind as you think?'

'I did a dummy run — last week — to prove it all to myself.'

'Okay.' Liam still didn't sound convinced. 'Well, what if the police are out and about when we're trying to get this great big volume back to the car?'

'Well, that's one of the main risks. The other is that they'll stop us in the stolen car. But if we just take our time and remain vigilant then we should each be £10,000 richer in just a few hours.'

'Mmm.' Liam was still mulling things over. But then his tone brightened. 'Look Francis, I'll level with you. The job does sound pretty straightforward. And I cannot deny that *I am* interested. What I don't understand is why you're not using somebody you know — somebody you could trust one hundred per cent?'

I'd been waiting for this.

'Well Liam. I have considered doing just that — asking *someone I know* — because, of course, anybody could assist me in getting the volume back to the lock-up. But I don't think there is anybody I could trust *one hundred per cent* — not when I'm asking them to commit a crime.

'Being honest, I hadn't considered using a stolen vehicle until I saw you going into the pub this afternoon. It prompted a memory of Maire castigating you about stealing a car...'

'She's always digging me out about that. I suppose it was that night in The Crown...'

'Er, yeah!' I lied, almost automatically and quickly returned to the matter in hand. 'Anyway, seeing you again sparked an idea in my head: what better accomplice than a relative stranger who knows how to steal a car? And actually, when I think about it, you don't even need to steal a car.'

'I would never risk using my own car,' Liam asserted. 'It's bound to be captured on CCTV — either when I make my way to the lock-up, or when we drive to meet our buyer. I guess that's why you're not using your own.'

'Precisely.'

'Although when I think about it,' Liam deliberated, 'why doesn't *our mutual friend* supply you with the help?'

'I asked him to. But Marcus says it increases the risk at his end.'

'Mmm. Makes sense, I suppose… Go on then!' Liam said suddenly; excitedly.

'You can check out the layout of the library on Google Maps before we meet — to give yourself a picture in your head — but I have a plan of the building and photographs of the actual artefact on my phone, so you can look at them before you make your final decision.'

'And what if the book turns out to be worthless?'

'Marcus takes the hit — he is paying us £20,000 to bring it to him. But he's seen the photos — and he thinks it might be worth ten-times what he's paying us. As I said, he's a friend of my late father's and he plays the game fair and square.

'We phone him the minute we have the volume in the boot of the car. He will then direct us to a designated meeting-point, and once his people have checked out *the goods*, they will give us our *finder's fee* and take it off our hands.

'Then all we have to do is dump the car somewhere and go our separate ways. I'll have to get the volume back into the library at a later stage, but that shouldn't prove too difficult. And anyway, it's not your problem.'

'I'm starting to believe our paths crossed for a reason,' Liam said prophetically. 'Do you believe in fate?'

'I do,' I smiled. 'And anyway, we're not risking anything by meeting up.'

'*You're* not risking anything, you mean!'

'I stand corrected,' I chuckled, then I became serious

again. 'Look, I'll be at the lock-up at 1.30. I'll hang back and wait for you. If you're not there by two, then I'll understand. There'll be no hard feelings.'

'I'll be there,' Liam insisted. 'But I won't be making a final decision until I've taken a look at those photos and those plans. And if I don't think it all adds up then I *will* bail out. I've never known a job to be as simple as this — at least, not for ten grand a-piece.'

'I can assure you it really is this simple — stealing that car is going to be the biggest risk you take tonight.'

'You leave that to me.' Liam was now *all business*. '1.30 at the lock-up, then?'

'Yeah!' I grinned, and I was about to reassure him further, but he hung up.

That must be when he phoned his brother.

Four

I lied to Liam on the phone: I have never believed in fate. It was just convenient for me to suggest that the gods were playing a part. And although there are times, even now, when I try to convince myself that there was a certain inevitability about everything that happened, destiny was never a factor.

I was not preordained to fall into a life of crime: I chose to.

Of course, there was an element of *chance* in it all: it was *by chance* that Liam was on his own when I followed him into The Crown, it was *by chance* that I had heard his sister shouting at him, it was *by chance* that I had been listening to the weather forecast just seconds before I saw him, and it was further *chance* that I discovered the lock-up on my way home from work, just a couple of weeks earlier...

There had been a *leaving do* at the library for one of my colleagues, and after a few too many Stellas, I got caught short on my way home. The 'urge' was upon me the moment I was out in the cold night air, and taking the first opportunity that came my way, I dashed down an alley that ran between two houses on a residential cul-de-sac.

As soon as I was out of *eyeshot* of the semi-detached properties, I got *it* out and *let the flow begin*, and with the desperation that such a situation brings, there followed a certain euphoria once release has been granted.

Having given *it* a cursory shake, I popped *it* back inside my pants, and was turning to re-trace my steps when I noticed just how dark it was — and how very quiet too; eerily so. A shiver ran down my spine at the thought that somebody could attack me from the surrounding gloom, but in the face of my fears, buoyed by the drink perhaps, I found myself creeping further down the alley — just for a *nosey*.

As my eyes adjusted to the dark, I was able to make out the two rows of garages at the very end of the lane, and as I approached, I could see that the last one on my right was unlocked. Nudging the door open with my foot, I stepped inside, and I remember catching a musty smell in the air before an unholy mewling had me scrambling back out the door in a panic.

I had disturbed a fox.

I thought the startled animal was going to go for me when it appeared at the door, but as I stumbled backwards, it bolted down a gap between the garage and the surrounding fence, and a few seconds later, I heard a splash as it landed in the small river — the Silkstream — that flowed behind the lock-ups.

In the face of common sense, I decided to slip down the tight space after him, and after just a few strides, I had reached the large hole in the mesh through which *Mr Fox* had made good his escape.

Peering down at the water a few feet below, I could see *him* standing there, contemplating his next move. We stared at one another for a few tense seconds before *he* leapt up onto the low, concrete retaining wall on the other side of the water and disappeared into the greenery, re-appearing a few moments later, in the orange glow of the streetlights on the next road along…

I would probably never have thought of the fox again had I not
seen Liam going into The Crown, but in that fateful instant, I
linked the poor creature to an argument between siblings, to a
forecast deluge and to the discovery of a lost Charles Dickens
publication.

Of course, a decent human being would have gone straight
to the Chief Librarian with the news of the lucrative find —
rather than to a felonious friend of his father's — but as I have
come to learn, I am anything but a decent human being.

When I arrived back home, having loaded my dirty kit into the
washing machine, I went upstairs to fetch down two clean bath
towels, a pair of flip-flops and my black leather driving gloves
from the bedside drawer (obviously I didn't want to leave
prints). I placed them all on the floor just inside the back door,
drew the curtains, and behind the arras, I stripped to my pants.

Only now did I feel a pain in my right calf. It was nothing
serious, and it struck me that I could easily have twisted an
ankle or a knee during the match — which would have
scuppered my plans entirely — but *by chance*, nothing like that
did happen.

For the next hour, I sat watching the television in my
boxers — Only Fools and Horses repeats on UK Gold that I
had seen dozens of times before. There were more re-runs of
the vintage sit com scheduled for the coming two hours which
would help form the basis of my alibi — under cross-
examination, I would assert that I had been at home, watching
television. It was the best I could do — but, of course, I was
hoping that the case would never get to court.

The wait took an eternity; it was like the countdown to an operation — I was full of nerves, anticipating what might go wrong, but all the while, knowing it was going to happen whether I liked it or not — until eventually, my watch said 1.10: almost time to go.

I stole a peek through the curtains at the neighbouring houses, front and back — there wasn't a light on in any which was good news for me: anybody awake was a potential witness — and having put on my *black outfit*, gloves included, I unpacked the padlock which I popped into my left trouser pocket along with the torch. The Nokia went into my right and the hammer into the pouch-pocket of my jogging top. Next, I took a bin-liner from under the kitchen sink and slipped it in with the phone; then, after picking up the roll of Sellotape from the table, I stepped outside.

I closed the French doors without locking them, and using my teeth, I tore off a strip of tape which I placed across the gap in between, and leaving the Sellotape on the doorstep, I walked to the bottom of the garden, unlocked the gate and took another look at my watch: 1.17.

At a steady pace, I reckoned I'd be at the garage at just before 1.30, and all I needed now was for Liam to be on time, because if I was made to hang about, even for just a few minutes, then there was every chance that I would *bottle it*.

Five

Brigid and I had bought our bijou little home in 2005, and we had lived happily in the quiet, yellow-brick housing development for almost eight years. It was the type of neighbourhood where people never made complaints about one another, simply because there was nothing to complain about — somebody using the wrong parking-space or someone playing music a bit too loudly was about as serious as it got.

Our property was one end of a four-house terrace, and as the house next-door was a buy-to-let, our closest neighbours had changed on something of a regular basis over the years. We'd managed to get on with most, but the Greenes' — who had only been living next-door to us for a couple of months — were the best we'd ever had.

Like us, Jonathan and Lisa had a young daughter who, like our Maeve, slept in the front bedroom. And *wee Jessica* was the reason I left the house by the back — the last thing I wanted was to have my neighbours woken by a fractious baby.

Noiselessly, I opened the back gate and cocked an ear — the whole estate was dormant — and as I set off to meet Liam, I knew that this was where circumstances might conspire against me.

What if I had an unexpected caller? What if we were burgled? What if there was a fire next-door? In such circumstances, I could hardly have claimed to be at home, but thankfully nothing like that transpired so, if called upon, my 'alibi' would remain 'valid'.

Dressed as I was, I realised I cut a decidedly suspicious figure, and if stopped by an officer of the law, I was ready to explain that, unable to sleep, I had decided to go for a late-night jog in order to clear my head. Of course, such a flimsy pretext would hold no water if the diligent constable insisted upon a body search — because with a hammer secreted about my person, I would surely have been arrested for intent (although even the most perspicacious of officers could never have guessed what that intent was).

Again, though, nothing like that happened.

With my hood up and my head firmly down, I was *all ears*, and having crossed the communal car park that backed onto our house, I made my way up a small slope to a second car park that serviced an adjacent apartment block — again no lights.

Soon afterwards I was on the public roads, and from here on, I had to be keenly alert.

The first part of my 'run' was uphill, and with the knock on my calf aching slightly, I was glad when I turned into Springfield Mount — the apex of my climb — and a minute later, as I closed in on Colindale High Street, I slowed my pace to a brisk walk.

This was where I was going to be at my most vulnerable (hence my earlier *reconnaissance*) and without lifting my head, I concentrated on the road ahead. I allowed a car to whizz past, then, as the sound of its engine faded to silence, I took my chance and sprinted as hard as I could, past Star Wines and across the High Street, and I was a long way past the car dealership and well down Woodville Avenue before I slowed back down.

Save the dying hum of the car's engine, there had been no other discernible sounds. I hadn't 'sensed' anybody close by, but that didn't necessarily mean there hadn't been someone about — a drunk tucking into his kebab under the bus shelter, or a couple having a sneaky grope in one of the shop doorways. I had kept my head down at all times, though, so how could anybody — or even any camera — identify me *per se*?

I would have to run the same gauntlet in reverse later on, but with the forecast deluge beginning to fall, I didn't dwell on it and carried on apace through another private residential area — another part of bourgeois suburbia — where again, not a single light was on.

Very soon, the mini-roundabout that I had used as a guidepost for Liam came into view, but my plan had always been to take the preceding right — the road along which *Mr Fox* had made good his escape — and as I turned into it, I relaxed just a little.

The proximity of this particular cul-de-sac to the Silkstream meant that houses bordered only one side of the road. The other side — the side nearest to the water — was used as a residents' car park, and having ducked down between two cars, I took a moment to gather my thoughts.

The lock-up was less than a hundred metres from where I sat, and after regaining my breath, I just went for it. I hurdled the low, metal fence that I had been leaning up against, scrambled through the light brush, and in a matter of seconds, I had reached the concrete ledge above the stream.

I could hear the water flowing fast a few feet below, and having eased myself down the sheer dam, I managed to contain a yelp as, first my feet, and then my ankles, entered the freezing brook. The water was soon up to my knees, and the current felt strong as I moved upstream. Progress was tricky with every rock seeming to shift under my weight. The algae made each step a slippery one, and with the rain turning near torrential, my clothes were starting to weigh me down too. I do not know how I remained upright, but somehow I did, and when I located the hole in the fence that *Mr Fox* had used, I stepped out of the surging water and onto on a small 'isthmus' of shingle, where I took another moment — this time to check my pockets.

I scrabbled to the top of the bank, climbed through the hole in the mesh and, as I slipped down the gap between the fence and the garage, I listened hard — for the purring of an engine — but I was met with stony silence. Then, above the stillness, there was a sound — gentle steps inside the garage; somebody pacing.

Suddenly paranoia kicked in!

What if it wasn't Liam? What if it was someone else? A drug-dealer perhaps? That hole in the fence may have been there by design — for surreptitious and illegal transactions?

I pinpointed a crack in the wall panels, and through it I caught a glimpse of Liam's face — lit up by the torch on his phone — but there was definitely no car, and it gave me one last moment of doubt.

Even at this late stage, I could have turned around and gone home.

But I chose not to.

And so, I sealed my fate.

Before that night, the only time I'd ever found myself on the wrong side of the law was when, as a teenager, I was arrested for being drunk and disorderly — but that was hardly a crime. Once, as a child, I was accused of stealing sweets — but I never did. As an adult, I was again accused of stealing — this time money — but again not guilty. I was never a saint, but nor was I a sinner.

Not until that moment: the point of no return.

Liam must have heard me as I stepped out from the side of the garage, because he had the door ajar. Then, in the next instant, he had a gun levelled at me and was pulling me inside by the sleeve of my hoodie, all the while checking to see if I was alone.

'What the fuck's the gun for?' I squealed. I had not expected anything like this. 'And where's the car?' I was panting. Snivelling like a child if the truth be told.

'Don't concern yourself with a car until I've had a look at those plans,' Liam said evenly. He was shining the bright light on his phone directly into my eyes, and although he reeked of booze, he was cool, calm and collected: a real pro. He was in total control.

'So? Where are they?' he snarled, with a gentle wave of his weapon.

And bang!

Six

Liam had made his big mistake when he invited me to go into my pockets, because despite my hands trembling violently (the gun had taken me completely unawares) as I delved into the pouch for those non-existent plans, I was thinking clearly, and in one fluid motion, I was able to produce the hammer from the front of my hoodie and strike Liam a fatal blow.

I whacked him with all my might, flush on the left temple, and for a very long moment, nothing seemed to happen — Liam just stood facing me, zombie-like, a glazed look in his eyes. Then his jaw slackened, and he slumped forward.

Liam's arms did nothing to prevent the fall and with his head hitting the concrete floor — hard — I felt it safe to assume that he was, at the very least, out cold, and having placed the hammer on the ground, I gave myself another few crucial seconds of thinking time.

I then went back outside and fetched in an old, discarded bucket that I had almost tripped over when Liam dragged me into the garage, and having tentatively opened Liam's mouth, I poured the contents in.

Liam gagged momentarily and his body arched. I thought he was going to counter. But no. It must have been a reflex reaction, because after that he never moved again.

I then placed the half-empty bucket beside the hammer and my thoughts turned to his mobile phone — our earlier conversation was traceable. I shone the torch on the corpse, but although I could see the gun still in his right hand, there was no mobile phone. Logic dictated Liam must have dropped it as he'd fallen, so I took out my own and hit re-dial.

Almost instantly, Liam's phone buzzed behind me — it had bounced up against the door of the lock-up. Picking it off the floor, I checked the screen — *unknown number* — and after switching off both phones, I lay them down on the ground between the hammer and the bucket.

Then I took a long, hard look at Liam's corpse.

This was the first time I'd actually seen a dead body, and although I remember feeling a little numb, in truth, it felt no different to seeing a dead person on the TV.

There was no overriding emotion: I didn't feel sick nor elated. There was no remorse nor any regret. There was no sense of achievement, nor any of loss. No emptiness, and no fulfilment.

It had been a cowardly deed yet, perversely, it had also been an act of personal courage, and whatever else it was, I suppose it was the defining moment of my life — because in that moment I became a murderer; something from which there is no turning back.

Still, I didn't have time to ponder the bigger picture — the job was only half-done, and the clock was ticking — and having pulled the black bag from my trouser pocket, I placed both phones inside and smashed them to smithereens using the hammer.

The bag of fragmented phone along with the *instrument of death* went into the pouch pocket of my hoodie, and I shone the torch all around the enclosed space to see if I'd missed anything — it didn't appear that I had.

Better still, the rain was finding its way in through the garage roof — with one leak pouring directly onto Liam's face — and although *all* material evidence was never going to be washed away, if Liam's body remained undiscovered for a day or two, then I was hoping the rainwater might just 'disturb' the crime scene enough to render any vestige of the perpetrator as forensically worthless.

As added insurance, I used most of what remained in the bucket to 'douse' the corpse, and walking backwards out of the lock-up, I poured what was left in my wake.

Before setting off for home, I said a little prayer (two in fact: one for the repose of Liam's soul, the other that his mortal remains would not be found for a few days) and after one last look at *my night's work*, I switched off my torch and closed the garage door behind me.

Finally, I took the padlock from my pocket, and having secured the door, I was on my way, fully aware that every footstep and every snagged fibre might yet be used as *evidence against me*.

I edged back along the gap at the side of the garage, and after carefully climbing through the hole in the fence, I scrambled down the slope to the water's edge. The tract of shingle had all but disappeared, and I could feel my heart pounding inside my chest as I crossed back over to the other side.

Before I climbed out, I tipped the contents of the black bag into the rushing water, watching with boyish glee as, bit by bit, the two phones set off on what I hoped was an untraceable journey, and although I realised that, via his phone's GPS, the police would probably be able to use Liam's network to approximate where his corpse lay, as they would discover his body within a day or two anyway, it hardly mattered.

Drenched and exhausted, I thought I might not be able to summon the energy to haul myself up onto the concrete ledge, but I managed it at the first attempt, and having crept back through the foliage, I was glad to find silence still reigning in the cul-de-sac.

After a quick dust-down I reversed my run, knowing that, if I was stopped on the way home, with the hammer about my person, then I had made a noose for my own neck. But it was a calculated risk, because *if* I could get back safely, then, in just a few hours, the murder weapon would be 'lost' forever.

Soaked through, I was starting to feel the cold, but adrenalin carried me home, head down all the way, and before I knew it, I was bolting the back gate behind me, relieved to see the estate still asleep.

At two o'clock in the morning, all of NW9's law-abiding citizens appeared to be tucked up snugly in their beds, locked safely in their homes, shielded from the world outside, indifferent to the misdemeanours being perpetrated in that wicked place. At least, that's what I was banking on.

At the back door, I took the hammer from the hoodie pocket and placed it on the doorstep beside the Sellotape. Then, after one last look around — no lights; no sounds — I did something which would certainly have aroused the suspicions of a nosey neighbour: I stripped.

My sodden clothes I left in a pile on the ground (they could hardly get any wetter!) and after checking that the strip of tape on the back door remained unbroken, I opened it and snuck inside, drying myself behind the curtain, away from prying eyes.

After putting on my flip flops, I went upstairs to the bathroom and climbed into an empty bath. I would have preferred a shower, but I needed to minimise the noise (not that there were any guarantees that I hadn't already woken my neighbours).

Releasing the water from the tap at barely a trickle, it took an age for the bath to fill, but this gave me the opportunity to replay events over in my head and to isolate any mistakes I may have made.

I had destroyed the two phones and I was certain that neither could ever be traced back to me. I was satisfied that I had 'washed away' any evidence from *inside* the lock-up, and with the rain still pouring down, I was fairly confident that any evidence left *outside* would be 'washed away' by the time the area was cordoned off as a murder scene. Most importantly though, I had worn gloves at all times, so I could *not* have left any fingerprints.

I still had to get rid of the clothes I had been wearing *and* the murder weapon, but if everything went to plan, then these would be taken care of before I started work (and hopefully before the corpse was discovered).

Every passing minute thereafter would count in my favour.

As I dried myself, I mapped out everything that still needed to be done: destroy the trainers, wash the clothes, get rid of the clothes, dispose of the hammer, dump any plastic bags I had used, and discard the packaging from the padlock (it could probably be linked to the lock on the garage door).

Before getting into my pyjamas, I went back downstairs and threw the towel and flip flops outside onto the pile of sodden clothes, and having washed my hands one last time in the kitchen sink, I dried them on a tea towel, locked the back door, switched off the television and the lights and went upstairs to bed.

As I slipped under the duvet, I checked my watch one last time: 02.24.

It had taken little more than an hour for me to commit the most shocking of crimes.

But apparently, it didn't weigh too heavily on my conscience, because I fell asleep, instantly.

Seven

The alarm clock woke me with a start, and despite just four hours sleep, I felt well rested.

I got up, brushed my teeth, dressed for work and then went downstairs for that crucial first coffee of the day, and while the kettle boiled, I switched on the TV.

It came as a great relief to me that there was no mention of a body on the news, although on reflection, that was only to be expected — after all, *Joe Public* would have to be up and about before *he* happened upon Liam's corpse.

I had looked upon my unpleasant task in five *acts*: the *first act* was to set my target up with a story that would appeal to an avaricious nature, *act two* was to get to the rendezvous, *act three*, if you'll pardon the pun, was to execute the plan, *act four* was to get home, and *the final act* was to take care of all potentially incriminating evidence.

I would not be resting on any laurels until this *fifth act* was complete, and so, as soon as I'd finished my coffee, I put on a pair of rubber gloves and got to work, and having grabbed the last two bin-liners from under the sink, I went out into the garden where *the real evidence against me* lay.

First, I wrapped the hammer in the black bag I had used the night before, and this I wrapped inside another (I was probably being a little OCD about 'transference', but better safe than sorry). Next, I put my rain-soaked clothes, the towels and my flip flops into the other *unsullied* bin-liner, and then I turned my attention to the trainers.

Having picked them up off the doorstep, I disappeared into the shed, and using a Stanley knife, I separated the soles from the uppers before dissecting the rubber and the black suede into dozens of small pieces which I brushed into a Sainsbury's bag that was *lying handy* on the workbench.

I took the carrier bag of debris back to the house and left it on the doorstep with the two bin-liners, and after another quick coffee, I gathered everything up, and having locked the patio doors, this time, I left by the front.

I placed the two black bags in the boot of my car, but I kept the Sainsbury's carrier bag on my lap, and driving with the window down, I had scattered every last fragment of trainer before I'd reached The Launderette (as it was innovatively named).

Then, having retrieved *my dirty washing* from the boot, I backed into the launderette door only to find it locked — it was supposed to open at seven (I had checked the day before), and it was already ten-past.

Peering inside, I could see a young man, a boy really, Romanian perhaps, sweeping the floor with his headphones on, and I had to rap the glass two or three times before he heard, but having let me in, the moustachioed adolescent went back to what he was doing and left me in peace.

I emptied the bin-liner into one of the large machines, paid for washing powder from the dispenser, and once the cycle had started, I walked across the road to Londis where I bought a copy of the Independent and a new roll of black bags.

On my way back, I was going to dump the *soiled* bin-liner and the empty Sainsbury's bag into a roadside dustbin, but then

I had another idea, and instead, stuffed them into my trouser pocket.

Back in the warm laundromat, as I watched the spinning clothes 'decontaminate', I perused the sports pages, and as soon as the half-hour cycle was up, I threw the 'clean' washing into the drier — along with three pound-coins — and settled down to do the crossword.

Once the clothes were dry, I retrieved my leather gloves from the mix and slipped them on. Only then did I unload everything else into a *clean* black bag from the roll, and this I safely stashed in the passenger foot-well.

Then, I set off for work.

It was just after 8.30 when I scanned my pass to enter the main staff car park, and I could feel myself getting twitchy as I took the double-wrapped hammer from the boot and stuffed it down the front of my trousers.

I scanned my pass for a second time — this time to enter into the main library building — and as I sidled passed the security desk, I acknowledged Trevor, the guard on duty.

Trevor uttered an automatic 'good morning' as I showed him my pass, but he was too engrossed in the morning papers to pay me any real heed, and from here on in, I knew it was going to be fairly easy for me to complete my business.

Set on six floors, British Library Newspapers was no ordinary library, and with separate photocopying and acquisitions departments, an annexed microfilm unit, its own bindery, a maintenance office and two prefabs (which were built after World War II as a *temporary measure* when the Luftwaffe mistook the library for the nearby Air Force base), it was always going to be easy to find 'a quiet spot' to work in.

My sanctuary of choice was the third-floor lavatory, and

having made my way up in the lift, I snuck in unobserved, grabbed a handful of paper towels from the dispenser, disappeared into a cubicle and locked the door behind me.

The early start on a Friday morning was a little out of character for me, but *flexi time* meant staff could start as early as eight or as late as ten, and nobody — not even my line manager — really cared about what I got up to so long as the previous day's replacing was done before the reading rooms opened for the day.

In truth, I needed just a few minutes to myself.

First, I took the hammer from the front of my trousers and unwrapped it. I stuffed the two black bags into my trouser pocket with the others and then grabbed a bottle of bleach from beside the toilet. Holding the hammer in my left hand, I smeared it thoroughly with my right, and after swapping the Domestos for a toilet brush, I softly scrubbed it until I was satisfied it had been 'cleansed' (perhaps not forensically but as much as was humanly possible). Then, after 'rinsing' it three times under the flush, I dried it with the paper towels and placed it on the ground.

Next, I took the plastic bags from my pocket, gathered up the paper towels and threw everything into a single bin liner. I then headed for the maintenance office, carrying the rubbish bag in my right hand and the hammer — *the murder weapon* — in my left.

When I appeared at the office door, the two workmen on duty looked up guiltily — no doubt, this was their second or third cuppa of the morning — but when Paul, the library's senior caretaker, realised it was only me, he smiled broadly.

'D'you piss the bed, Frank?' he asked, in his usual cheery manner

'Something like that!' I laughed falsely, and then, holding up the hammer, I suddenly found the words sticking in my throat.

'What's the problem?' Stephen, Paul's deputy, asked, giving me a curious stare.

'I, erm, borrowed this last night for a job up on the third floor,' I explained, 'but I need a bigger tool.'

'Don't we all!' Stephen roared with laughter — and this time my laugh was genuine.

'Get another one from that green bag in the corner,' Paul instructed before he returned to their conversation about *some bird* Stephen knew.

I walked slowly over to 'the green bag' which contained at least eight other hammers and a whole host of other tools. All staff were free to avail of this collection, which had built up over the years, for any small jobs or repairs on site, and having dropped *my* hammer into the mix, I pretended to rummage for another. Only when I felt certain that *mine* was indistinguishable — lost forever; never to be found — I announced that *I might have to leave it until later*.

'For fuck sake!' Paul shouted, exasperated at yet another interruption. 'We're trying to have a conversation here, Frank!'

'Sorry,' I smiled apologetically, leaving them to it, while I wandered up towards the library's reading rooms, knowing precisely how I'd be taking care of the paper towels and the plastic bags.

Friday was 'bin day' at the library and the dustmen usually arrived on site at 8.45 to empty the bins, and I'd timed my walk to perfection, because the lorry was just reversing in as I headed back to the main building.

Having tossed my black bag into one of the library's massive industrial steel bins, I removed the gloves and tossed them in too, and a few moments later, I watched triumphantly as the mechanical arm of the lorry tipped the bin upside down and the last of *my rubbish* disappeared forever.

After that, I carried out all of the mundane duties that I was paid to do with my usual lack of enthusiasm, with the previous night's *life-changing event* seeming to have no discernible effect.

I had assumed the murder would prey on my mind, but I got through the day without having to put on an act, and I reckon, even a 'professional' would have had trouble telling that, only hours earlier, I had taken a human life for the first time.

I made a point of avoiding the news throughout the day, but the moment I arrived home, I switched on the television to see what was being reported. The murder had yet to make the headlines.

I felt in desperate need of a drink and I slaked the two cans of premium American lager that I had purchased the night before. I was considering going back down to Star Wines to grab a few more, but no sooner had I drawn the curtains and lay down on the sofa, than I was sound asleep, and I must have been completely shattered — mentally as much as physically — because I didn't stir again until eleven o'clock the next morning.

Eight

I worked alternate Saturdays. Not out of want but necessity. Saturday overtime made an acceptable pay-packet into a decent wage. But on the one Saturday I could have done with the distraction of my job, I wasn't on the roster to work, and so, still lying on the sofa, I again replayed the whole drama over in my head and contemplated *the case against me*.

There was virtually nothing to link me to Liam, and this had been at the forefront of my mind when I saw him going into The Crown — because if his murder appeared random, then the police were left with the task of finding one of the few cryptic signposts to direct them from victim to culprit.

I realised witnesses could place Liam and me in The Crown together (or failing that, CCTV) but even then, it could only be asserted that Liam and I had gone to the toilet at around the same time. On that evidence, I was no more indictable than the barmaid, the raucous group of lads or the old men at the bar.

Of course, the municipal CCTV could certainly be *used by the prosecution*, but that would only come into play if the police managed to pinpoint precisely when the murder took place, and even then, an image of a male in dark clothing, running across the High Street half-a-mile from the murder scene, could hardly be construed as *proof* of my guilt.

Of more immediate concern were my neighbours, because

if just one had been peering out of their window at the right moment, or from my perspective, the wrong moment, then if reported, my impromptu striptease might just be enough to set the police off on the right trail once the body was discovered.

I had done everything in my power to leave *nothing* at the crime scene — certainly no prints. I never touched Liam (even when I *whacked him* with the hammer I'd done so at a full arm's length), and I was confident that there had been 'no transference of DNA' in either direction.

Of course, it would take just a single fragment of Liam's skin or a single hair from his head — inadvertently 'relocated' by me onto my bed linen — to see me banged to rights, and for that reason, the chances of me being caught out by forensics could never be zero, but I was satisfied that they couldn't be much smaller, and with each passing hour, any trace evidence in the lock-up was becoming less and less valuable to the police.

'Washing' the corpse with the bucket of rainwater had been an inspired idea, and having 'taken care of' the other crucial pieces of evidence — the murder weapon, the phones and my trainers — all that remained to be disposed of were the clothes I'd worn on my *midnight run*.

After brushing my teeth, still dressed in the clothes I'd worn to work the previous day, I paid a visit to the charity bins on the forecourt of our local Sainsbury's petrol station where I emptied my laundry into the jumble.

I held onto the bin liner, though — I'd forgotten to wear gloves — but as soon as I arrived back home, I filled it with rubbish from the kitchen and jettisoned it into our wheelie bin which was due for collection on Monday.

There was now nothing more I could do to distance myself

from the murder, and after a quick shower, I got dressed and phoned Brigid in Ireland.

After a brief chat with my daughter, my wife gave me a list of chores to complete before she returned to London, and having cheerfully promised, through gritted teeth, that I would have everything ready, I sat down with a tuna sandwich and a coffee and remember thinking it strange how normal everything felt.

With no news of a body on the lunchtime news I couldn't settle, so I phoned my brother to see if he fancied going out for a pint. Tommy, though, was off to see Spurs with his best mate Mark, and Sod's Law dictated that there were no spare tickets.

To pass the day, I went into Colindale to have a few bets, and apart from the fact that I left the house by the front door, I followed the exact route I'd taken in the small hours of Friday morning.

It gave me the opportunity to check if I'd missed anything, but everywhere I looked for potential danger, I just found greater certainty, and while in retrospect, I can see that there is no such a thing as *the perfect crime*, when I walked into the bookies on that Saturday afternoon, I truly believed I had committed it.

And sometimes, when you're feeling lucky, you are lucky!

I would be a liar to suggest that every bet I placed that day was a winner, but what I can say is that, I went into William Hill with about £40 in my pocket and left with over £600 in it.

And as I was being paid out on a greyhound called Killeen Machine — who strolled in at odds of 7/1 — I finally saw a familiar face: Jimmy Evans.

Jimmy was a regular in Erin's Hope: the sort of punter

every pub needs, a bloke's bloke. The type of person who doesn't have to try too hard to be liked. A decent footballer in his day, Jimmy was one of those lads who *could have made it*, but by nineteen, he was too fond of the drink to ever become a serious contender.

Jimmy's afternoon had not been quite as fruitful as mine and so he was only too happy to take me up on my offer of a pint. No sooner had we sat down though, than Jimmy was bending my ear about his fiancée, Karly, and I began to wish we'd not bumped into one another.

I listened patiently for more than an hour as Jimmy banged on about how in love the two of them were (so much so, that after six years together they still lived with their parents!) but when I enquired *when* they were going to get hitched, his tone suddenly hardened.

'Not until Karly learns to save some fucking money!' he fumed, then reliably informed me that, while he had saved fifty grand since they'd been together, Karly hadn't managed fifty pence!

As Jimmy raged on, I got the impression that the real reason he was so angry was because Karly had gone into London for a girls' day out, while he was stuck in his dingy local with me.

Happily, after a visit to the gents, Jimmy re-appeared in much better form — a line or two of *Charlie* does wonders for your state of mind — and, at the fourth time of asking, he finally stood me a drink.

When he returned to the table with my pint, Jimmy was grinning like *the Cheshire cat that got the cream*, and with a raised eyebrow, he asked if I could keep a secret. Always one for a bit of scandal, I reassured him that I could.

Jimmy was itching to divulge the news that he had just asked out the barmaid, and shortly afterwards, as Eileen waltzed away with our empties, I asked Jimmy directly what the point of staying with Karly was.

'I love her,' he replied; with absolute sincerity.

Faces came and went as afternoon became evening, but by seven o'clock, with too much drink having been taken, I was getting bored. Then, when Eileen slipped away without Jimmy noticing, his mood again darkened, and I decided that enough was enough. But just as I was standing to leave, my brother and Mark staggered in through the door, so I changed my mind.

I left them with Jimmy to talk about Spurs' convincing victory and went to the bar, and as I was waiting to be served, I felt a gentle nudge in my back. Turning around, I found myself standing eyeball-to-eyeball with Maire — she was out with a couple of girlfriends — and I could hear myself swallowing hard.

'All right Maire?' I ventured, nervily.

'Fine thanks,' she replied, looking at me a little sheepishly.

'Glad to hear it...' I smiled before I set about venting my spleen.

'However, I hate to tell you, but your brother isn't... *Fine* that is... Have you seen Liam this weekend...? No...? I didn't think so... You see, Liam had a little bit of business to attend to... Or should I say *I* had a little bit of business to attend to with him — very early on Friday morning...

'Can I ask if you parted on good terms the last time you saw each other...? Yeah? Oh good...! And what was the last thing you said to him...? *'Take care'*...! Oh, how sweet...!

'Unfortunately, he didn't... *Take care*, that is... He's a greedy little bastard, you see... Or should I say he *was*... Because his greed cost him his life... Thought he was going to earn a few quid... Actually, he thought he was going to rip me off... But I killed the ugly scrote...! Whacked him with a hammer...! Sent the dirty weasel to meet his Maker...! A little prematurely perhaps, but I see nobody's missing him...

'When...? Two nights ago... Well almost... And I'm just hoping Mother Nature is *taking care of him* as we speak...

'Where is he...? Now come on Maire! That would be telling...

'Why...? Why do you think...? You don't know...? Well, let me enlighten you...

'You remember not so long ago when you lived next-door to me...? Yes...? Well do you also remember that Friday night in January...? The last of the month: pay day, I presume — when you and your cronies landed home, full of drink... Absolutely rat-arsed...! You do...? Well Liam is dead because of that Friday night... Or Saturday morning to be precise...

'Remember...? It was almost *three a.m.* when the carry on started up... I might have put up with the roaring... But then you put the music on... Full blast, *full fucking blast*...!

'And you knew full-well that we had a little girl... And that our little girl would be sleeping... Well, it was three o'clock in the morning...!

'Now, in my book, that sort of behaviour is pure fucking ignorance...! So, I felt obliged to knock on your door — to tell you to turn the music off...

'It was your dopey-looking brother who answered... He did apologise... But obviously he didn't mean it, because although the music was switched off, the respite was short-lived... And ten minutes later it was back on...

'So, when I banged on the door for a second time, I was fucking livid...! This time it was *you* who answered: pissed as usual, you useless fucking sot...! I threatened you with the police and although you complied, no sooner had you done so, than the singing commenced...

'If I'd not drunk a bottle-and-a-half of wine myself that night I would have driven to the police station there and then... And if my daughter had woken, I would have called them... But I didn't dial 999 because it was hardly an emergency. It was just one more inconsiderate fucker in a society full of them...

'I must admit I'd forgotten all about that night until I saw your brother on Thursday last — going into The Crown... But it must have been festering within me, because in that split-second I concocted a plan that would see Liam paying the price for his ignorance...

'Your brother is dead because...'

'Sorry?' Maire was evidently too drunk to listen properly, so I repeated myself.

'Can I get you a drink?'

Come on! You don't really believe I went to all that trouble of covering up the murder just to blab it out to my victim's sister! I thought all those things, but I never said them. I'm stupid, but I'm not that stupid!

I could see Maire was embarrassed — we'd not spoken since the night I'd told her I would call the police.

'I'm with my mates,' she shrugged, awkwardly.

'I'll get *you all* a drink,' I proposed, magnanimously.

'Ah go on then,' she grinned. 'Two bottles of Bud and a

vodka-and-coke.'

Maire and her friends helped me bring the drinks across to the table where they sat themselves down with Tommy, Jimmy and Mark and with everybody vaguely acquainted and everybody well-oiled, *the craic was mighty*. At least it was until Jimmy began talking politics — always a minefield, especially in pubs.

The topic up for discussion was Northern Ireland, and with opinions at opposite ends of the spectrum, things became tense. A staunch Englishman, Jimmy had been spoiling for a fight all afternoon, and when Grainne, one of Maire's friends, started to delineate the rights of the 'occupied six counties' Jimmy bit, but Grainne easily outwitted Jimmy, and in the end, he left the table and went over to the fruit machines.

To give my own head peace, I got up and went to the toilet.

I didn't notice as Maire followed.

'Sorry,' she grabbed my arm, apologising, I assumed on her friend's behalf.

'Ah don't worry,' I shrugged. 'They're both adults. And Jimmy loves a barney.'

'No. Not for that,' she corrected me. 'For the night we made all that noise. You're a decent fella, Frank.'

How ironic!

It had been bad enough them making all that racket when she knew we had a baby, but what really made my blood boil, what really added insult to injury, was the fact there was never an apology.

All somebody had to do the next day was knock on our front door and say sorry, and if Maire had managed to say that one simple word thirteen weeks sooner, then her brother would still be alive.

'Not to worry,' I shrugged guiltily. 'It's history now. We all push the boat out once in a while. It's just a shame you couldn't have apologised sooner.'

'Well, I'm apologising now,' she slurred in her Dublin lilt. 'Really Frank, I'm truly sorry.'

Then Maire toppled forward and went to kiss me, but I moved my head to one side and she only caught my cheek. In my own state of insobriety, I was wondering if I was overplaying the situation, but then Maire made it clear there was more to it than friendliness.

'Look Frank. Me and my friends are going to a party in Neasden. *You* could come too. I could meet you across the road in, say, twenty minutes? I could get something to eat while you make your excuses.'

It was on a plate, but unlike Jimmy who had no conscience where women were concerned — whose bedpost was undoubtedly scored ragged — I believed in fidelity.

'I'm afraid I can't,' I smiled apologetically and tried to make light of it. 'I'm with them losers tonight.'

'Oh well, suit yourself!' she huffed, slighted; and by the time I'd returned from the toilet, Maire and her friends had left.

'That looked a bit serious,' my brother observed when I eventually sat back down — obviously he'd been *keeping an eye on me.*

'She was apologising for the night they made all that noise.'

'Looked more intimate than that,' he pressed.

'Well, I can't help it if she fancies me!' I retorted.

'Got the beer goggles on more like!' he laughed.

'Well, whatever. *She* made a play for me. Cheating ain't

my style.'

'Not with a slag like that!' Mark interjected, viciously.

'She's all right.' I felt a little sorry for Maire. 'She's just pissed.'

'She's a fucking *alkie*!' Mark snarled. 'And she'd have her knickers off for anyone.'

'Well, we didn't make it that far!' I said pointedly.

'Only 'cos *you* put the *kibosh* on it!'

'We should never have started talking politics,' I joked, hoping to change the subject. 'It always leads to arguments.'

'That's religion,' my brother asserted.

'No! It's slags like Maire who cause the most rows!'

Mark really wasn't letting up on her — I sensed Maire had perhaps rebuffed him in the past — but I said no more on the subject.

With a few more pints inside me I might have 'forgotten' about my wife, but with her big droopy eyes, her lank, mousey hair and her tortured complexion, Maire simply wasn't that attractive.

Mind you, even if she'd looked like Marilyn Monroe, how could I have slept with her?

After all, it was less than forty-eight hours since I'd killed her brother.

Whether it was Maire's pass, or the argument between Jimmy and Grainne, all sense of bonhomie had gone, and I told Tommy and Mark I was calling it a night. And this time I was true to my word.

I was wary that Maire might be hanging about — and worried that I might yet prove weak — so I was glad when Tommy came up behind me in the kebab shop, and as we walked back to mine, *chewing the fat* — literally as well as metaphorically — Tommy told me about a teaching opportunity in Dubai.

'…With you moving to Ireland and mum and dad retiring to the Essex coast next year, I'm giving serious consideration to a more exotic move of my own,' he informed me, before inserting a cautious proviso. 'Maybe just for a year.'

'Go for it!' I encouraged.

But I knew he never would; Tommy was just too stuck in his ways.

Match of the Day was on when we got in, and although Tommy said he needed to go home — he was playing football again the next morning; Tommy loved playing football — he had soon fallen asleep on the sofa.

Unable to hear the television for my brother's snoring, I switched it off, threw a sleeping bag over him and went upstairs to bed, and when I came downstairs the next morning to wake him, Tommy had already left

All things considered, I was feeling fairly fresh, and after brushing the taste out of my mouth, my thoughts turned to my wife and child who were due home in a matter of hours, and as I tidied up, I wondered if Brigid would notice a difference in me, because nobody else seemed to have done.

On the surface, I supposed, I was the same person, and anyone who had seen me since the events of early Friday morning, could not say I had acted out of character in any way, shape or form.

I realised that this might change when Liam's body surfaced, but after an hour spent flicking between news channels, I was heartened, if a little mystified, to discover there was nothing to report — Liam must have still been lying in the lock-up, wondering for all eternity about a non-existent

Charles Dickens' first edition.

But while time had stopped for Maire's brother, for me, like everyone else, it continued apace, and every passing second put greater distance between the murder and the murderer, reinforcing my growing conviction that my actions were never going to catch up with me.

Well, not in this life.

Nine

I was brought up a Catholic, indoctrinated at school, and the 'brainwashing' must have served its purpose, because despite the hopeless eternity that my Faith promises, I still *believe*.

For obvious reasons, I was not too keen on going to chapel on the Sunday after the murder, but I had to keep up appearances, so on bended knee, I 'confessed' my sin to my God (the New Testament's *all-loving adaptation* who might just forgive me, who might just spare me, rather than the Old Testament's *fire and brimstone version* who would see my soul cast to Hell for all eternity).

I felt absolutely no remorse though, which left me in something of a *Catch-22*, because as every good Catholic knows, without repentance in this life, there can be no forgiveness in the next.

Still, I was glad I went; it felt cathartic.

After Mass, I paid my customary Sunday morning visit to Starbucks, and as I nursed a *mocha venti*, I tried to stop thinking about Liam and instead, tried to focus on the fundamental change that was about to happen in my life: the family move to Ireland.

Almost from the day I met her, Brigid had been angling for a move 'back home', and she really upped the ante when she found out she was pregnant for the second time, constantly protesting that living in a two-bedroom house was all well and good with one child.

'... But it's going to become a whole lot harder with four of us under this one tiny roof!'

'*If* we do move to Armagh then *you* will have to find a job,' I asserted on one occasion, believing I was calling my wife's bluff.

But fair play to Brigid, because she called mine.

During her previous visit *back home* in February, Brigid had interviewed for a well-paid position with a brand-new, public-funded, cross-border agency, and when she opened the letter confirming her selection, I cannot deny my heart sank. But the more we talked it through, the more I began to warm to the idea.

With Brigid 'expecting' in August, her role within the quango was to be put on ice until November, and so, to give me time to settle in, Brigid suggested that I play 'house-husband' until Maeve started primary school in September 2014 — and that was what ultimately clinched the deal.

When Brigid's parents heard the news, they 'bequeathed' us a site on land they owned close to the border, and although I would come to see that my in-laws must have been plotting Brigid's homecoming for years — planning permission to build a five bedroom, two-storey house on the site had been granted eighteen months earlier — I didn't kick up a fuss.

During the weekend in question, Brigid had been in Armagh for two reasons: firstly, to ensure that the architect's plans were signed off — meaning construction of our new home could begin as soon as Brigid moved across in June (on paid maternity leave from her *then current* employer) — and secondly, to find us a property to rent while the house was being built.

It made financial sense for me to remain in London until just before Brigid started in her new job, partly to ensure we still had some money coming in, but more importantly, because I was due to receive a sizeable lump-sum from the British Library in late October.

I should probably explain that the British Library had sold its Colindale site to property developers, and all members of staff who worked there, myself included, had been given the option of moving to one of the other main British Library buildings, or of taking severance pay. And the timing could not have been more perfect for us — because the sale was announced just days after Brigid had been offered the new job.

At that stage, family aside, nobody was privy to our plans, so it came as a shock to everyone at work when I told them that I would be taking the money, and although the settlement figure was hardly life-changing, after thirteen years of service, it was generous enough.

Most of the money, along with the positive equity from the sale of our house in Colindale, was to be ploughed straight into the new-build, and as the site had cost us absolutely nothing, we only needed a modest mortgage to create our dream home.

Brigid and I had done the maths as soon as she had received the job offer, and we had calculated that, while our gross income was about to plummet, with our mortgage repayments reduced by more than half, and with no child-care costs, our disposable income would be only marginally less than it was in London.

The move to rural Ireland was going to mean a great upheaval for me personally, but bored as I was with my job at the library, and with the prospect of becoming a stay-at-home dad for a year, I had, over time, become almost as enthusiastic as my wife about it.

This was an opportunity to bring up the children away from the pollution of the big city, in the fresh country air, and if government statistics were anything to go by, then Maeve and the new arrival could expect a better standard of education too.

When contracts were exchanged on our London home, we stipulated that the sale would not be complete until November 1st (which suited the buyer as much as us) and with Brigid's father more than happy to bankroll his daughter until then, each stage of the new-build went ahead without delay; and the final piece of the jigsaw would fall into place when our second child, a son, was born in August.

On the short drive home from Starbucks, I was thinking about what car I might get — Brigid was allowing me £3,500 of my severance pay-out to buy a second car — and I was wondering if we would ever make use of the double-garage that Brigid had insisted on building, when suddenly, I was 'back in' the lock-up.

Not surprisingly, Liam was infiltrating my every unconscious thought.

Could he still be alive? What if I hadn't actually killed him? What if he had somehow survived the attack? But then, surely, he would have gone straight to the police? Surely, he would have told them everything from beginning to end: the whole lie?

These doubts continued to creep around my head throughout that Sunday afternoon, and when Brigid finally messaged to say her flight was about to take off, I was glad to have something else to think about.

Ninety minutes later, I was at Luton Airport, welcoming home my heavily pregnant wife and our adorable little daughter, and as I recall, we had a lovely evening together. Brigid and I shared a Chinese takeaway, and once I'd put Maeve to bed, we watched a film together on Netflix.

For once, we chatted rather than bickered, and I distinctly remember Brigid saying we were going through two of the three most stressful things in life: a birth and a house move.

'Perhaps we should get a divorce?' I joked, thinking about that other very *stressful experience* I had recently been through.

Unbelievably, Brigid laughed too, and as she did, she remarked upon how much calmer I seemed. I put it down to having her and Maeve back home. But deep down, I knew my newfound tranquillity was born of pure relief: relief that I'd got away with murder.

Perversely, I wanted some credit for the killing — there is no kudos in committing the perfect crime unless the world knows you've done it! — but I had to accept that, even when it came to light, unless I confessed to it, my *noble deed* would remain something of a pyrrhic action.

There had, of course, been no need for me to kill Liam, but that most brutal and primitive of human instincts must have always lain within me. Perhaps it hides within us all? Most people, though, choose not to make reality of their ephemeral violent thoughts. So, what made me different? And why was I not being eaten up by guilt?

I went to sleep that night without being haunted by the image of my victim, and again, I could only put my inner peace down to my growing certainty that I had got away with murder

— a conviction that was reinforced the next morning when I discovered that there was still nothing being reported on any of the news channels.

Shortly after her mother had left for work, Maeve woke, and when she'd finished her breakfast, she brushed her teeth and I got her ready for nursery. As I listened to my daughter chirruping away in the back of the car, I can still recall saying to her (or maybe to myself): 'I think that this move to Ireland is going to be good for us… All of us.'

And they were not hollow words; I truly meant them.

At least, I did at the time.

Ten

And so it was: one spring evening I was driving home from Cricklewood, worried if the screws I'd bought were the right size to re-attach a panel to the bath, and by the next morning, I'd killed a man.

I doubt even a qualified psychiatrist could fathom out what drove me to piece together the random snippets of information that were lurking in the dark recesses of my mind and cross the ultimate boundary. Perhaps there is no rational explanation as to why this law-abiding citizen, suddenly and without warning, came up with a plan for murder. But the fact is I did.

I was driven, not by fear nor lust, nor even hatred but only by anger. An anger that had been 'awakened' by loud music — an intense anger and a senseless anger. And perhaps the most senseless thing about it all, is that my gripe hadn't really been with Liam, but with Maire — *she* was our neighbour and *she* should have had some respect for us.

In my warped mind, I like to think that I killed Liam, not just for myself, but for everybody who, for fear of the consequences, feels unable to stand up for what is right. I like to believe that Liam's murder was payback for each and every one of society's ignorant bastards.

Liam paid the price for those thugs on the tube, who with a gallon of courage inside them bully fellow-passengers only because they know their victims are never going to fight back, he paid the price for all the 'street artists' who think graffiti on the walls brightens the place up, he paid the price for all the rubbish left behind by the litter-louts who have no consideration for anybody else, he paid the price for all the vandals who get inane pleasure from smashing up shop-fronts or bus-shelters, and he paid the price for the gangs hanging about on street corners who make decent people scared to venture out of their own homes and have women living in fear of rape.

Liam was the sacrificial lamb who paid the cumulative price for them all.

I'm sure there are millions of other people out there who have thought 'murder' when the loud music has started up next-door, and for the majority, the moment soon passes. But like the myriad of seeds that fall to the ground, one or two must inevitably take root, and when they do, who can tell how destructive the weed is going to be?

Once you have killed (in this country, at least) there is nothing left to fear in this life, because regardless of how many times you repeat the action, the punishment can get no worse than a life of incarceration.

Perhaps, if the death penalty existed, then maybe none of this would have happened, because I have since proven, time and time again, that no matter how worthy the cause, I will never give up *my* life.

On the Monday after my first murder, I dropped my daughter off at nursery, went to work, did my shift, picked Maeve up, went home, made the dinner, watched some television and went to bed. Ditto Tuesday. Ditto Wednesday.

Life simply fell back into its routines, and as the days passed, the murder simply became something which had happened: something which could be put to the back of my mind.

It felt no different to my daily outbursts of road rage — incandescent fury that calms to nothing almost as quickly as it erupts — and because I felt no guilt, the murder never preyed on my mind.

There was still no news by Thursday (when I had a blinder at five-a-side) and by Friday, with a full week having passed, Liam's body had yet to be discovered. Then one week became two, and two were soon three. Then a month had passed, and while I still thought about him sporadically, Liam no longer hung about the peripheries of my every thought.

In late May, just after Brigid had started her maternity leave, we went on a 'family holiday'. Five nights camping with a group of expectant mothers, their partners and their children; our days spent learning meditation, yoga, Pilates, reiki and 'mindfulness'. Technology was banned (I wasn't even allowed a book!) and the only news that infiltrated the camp during our imprisonment was the shocking report of a young soldier being barbarously slain on the streets of London.

May he rest in peace.

As you may have guessed, it wasn't much of a holiday for me, but as everyone else seemed to be enjoying their time *away from it all* — even the men, especially the men — to keep my wife happy, I played along.

On the second evening, as we all sat around the campfire, Brigid gave me a hug and told the group that she was delighted to see her husband so in touch with his spiritual side. I joked that the only spirits I was interested in were bottled and labelled Smirnoff!

Nobody else found it funny.

It was only three days since I'd last had a 'drink', but I had been thinking about little else since we'd arrived 'at camp', and my opportunity finally came on day four when, after a gentle hike, I volunteered to get the salad for the evening's 'pescatarian BBQ'.

Along with 'the green stuff', I also purchased four bottles of red wine (screw tops) which I secreted close to a badgers' sett I'd located in the woods, about a quarter-of-a-mile outside camp — the badgers were to be my excuse for a midnight ramble that I knew Brigid would have no interest in.

However, much to my annoyance, my wife announced my discovery to the rest of the group during the barbecue, and inevitably, one of the other husbands invited himself along; and I was raging, because Malcolm was not the sort who'd enjoy a sneaky slurp (and even if he had been, I didn't want to share).

For two long hours, as we waited for the cubs (if that is the correct term for baby badgers) to appear, I was forced to make small talk with one of the most boring people I've ever had the displeasure of meeting, but finally, at just after one o'clock, with no sign of life, Malcom gave up the ghost and headed back to the camp.

I told him I would hang on for a bit longer.

For ten torturous minutes (just in case Malcolm decided to make a re-appearance), I resisted the urge to retrieve a bottle from the hollow of a tree. Despite the cool, night air, I was sweating buckets, but once I'd counted to 'six hundred', with a shaky hand, I unscrewed a bottle and gulped the wine down like a man drinking water after a week in the desert.

I managed to stop at two bottles — after all, I had another night to get through — and having rinsed my mouth with a travel-size bottle of Listerine (which I'd also purchased at the Co-Op earlier in the evening) I returned to the tent, where Brigid and Maeve were sound asleep.

My fuzzy head the next morning I put down to a chill, but needless to say, my 'head cold' did not stop me going out *badger watching* on the final night of our stay.

After our 'holiday', the move to Ireland began to take real shape.

Brigid and Maeve moved across in mid-June and soon settled into the cottage we were renting. The property was 'fully furnished' (well, it had to be as our furniture would not be travelling across the Irish Sea until October) and I travelled across to stay there on alternate weekends.

When Joe came along in August — with paternity leave *plus* annual leave *plus* 'flexi-time' — I was able to spend three full weeks with my wife and children, and I was both amazed and delighted at how seamlessly everything was falling into place.

With work on the new house well under way, I was now keen to move across and get started on the next chapter in my life, and just after Tommy and I had ferried the furniture across — storing it all in the huge double-garage — Brigid tendered her resignation in London.

In the event, her boss proved very accommodating, and as a 'thank you' for her nine years of service, Mr Andrews did not make Brigid return to London to work out her notice and paid the last few weeks of Brigid's maternity entitlement — in full.

It was now the best part of six months since I'd killed Liam, yet there had been no word of a body.

By this stage, I rarely thought about him (whether it was a conscious or subconscious decision, I cannot say) but when I bumped into Maire again (not surprisingly, in the pub), automatically Liam sprang to mind.

I wondered if I should ask an obscure question about 'family', or maybe mention a vague fact about 'murder', but thankfully I didn't take the opportunity to regret something I said, because just a few minutes after I'd arrived, probably still embarrassed about the last time we'd met, Maire left with her friends.

Then, on two occasions, I thought I saw him: Liam, I mean.

The first was on a Saturday night when I was out with the football lads in a Willesden nightclub. True, it was past one in the morning and I was steaming, but I could have sworn it was *him*, leering across the dancefloor at a group of twenty-somethings.

As my jaw dropped, though, so unfortunately did my pint — and all over a behemoth of a Corkman who went absolutely ballistic. Not wishing to have my face 'put in', I offered to buy him a large whiskey and we negotiated a dry-cleaning fee. I then spent the last half-hour of the night hunting for Liam. But there was no sign.

Well, how could there be?

Then, just a week before I was due to leave for Ireland, circumstances conspired to make my mind play tricks again. You see, I was driving home from the builders' merchant in Cricklewood — this time with a replacement door handle; we didn't want any complaints from our buyer — and as I passed

The Crown, I froze in my seat.

This time, I was *absolutely certain* I'd just watched Liam stroll into the pub.

A toot from behind woke me from my reverie, and wisely, I resisted the temptation to turn back around. But the very next night, with 'the sighting' fresh in my mind, I decided it might be a good idea to take a detour via the murder-scene — a place I hadn't dared walk past since that fateful April night.

Experts do say that criminals often return to the scene of a crime, and I could not believe that I was conforming to type, but for my own peace of mind, I needed to see if the garage door was still locked: it would be proof that Liam was still inside.

However, I never took a single step down that lane, because, as I was about to turn into it, a car came tearing out, and whatever he had been up to, the boy-racer spooked me enough to deter me from re-visiting my past.

Then, after one final weekend of partying, I left London behind, and with Brigid eager to start her new job and me eager to spend the next year at home with my children, I genuinely believed that this new beginning would bring us closer together.

How wrong I was.

Part II
November 2013

One

Our new house on the outskirts of Keady, a border town where the tricolour has always flown high, was nearing completion when I arrived in Northern Ireland. But for my first six weeks there, we continued to rent the quaint, three-bedroom cottage where Brigid and the children had been living since June.

The Monday after I joined my family, Brigid started in her new job, and despite my wife's initial reservations about me playing 'house-husband', she was soon applauding my efforts, as every evening, Brigid would come home to a clean and tidy house with dinner on the table. Those first weeks literally flew by, and as projected, we were into our new home in time to celebrate Christmas.

Having upsized from two bedrooms to five, we now had 'space' to live in. The house itself was a grand, two-storey affair, painted grey with black cornerstones. The front door opened into a porch which in turn, led into a huge, red and black tiled hallway. On either side of the grand entrance were two reception rooms — a lounge and a TV room — both painted in neutral creams and carpeted in a thick, brown Wilton weave. Beyond the mahogany staircase, behind a great oak door, was the kitchen-diner with an adjoining utility room, tiled in the same red and black check as the hallway.

At the top of the staircase, the landing formed a square balcony overlooking the entrance hall, and behind the door at the top of the stairs was a modern-looking, white-tiled bathroom. Behind four of the other doors were the bedrooms, two *en suite*, all carpeted in a deep, cream shagpile with papered walls and spectacular views of the surrounding countryside, while the fifth bedroom was designated a playroom for the children.

The surrounding plot had been landscaped into what we hoped would become a delightful garden where Maeve and Joe would be able to play — away from the danger of urban traffic, far from any discarded needle, at a distance from any nuisance neighbours and without the constant fear that every queer-looking passer-by might be a paedophile. Obviously, these societal problems still existed in the countryside, but in our own little fortress, we could keep them at a very long arm's length.

In London, Brigid and I had earned a combined income of roughly £65,000; in Northern Ireland, this had been reduced to a single income of less than half that figure, but as forecast, in real terms, we were only marginally worse off.

After HMRC's unavoidable deductions, we were approximately £2200-a-month down in nett income, but this sizeable discrepancy was virtually negated by two factors: one, we no longer had to find child-care fees (in London, for Maeve alone, they had been touching £1000 per month), and two, our mortgage repayments had been slashed by almost two-thirds. When one also *factored in* the reduction in council tax — and the fact that we had to pay no water rates whatsoever — and *factored out* the exorbitant cost of travel on the London Underground, it was clear how the household finances could be balanced. There were two *drains* that I'd not legislated for, though — oil to heat such a large house and diesel to run *two* cars — but these were largely offset by my Jobseekers Allowance and the generally, cheaper cost of living.

Not that money had been my motive for moving; that had always been my children. And as Maeve and Joe were thriving, I could satisfy myself that, while I had my own issues, in the overround, the move had been for the best.

Maeve, like all children her age, was entitled to a part-time place in a State nursery. In London, given that both Brigid and I would have been working full-time, this would have been of no real use, but in Armagh we were able to take full advantage.

Brigid's new boss, Peter, a Sinn Fein councillor, had *advised* us how to *work the system*, and we managed to finagle a place for Maeve at a nursery, right in the heart of Armagh's most Republican housing estate; and in March, she took her first, formative steps into the world of academia.

I was always a little sad when it came to saying goodbye to my daughter in the morning, but I knew it was for the best — a child's social development can only be enhanced by interacting with his or her own peer group — and once she had settled in, it was wonderful to see Maeve blossoming into her own, little person.

Unlike his older sister who did not develop a regular sleep pattern until she was fourteen months, Joe had been sleeping seven hours through the night from just five weeks of age. This meant *dada* was always well-rested too, and as such, it was easy for me to establish a weekday routine.

Every morning, I would be up at 6.30 with the wee man, and while he took his bottle, I took my caffeine fix. Brigid would rise at about 7.15 and after a shower, would come down the stairs, usually with our daughter in tow, and while I made breakfast, my wife endured the torture that is *Cbeebies*.

As I remember, the morning scene in the Kelly household was a very homely one.

Brigid would leave for work at eight, and once she'd gone, I'd make the kitchen respectable before taking Maeve upstairs to brush her teeth and get dressed. After dropping my daughter off at nursery, Joe and I would go to LIDL — or sometimes M&S — to buy whatever groceries were needed, and weather permitting, after we'd returned home, we'd go for a morning *constitutional*.

Joe would invariably be asleep by the time we'd completed our three-mile loop, which gave me the chance to clean the house properly and prepare the evening meals. Most days, I managed to squeeze in a little daytime television before my son woke for his lunch, and after Joe had been fed and changed, we'd head back to the nursery to collect his sister.

Afternoons, especially when it was cold or wet, were spent in the playroom where I indulged my daughter by playing whatever games her imagination dreamt up, but as the seasons progressed, I would either drive out to a fantastic, little play-park in Glaslough that Maeve never seemed to tire of, or to the leisure centre in Armagh where the three of us would spend a half-hour or so splashing around in the paddling pool as I tried to teach Maeve and Joe to love the water.

After the children had eaten their evening meal, Maeve would invariably make a beeline back to the playroom where she was free to be as messy as she wished (everything in it was child-friendly and child-resistant) and while his sister played upstairs, Joe amused himself on his activity-mat while I got the grown-ups' dinner going.

Maeve was allowed an hour of television when her mother

arrived in from work at around six, and after a soak in the bath, Brigid would come down to a glass of cold Sauvignon Blanc or a full-bodied red, depending on her mood and the dinner menu.

Brigid liked to put Maeve to bed, reading her stories until she dropped off, and then, with our son on my knee, Brigid and I would watch some television together. Once we'd put Joe down, we might indulge in a few more drinks, but Brigid would always be in bed by ten, and as she was usually sound asleep by the time I joined her, sex became something of an occasional pastime.

With the benefit of hindsight, I can see that although it wasn't perfect, our marriage was probably better than most. But at the time, I didn't appreciate what I had.

I had always known that the move from a London suburb to rural Ireland would mean a change of life and a change in lifestyle, but I had grown resentful of all the compromise and sacrifice I felt *I* was making.

What I had not anticipated was the sense of isolation that would come with the move, and having quickly lost touch with all my friends, I felt I was losing touch with *my* family too. True, I had been back to England twice — in January and then in March, just before my mum and dad moved to their retirement home on the Essex coast — but nobody had come to visit me, and I lost many-an-hour mooching around the house, hankering for the life I'd left behind.

What made matters worse was that, while my life had flat-lined, Brigid's was flourishing, especially on the social front: there was regular 'zumba' or 'pilates' with *the women from work*, Friday night drinks with *the girls*, and when she wasn't out gallivanting, she was spending most of her free time at the

Sinn Fein offices trying to get a foot on the first rung of the political ladder.

In April, I did start playing five-a-side with Brigid's cousin — and it was *good craic* — but after my wife forbid me from going out for a drink with the lads on Champions League Final night, my heart went out of playing and I soon stopped the one social activity I had.

At home, Brigid was always too stressed about work or too preoccupied with *the campaign* to lighten up, and our sex-life reached a complete hiatus as, without noticing, we had drifted apart.

And as the end of my time as a full-time father loomed, I could not help but feel anxious about what the future held in store for me.

I constantly argued that finding a job in Northern Ireland was not going to be as easy as finding one in London, but my wife cut me no slack. I had hoped Brigid would be more understanding — particularly as, once I started work, we'd have to find full-time child-care fees for Joe, so me going back to work was hardly going to be cost-effective — but she constantly reiterated the *agreed* deadline, 'You said September, Frank!'

Money was Brigid's new stick with which to beat me — especially after a few too many Merlots — but while she was correct to point out that *she* had been paying all the household bills since moving to Ireland, I felt justified in my counterargument that I had *never once* made any demands on *her* money.

I also felt obliged to point out one night, that when she was bringing up our daughter in London, she had said it was the hardest work she'd ever done. And seeing that I'd hit a nerve, I rammed my point home.

'Of course, I've been bringing up *children*!' I mocked. 'That's *children*: plural!'

'You need to find a job, Frank,' Brigid bellyached, wilfully ignoring my point.

'There's no work out there,' I countered.

'There are jobs if you look!'

'Not proper jobs! Nothing that pays a decent wage! Not here in this backward, little country!'

'Don't start all that!' she fumed.

'Anyway...' in the moment, something else had crossed my mind, 'I was thinking I might go back to study.'

'Ha!' Brigid sneered. 'You've never bothered trying to better yourself in all the years we've been together! Why start now? You're just looking for an excuse not to go out and work: you're just being lazy!'

And Brigid had a perfectly valid point — because after graduating I had only ever done one job, spending more than a decade in the same dead-end post, because the work was easy and the pay adequate. I simply didn't have the application or ambition to find 'a career' for myself.

Before moving to Ireland, I had promised Brigid (and myself) that this would change — that I would find a job with a purpose; a job that gave my life meaning. And in a way I did. Unfortunately, being a full-time dad didn't fit Brigid's agenda.

One late-summer's evening, as we were enjoying a bottle of wine in the garden, in an effort to prolong the status quo, I suggested another child.

'No way!' Brigid raged. 'I'm not going through *that* again!'

And so, the end of my blissful existence was confirmed.

In the end, I found a job with a security firm in Belfast just before Maeve started school — Monday to Friday, seven-to-seven, seventy hours per week if you included travelling time — and when petrol was added to child-care fees, I was effectively earning less than a pound an hour.

I often wonder if we could have lived happily ever after (well, perhaps not happily ever after but relatively happily) had Brigid not been so bloody-minded about me finding work. Although in truth, the marriage was probably already in terminal decline, and things would have panned out the same, regardless.

Two

On a practical level, the difference between life in rural Ireland and life in London hit home the first time I forgot to buy milk and I was forced to 'load' the children into the car, drive into the village, buy the forgotten lactate, drive back home, 'unload' the kids, and all to satisfy my caffeine craving.

There was no popping into Starbucks!

The real difference, though, was in the lingering atmosphere.

Undoubtedly, things have moved on since the Good Friday Agreement was signed, but it remains 'a work in progress', because while most people have learned to accept (at times begrudgingly) that a resolution will only be reached by engaging with their neighbour, there still exists a sizeable minority who don't wish to move on: the cardboard martyrs who 'perpetuate the cause' because, put crudely, there is plenty of money to be made from living in the past.

With my Irish-Catholic heritage and my English accent, I never truly fitted in with either 'culture', and while the anti-Catholic sentiment pervasive in Orange doctrine, made me instinctively wary of *the other side*, it was *my own side* that I truly feared.

In the pubs of Keady, of Middletown and of Armagh that we frequented, I was always afraid to open my mouth, because the minute I did, the glowering looks would arrive: bullets across a crowded bar.

My accent meant I was to blame. I was a Brit: the self-same Brit who brought bloodshed, internment, murder and war to the Catholics streets: the self-same Brit who sided with Thatcher in support of the Unionist cause.

It was my new job as a security guard, though, working access-control, twelve hours a day, on a building site on the Falls Road, which gave me the truest insight of the grudge still borne by some.

I didn't suffer the same overtly racial abuse that the Afro Carribean, the Asian and even the Irish immigrants suffered down the years from Little Britons, just the drip, drip effect of snide comments and smart remarks that served to remind me that I didn't really belong. It cut absolutely no ice when I pointed out that I am a Catholic of Irish descent — in fact, whenever I did lay claim to my heritage, I suddenly became one hundred per cent plastic! — and over time, when you have to listen to it all day long, it really gets to you.

I did try to find alternative employment, but permanent, full-time positions in Northern Ireland were few and far between, and as I quickly discovered, my library knowledge and experience didn't really translate into many other professions. What I would have given for a job like my old one!

So, I just had to get on with it.

I was up every morning at 5.45, rarely getting back home before eight. It meant I was always ratty and rarely pleasant to my wife, and as irritation became anger, as petty squabbling and bickering descended into full-blown rows, and as love evolved into something akin to hate, it became harder and harder to maintain the pretence of a happy marriage.

Brigid *adroitly* steered almost every argument onto the subject of my drinking — probably because she knew it always hit the rawest of nerves. Not that I ever acknowledged my growing dependence. Not until one evening when I arrived in from work; knackered, as usual.

Brigid literally passed me in the hall on her way to a yoga class.

Or, was it circuits?

To be honest, I wasn't listening!

'Joe's in bed. Maeve's watching *Dumbo* and your dinner's in the microwave!'

Then she was gone.

When she had said that *my dinner was in the microwave*, my wife simply meant that a ready meal from Sainsbury's was waiting for me to heat up, and as I switched on the appliance, I helped myself to a beer from the fridge which I took with me as I went to find Maeve.

Maeve had just that week started her second year at school. Bright as a button and oozing confidence, she was an absolute star, and I found her sat on her miniature leather armchair, engrossed in the movie, a picture of beautiful innocence, a darling — *my* darling.

As I sat beside her, asking about her day, Maeve hushed me dismissively. It stung. But it was never hard to forgive my daughter. And not wishing to annoy her, I left her to her own devices and crept upstairs to look in on Joe.

Like his big sister, Joe was growing up fast; too fast. In the year since I'd started back to work, I now only saw my children in snatches — evenings and weekends mainly; I had become a bit-part player in their lives — and as I stood over my son, it suddenly dawned on me that I rarely saw him awake anymore.

Downstairs, alone in the kitchen, I washed down my Rogan Josh with two or three more bottles of Stella before I ventured back into the TV room — with another bottle of Belgium's finest export in my hand.

I sat in total silence watching Maeve watch her film, and when it was over, we 'chatted' briefly, before she fell asleep in my arms. I tucked her in and kissed her forehead, and as I told her to *have beautiful dreams*, I remember wiping a tear from my eye.

Back downstairs, I went to fetch myself another beer from the fridge only to find the case was empty. I was shocked: I had been home little more than an hour, and I'd drunk twelve bottles. Still, it didn't stop me opening a bottle of Brigid's wine — and the spiteful child within me was hoping it was one of her more expensive Clarets.

Then, the next thing I knew it was 5.30 in the morning.

Having crawled off the sofa, I snuck up to the bathroom for a shave and just as I'd finished brushing my teeth, Brigid appeared at the door to give me a whispered lecture about where my life had gone wrong.

'Fuck off!' I screamed, as I stormed past her and down the stairs.

'It's *you* who needs to *fuck off*!' she raged after me, as she followed me out to the car.

It didn't seem like such a long time ago that I thought we were thriving on this country life.

When I got in from work that same night, I took a long, hard look at my reflection: podgy and scruffy, I had developed a jowl and a paunch, and I hardly recognised the shaven-headed thug staring back at me.

The scales informed me that I had put on almost four stone in the past twelve months — a result of a sedentary job, an absence of exercise and a diet of junk food and ready meals — and as I *grew into* middle-age, my wife was doing her best to reverse the process.

Brigid was now living life by the mantra that a healthy body meant a healthy mind, and it appeared to be working, because not only had she gained a promotion at work, but her political career was taking off too.

Despite our morning spat, Brigid could not rein in her excitement that night when she returned from the Sinn Fein office, with the news that her boss was about to rubber-stamp her candidacy nomination in the forthcoming council elections.

'…We'll be *entertaining* Peter and his wife on Saturday,' she cooed. 'So, I need you to be on your best behaviour.'

I promised I would be.

It was decided that I should cook: 'a seafood chowder as a starter, chicken with ginger and chilli as the main, and a white chocolate cheesecake for dessert,' I informed my wife on the Saturday morning.

'Just make sure it's edible!' Brigid barked, reverting to type.

For once, I bit my tongue, and while my wife went to Sainsburys to select the wine, I set to work. I had the 'prep' done by lunchtime, and defying the demons within, I made myself a coffee.

As I waited for the kettle to boil, I rifled through a copy of the Irish Times from earlier in the week, and my interest was piqued, by an article about an ongoing drugs feud in Dublin. The report focussed on the arrest of a man named

Michael Breen. Breen had been charged in relation to two shootings in Dublin and a third in Limerick. Then, as I turned the page, my head started to spin.

In amongst the various photographs accompanying the piece was a shot of Liam.

Sitting down, I read on and discovered that London's Metropolitan Police Force had come across to Dublin to question Breen about Liam's murder. Breen denied all knowledge (quite reasonably) and as no formal charges were brought, Liam's murder remained *'a live investigation'*. But while the report may have reassured me that the police were probably never going to apprehend the right man, the police were no longer my primary concern: Liam's family was.

The Carrolls were obviously much bigger players than I could ever have imagined, and if they ever put the puzzle together, then my fate was sealed. Enemies of these Dublin gangs had been executed over far less than a murdered sibling.

What had I got myself into?

My need for a drink was urgent and I poured myself a glass of brandy: a large one, then another and another.

I had to keep telling myself that, *if* the Carrolls suspected me, then I'd already be dead, and I was about to pour myself a fourth glass, when a terse phone call from my wife brought me back to the present.

With a dinner to make, I took a very cold shower, and after two cups of very strong coffee, I felt back in control. However, when my wife arrived in at 5.30, she must have smelt it on my breath and accused me of drinking (which I was hardly in a position to deny).

I insisted it was only a small glass of brandy while I'd watched the racing, but an ever-suspicious Brigid went straight to the drinks' cabinet, and holding up the half-empty bottle of Courvoisier to the light, she was adamant it had been full.

I reminded her that her cousin had called around earlier in the week — Austin loved the drink more than me — and although Brigid wasn't convinced, she was forced to give up the interrogation because we had to get ready for dinner.

While my wife made herself beautiful, I took a second shower (this time, hot) and changed into something more formal, and by the time our guests arrived at 8.30, I felt relatively sober.

To begin with, it was all quite civil. Peter and Brigid *talked shop* while I chatted to Collette (mainly, as I recall, about her: Collette was a marketing manager for the food industry) and although she did compliment my culinary skills, I sensed a distinct note of condescension in her tone.

Collette did nothing to disguise her displeasure at being omitted from the *main exchange*, and I caught her glaring at her husband on more than one occasion, imploring him to *get her away from this boring, little man.*

But Peter was too engrossed in political debate with my wife to notice.

Eventually, Collette created an angle in, and by dint of the fact I had nothing relevant to contribute, I withdrew into my shell, and I guess I must have been exceedingly drunk by the time we retired to the sitting room for coffee, because no sooner had we sat down than Peter and Collette were racing out the door at almost breakneck speed.

When they'd gone, Brigid had no trouble in letting me know how *I'd fucked up... again!*

'...You're drunk!' she asserted reasonably.

'I've had no more than anyone else,' I countered.

'Are you really that blind?' Brigid retorted resentfully.

'What?'

'Peter had one glass. Collette and I had just two. Yet we have three empty wine bottles...'

I was lost for words.

'...You've embarrassed me, Frank. I don't know what Peter and Collette must think.'

'That's all you care about ... What other people think!'

'You're a disgrace, Frank!' Brigid was raging, her eyes brimming with tears. 'You sleep in the spare room tonight!' she sobbed.

After that, we never shared the same bed again.

My sleep that night was fitful. In every one of my drink-fuelled imaginings, I saw *the shadow of a gunman*. But no avenging angel arrived to put me out of my misery, and at the crack of dawn, I had to listen to *the devil incarnate* re-hash her words.

'... I can't take much more of this,' she concluded.

'Nor can I,' I replied dolefully. Then I took a deep breath. 'I have something to tell you...'

I had wrestled with it all night and had come to the conclusion that I needed to confess everything to Brigid. My mind was made up, and calmly, I asked her to sit down.

'Are you still drunk?' I can still hear the contempt in her voice.

'Probably,' I shrugged. 'But you're not going to like this.'

'Go on.'

For once, Brigid actually sounded interested in what *I* had to say.

Then, right on cue, the phone rang — her mother. Those two could talk for hours, and I had the dishwasher emptied and the debris from the previous night cleared up, before Brigid finally hung up.

'So, what was so important?' she scoffed; her interest hadn't lasted long.

'Oh nothing.' I sighed; the moment had passed for me too. 'I just wanted to say I was unhappy with the way life is working out for me.'

'Well, do something about it then!' she retorted. 'You've been trying to re-write history, Frank. But you agreed to this move.'

'I know, I know,' I conceded.

'And you'll need cut down on the drinking.'

I'm sure there was actually a small note of concern in Brigid's voice.

'I'll try,' I replied, unconvincingly.

Truth be told, while Brigid had been on the phone, I had necked the dregs from one of the previous night's bottles, and shortly afterwards, when Brigid went to collect the children from her mother's, I opened up another, and with a mug of Malbec in my hand, I re-read the relevant tracts from the previous day's newspaper article.

What I recall:

On Thursday 24th April 2013, Liam Carroll arrived into London Luton Airport from Dublin ... A taxi driver confirmed he took Mr Carroll to Kilburn from McGowan's, a bar in Cricklewood, at around 6.30 that evening... The last definitive sighting of Mr Carroll was at 11.54 that night when he was pictured on CCTV leaving the Brondes Age bar in Kilburn... It is believed Liam had arranged a meeting with an unknown associate for the next day... It is not clear whether the meeting took place...

It was almost a month later that the body of Liam Carroll was found in a disused garage in Colindale, north-west London... The door was padlocked... The autopsy revealed the cause of death to be a subdural haematoma to the brain by means of battery with a blunt instrument... Police are confident that the victim was murdered on, or just after, Friday 25th April 2013...

It is unclear what the motive may have been... Police are still trying to identify the man who Liam had arranged to meet... They believe that Liam Carroll's murder is linked to a gangland feud in Ireland, that has seen eleven people killed in little more than two years...

For a time, I wondered how the news could have passed under my notice, but thinking back, Liam's body must have been discovered when I was 'on holiday' with Brigid, and a quick Google search revealed his murder must have been a mere footnote on the news pages, because Liam's corpse surfaced on the same day that Fusilier Lee Rigby was brutally slain.

God rest his soul.

I re-read the article and given that they had the correct date of Liam's murder, I couldn't understand how the police hadn't picked up a single image of me on CCTV — either in the pub where we'd met, or from the street cameras later that night. But the fact was, they hadn't. And so far as the criminal case went, it appeared that I was in the clear.

In one way it was a bonus that Liam's murder had been linked to a gangland feud, but in another, it was very bad news, because his family would *never* stop hunting for his killer.

Another drunken Sunday eventually passed into the annals of history, and soon, another week had passed too. Then another and another. And with the passage of time, I realised that, perhaps, I had overreacted.

In spite of my promise to my wife, I was drinking more than ever, and my life was now one complete blur. Miserable as sin, I spent most of my time wondering if it might not be best all round if I went back to London — if nothing else, it would at least put an end to endless wrangling at home that must have been having a profoundly detrimental effect on our children.

I was never foolish enough to drink at work, but I was forever nursing a hangover, and I was only able to function, thanks to a massive intake of caffeine. Still, so long as I turned up on time, nobody seemed to care.

Not until one Thursday, about a month after our infamous dinner party, when the inevitable happened.

I wasn't late for work that morning, but I was cutting it fine, and the traffic light had turned red when I went through it. Normally, I would have got away with this minor transgression, but unfortunately for me, the vehicle behind, was an unmarked police car.

When the blue lights went on, I knew I was done for, and when I was asked to blow into a breathalyser by a smarmy, young constable we both knew it was a foregone conclusion — the previous night I'd drunk a bottle of rosé, six Stellas and a couple of vodkas for good measure.

The whole experience was a mortifying one: being led away in handcuffs, sitting in the cell, and worst of all, listening to the policemen take the moral high ground, insinuating within my earshot that I was an unfit parent.

In the interrogation room I admitted my guilt. There was no escape. The case was cut and dried. I did try to put forward the extenuating circumstance — *I didn't realise I was over the limit, I'd had an old friend around, it was a one-off* — but the truth of the matter was, that by that stage, I had been driving drunk, day-in and day-out, for more than a year. The only saving grace was that I hadn't injured anyone.

The police, I could deal with. Losing my licence, I could deal with. I could even deal with losing my job. It was my wife that I could not face. But eventually, at 3.30 in the afternoon, I was forced to make the call.

Dutifully, Brigid came to the station to pick me up, but she said nothing to me — not one word! — as she drove my car from Lisburn to Keady. With every mile, I could feel her hatred of me intensifying, and when we got home, there was no suggestion that we would *talk it through*. Instead, a contemptuous Brigid went upstairs, fetched her kitbag and sauntered off to yoga.

My whole life was falling apart, and unable to remedy the situation, the moment Brigid was out the door, as I'm sure you've guessed, I opened a bottle of wine, and I had downed two large glasses before I thought about Maeve and Joe, and only as I looked into their empty bedrooms, did I wake up to the fact that my wife and my children had left home.

Life changes gradually, I suppose. It does not change in one single moment. Nevertheless, certain moments are life-changing, and although in itself, a drink-driving charge is not necessarily terminal, it was at the very least, the catalyst for Brigid to call time on the marriage.

I put on some music — songs to remind me of happier times. But there was no solace in lyrics that no longer meant anything, so I switched the stereo off and opened a second bottle of Brigid's wine.

Sitting in the dark, in total silence, I could do nothing to thwart my mind from flashing back to the moment I saw Liam going into the pub — the moment I hatched a plan that will haunt me to my grave — and I fell asleep where I sat, wishing I could turn back the clock.

Three

You can take the man out of Ireland, but you can't take Ireland out of the man!

Well, let me tell you, you can't put Ireland into him either.

To begin with, I was more than happy to move there — away from what I'd done. The hope was that life in a big house in the Irish countryside would bring me sanctuary, but my home had become my prison.

I had no friends and no interests; I had allowed my marriage to disintegrate before my very eyes, and worst of all, I had lost the close bond with my children.

All I had was the drink.

The next day, I woke in the same black, velvet armchair, drool washing down my front, and for a few dizzy moments, I genuinely believed I was waking from a nightmare. But as my head cleared, reality bit.

Brigid had not said it explicitly — in fact, she'd not said anything at all — but I knew the marriage was over.

Too yellow to pick up the phone, for something to do (other than drink), I cleaned the house from top to bottom. But if the process was meant to be cathartic, then it failed, and I spent the rest of the afternoon pacing the house in painful silence with only my thoughts for company.

My purgatory was intensified when the phone rang — I

had no choice but to answer it. It wasn't Brigid, though. It was Bison Security, calling to tell me that my contract had been terminated.

I cannot recall if they had found out about my arrest, or if I was simply sacked for not turning up to work, but whatever the reason, the outcome was the same. It would give my *soon-to-be ex-wife* something else to hate me for.

After I'd hung up, I drove to Sainsbury's in Armagh (I wasn't sure if legally I was allowed to, but to be honest, I didn't care) and although I did purchase ready meals, milk and coffee, bread and butter, cheese and ham and even some fruit, my main reason for being in the supermarket was, indubitably, the off-sales.

I picked up two cases of Stella, six bottles of Chardonnay, a bottle of vodka and a dozen cans of Red Bull, and as I paid with my credit card (a bill which would go unpaid), I vividly recall thinking, *you're not going to drink all that!*

Of course, I did, and after a weekend spent in an unremitting daze, I was finally brought out of my self-indulgent paralysis on Monday evening by the sound of tyres crunching on the long, gravel drive: Brigid's SUV.

Like any self-respecting alcoholic, I raced out to the kitchen to hide the empties, and having splashed my face with cold water, I rinsed my mouth with Listerine and had managed to open the door before my wife had her key in the lock.

'After all you've put me through!' she snarled contemptuously, as she stepped inside — my feeble subterfuge was never going to pull the wool over Brigid's all-seeing eyes.

'I'm so sorry Brigid!' I cried. I could feel myself cringing at my slurred response.

'Don't!' She was holding up her index finger,

admonishing me like a child. 'My mother always said you were no good...'

'Your bloody mother!'

'Don't try and blame anyone else for the mess you're in, Frank!' she chastised. 'This is entirely down to you, and I'm not putting up with it any longer.'

'You're leaving?' I asked, aghast.

'No, Frank...' Brigid allowed a moment for the penny to drop. '*You* are leaving,' she clarified, before she set about giving me a few home truths. 'You need to face up to the fact that you're an *alcoholic*, Frank,' she added weight to the word with a momentary pause. 'And your *problem* is having a detrimental effect on me and my children.'

I couldn't respond. What was there for me to say?

'I've had to tell my family that it's *irreconcilable differences*,' Brigid was standing with her arms folded, staring daggers, 'but I've said it's amicable. Nobody else needs to know about the drink-driving — although they all suspect the drinking.'

I hung my head in shame as the truth hit home.

'And I can't let you see Maeve or Joe again,' she added mournfully, 'not until... not unless you quit the booze.'

'*You* don't decide what access I get. I have rights!' I harrumphed.

'No, you don't, Frank!' Brigid replied matter-of-factly. 'Did you learn nothing from your afternoon at the police station? I had hoped it would have been a wake-up call for you: your *moment of clarity*. But obviously you're still too busy playing the martyr to care about the damage you're doing to anybody else.'

'I never wanted us to move *here*...' I offered limply. 'If

we'd stayed in London...'

'*We* discussed it and *we* agreed!' Brigid retorted loftily. 'You said it would be in the children's best interests and you also said you hated your life in London...'

'No, I didn't!' I lied.

'You did Frank,' Brigid asserted calmly. 'Anyway, I'm not here to go over old ground. Let's do this like adults. I'll give you until Saturday to pack your bags. But you'll need to be sober if we're to have a meaningful discussion about how we move forward.'

'We're still married, Brigid!' I argued.

'More fool me!' she laughed derisively, as she turned on her heels and walked back out to her car.

'Marriage is for better *and* for worse,' I reminded her in desperation, even though I realised a clean break was best all round. Certainly, as far as Brigid and the children were concerned, and in many ways, it was what I *wanted* too. But when it's not your decision, when it's foisted upon you, a divorce doesn't feel quite so liberating.

'Where will I go?' I called after her

'To hell!' she shrieked, and that was when I snapped and did the most cowardly thing a man can do.

'Sorry!' I squealed, almost before I'd lashed out. But it was too late.

'Stay away from me!' Brigid howled, as she fumbled in her bag for her keys.

I dropped to my knees, begging for forgiveness; ashamed of what I had done, ashamed of who I had become; but as Brigid sped off into the night, the tears streaming down her face, I knew that I'd gone too far.

I could only pray that what went on behind closed doors

stayed there.

Back inside, I went upstairs to take a bath, and as I lay in the warm, soapy water, *my moment of clarity* arrived: 'I am Frank, and I am an alcoholic.'

In just two years, I had descended from social drinker to heavy drinker to alcoholic, and we all know the reason.

I realised my marriage was over, but if I wanted some sort of meaningful relationship with my children, I had no choice other than to stop drinking — and, in that one regard, my life has been a triumph, because despite finding myself in some truly awful places since that shameful, shameful day, not another drop of *the hard stuff* has passed my lips.

The first twenty-four hours of abstinence were particularly cruel: physically I was a wreck, and the compulsion to drink was constant. But I quickly taught myself that, if my thirst was quenched, then the craving dulled.

I survived *Day One* on a diet of water and coffee, and when I weighed myself the next morning, I realised it wasn't just my liver which had suffered as a result of my drinking: the bathroom scales were showing sixteen stone exactly — my *ideal weight* was just over twelve.

So, as well a strict calorie-counting diet and a healthy-eating plan, I also laid out a simple daily fitness programme: one hundred sit-ups, sixty press-ups and a three-mile run.

On my first attempt, I completed just seventy-three sit-ups and twenty-four press-ups, and about half of the three-mile 'loop' that I used to walk with Joe, but undeterred, I made up the shortfall in sit-ups and managed another twenty-one press-ups later in the afternoon.

Even though I had fallen short of my targets, I felt good

about myself — it was a start.

The next morning, I completed the run (admittedly, at a snail's pace) and the sit-ups too; I was still struggling with the press-ups but managed to hit my target by doing three sets of twenty across the day.

By the Friday I was finding the exercise noticeably easier — so much so that I added a lap and fifty sit ups to the daily regime. I had adhered to my strict diet too: a large bowl of porridge for breakfast, 'fruit only' during the day, dinner was a single portion of meat or fish accompanied by three 'veg' and a small portion of 'carbs', for supper I would eat a small bowl of muesli, and before going to bed, I would have a cup of tea and two plain biscuits.

Coffee was now my only vice: three cups per day.

I was drinking water by the gallon and I hoped that, if I continued to stick to the programme, my body would eventually recondition itself back to something like its former *glory*.

And the initial signs were good because, by the Friday afternoon, having weighed myself immediately after I'd completed my *second* three-mile run of the day, I was delighted to discover that I was eight pounds lighter.

As I showered, I felt something I'd not felt in a long time — optimism — and that evening, I phoned Brigid on her mobile to apologise. She was understandably frosty and was steadfast in her assertion that the damage *I* had done to the marriage could never be repaired, but she said she was glad to hear me sounding sober and agreed that we needed to 'talk things through and set out a plan for moving forward.'

I proposed making dinner for eight o'clock on the Saturday evening — when we could discuss the future in a civilised manner — and I reassured her that I would leave on Sunday morning unless we came to an alternative arrangement.

'There will be no alternative arrangement!' she insisted, and I knew she meant it.

So, my sole focus became the children — Maeve and Joe were all I had left.

Alas, I haven't seen them in years.

Four

For a long time after I'd murdered Liam, I managed to get on with my life by acting as if it had never happened, and although outwardly, I may have seemed like the same person (murderers often make the best actors), on the inside, I could feel myself changing.

I suppose a latent, primitive evil must have always been festering deep within me, and once I had crossed the ultimate line, it continued to grow like a cancer, gradually eating away at any residual goodness, until eventually, like a rock eroded by the rain, I had changed beyond recognition.

In the immediate aftermath of Liam's murder, I had the move to Ireland to distract me. Then I had my children, but once I started work as a security guard, with so much time to brood, Liam was all I ever thought about.

At night, I blocked *him* out by drinking, and another line — the line between heavy drinker and alcoholic — was crossed the day of the dinner party, the day I saw Liam's picture in the newspaper, the day I started to live in fear of my life.

After that, the drink had control of me. And I suppose it still does, because while I have managed to bring my addiction under control, every day I still have to fight my demons. I am and always will be, an alcoholic. But that's my cross, and I will have to bear its weight until the day I join Liam.

As a Catholic, I have always had another 'way out', another way to exorcise my soul.

But I simply don't believe in the sanctity of the Confessional.

I mean, how can it be morally right for a priest to remain silent when he listens to the worst sins of all?

Let me illustrate the point.

A child goes into 'the box'. The usual: 'I stole a sweet... I lied...' Then: 'My school teacher makes me do things that are wrong ... He says it is my fault ... He gets me to...'

Well, I don't need to be graphic. You get the picture. The child knows a sin is being committed and the teacher makes the child believe that he (or she) is the sinner. Now the priest knows too. But if the cleric acts against the teacher, then he is breaking the Confessional. Yet surely, it is the right thing to do.

It's what I would do.

The moral question aside, there is a practical aspect too — because Catholics are taught to believe in an 'all-knowing' God. So, if this is true, why then, does God need a human intermediary?

He must know I am not truly contrite. He must know that Liam's murder has never troubled my conscience, and He must know that, in my heart, I continue to justify my actions with the heartfelt belief that Liam got what he deserved.

So, what then, is the point of a man like me, receiving the Sacrament of Penance?

In all honesty, it would be better for me *not* to believe.

But in the face of the scientific evidence put in front of me, I cannot deny my Faith.

And so, I live in in a limbo between this world and the next — in a place where fear is my constant companion — and when I get down on bended knee, I pray that, as well as being 'all-knowing', God is 'all-loving' and 'all-forgiving' too.

Five

I woke to a chorus of birdsong on what was a glorious Saturday morning, and as I *hit the roads*, I was feeling positively positive. I had only been 'dry' for a matter of days, but I felt a strange certainty within, that I was never going to 'drink' again.

For me, it had to be all or nothing — there could be no exceptions to the rule. This was not a matter of cutting down, because if I was under the influence of alcohol, then my life was under its control.

Abstinence would not equate to forgiveness, though. For that, I had to accept responsibility for my actions and apologise again — face-to-face; like a man — and I told myself I would do whatever my wife asked of me.

Best case scenario: we would rebuild the marriage.

Worst case: Brigid would not allow me to see my children again.

The reality, I guessed, would lie somewhere between the two.

I could not undo what had been done, and if, as was likely, Brigid pushed for a divorce, then there would be no running back to England and hiding from the mess I'd made; I would have no choice but to content myself with the role of part-time dad.

Of course, I still had to stand trial, which would mean

losing my licence, but as it was my first offence, I was hoping to receive nothing more than a ban (at worst, community service).

Whatever the judge decreed, it would mean a criminal record, so finding gainful employment in a land of few opportunities was going to become harder, and I decided that, come Monday, I would chance my arm and phone Bison Security — they were desperate for guards, and I'd never let them down before.

If they knew about the drink-driving charge, I planned to tell them that *my sister* had been killed in a road traffic accident and that I hadn't been thinking straight. I'd beg for a second chance, and if they gave it to me, then I would find myself a place near Belfast (where the company had virtually all of its sites) and commute to work by foot or on public transport.

What did I have to lose by making the call?

Before getting into the shower, I did one hundred sit-ups and sixty press-ups on the bathroom floor, and once I'd towelled myself down, I stood on the scales — fourteen stone and seven pounds. I had lost a stone-and-a-half in under a week. Most would have been water retention, and although I could not expect to see a similarly dramatic drop in the weeks to come, so long as I stuck to the diet and exercise regimen, I believed I could get down to something like my *ideal weight* before the year's end.

I went into the bedroom and smiled as I admired my trimmer self in the full-length mirror on Brigid's side of the bed, and as I put on a pair of khaki combat trousers that I thought I'd never fit into again, I noticed a few photographs on Brigid's bedside table that her mother must have taken at my brother-in-law's fortieth birthday party a couple of months earlier.

In one, I was all alone at the bar, raising a half-empty pint glass, and I looked truly dreadful, a treble chin, a scarlet face, greasy skin and a shaven head. I looked the thug that I had become.

Making a direct comparison with the man in the mirror, I could see a marked difference: my skin appeared fresh and clear, my face had lost its jowl, and my hair, although speckled with a little more grey than I would have liked, was gaining length for the first time in years, and it looked healthy and sleek.

Vanity gratified, I slipped on a polo shirt and went down to the kitchen, and after a cup of strong coffee, I drove south of the border to Tesco's in Monaghan. I still wasn't sure if I was allowed to drive, but from a little (unreliable) internet research, my understanding was that a ban only kicked in once I was convicted, so I decided to risk it.

As soon as I arrived back home, I set about preparing the menu: shellfish linguine to be preceded by a curried parsnip soup and followed by a chocolate orange mousse.

By six o'clock, the dessert was chilling in the fridge and the soup would only need re-heating once my guest arrived. The pasta would be made fresh later on, and after a shave and a shower, I got dressed for dinner.

I wasn't happy with the shirt and tie I'd chosen, though. It looked much too formal, so I changed back into the combat trousers I'd been wearing all day and put on a clean, black, woollen, V-neck jumper over a white, crew-neck t-shirt.

Having slipped into my favourite pair of Adidas trainers, I went to the bathroom and toyed with idea of wearing glasses.

Brigid had chosen the frames many moons earlier — she always used to say how much they suited me; she felt they made me look intelligent — but I'd not worn them since Maeve was born, and when I tried them on, I could see why.

They looked ridiculous: the tortoiseshell frames were too big, too round and too unfashionable.

Unthinkingly, I slipped the glasses into the right leg-pocket of my trousers, and I let out a squeal of delight when I found two £20 notes — English notes; not the Northern Irish bank notes which London shopkeepers tend to turn their nose up at — which meant I must have last fitted into the trousers when I was in London some six months earlier.

Having popped in a fresh pair of monthly contact lenses, I splashed on plenty of after-shave — Issy Miyake: Brigid's favourite — before going downstairs to wait for the guest of honour.

As I fidgeted on a stool at the breakfast bar, I tried to pre-empt what 'conditions' Brigid might set out. I would have to work hard to win back my wife's trust, but my ploy was to surprise her with a composed and even-tempered approach, and if I *proved myself* (and I would agree to make whatever concessions Brigid insisted upon; AA would undoubtedly be top of her list), then I felt certain she would not cut me out of my children's lives completely.

At a quarter-past-seven — 7.13 to be precise — the phone rang.

'Have you packed?' my wife was nothing if not direct.

'Not yet.'

'Why not?' Brigid did not sound as if she was in a compromising mood.

'Look, Brigid,' I said, tentatively. 'Just come over. I've

made dinner. There can be no harm in sitting down and talking over an agreeable meal. And who knows? We might be able to map out a way forward that is acceptable to both of us.'

'That's as maybe, Frank. But what you did the other night — that was unforgiveable.'

'I know. And I'm truly sorry.'

'Hollow words Frank!' Brigid was predictably spoiling for a fight.

'I mean it, Brigid,' I insisted evenly. 'If I could turn back the clock I would. I'm hoping you'll see a change in me, because I have changed. Changed for the better, changed for good.'

'Talk is cheap, Frank,' Brigid persisted; but then *her* tone softened. 'Look, I'll be over at eight and we'll take it from there.'

When she'd hung up, I went upstairs and packed a suitcase — just some clothes and a few photographs. I left it on the bed with my wallet, my passport, my mobile phone and my car keys, and having splashed on a little more aftershave, I went back downstairs to lay the table.

A stickler for timekeeping, my wife arrived at eight o'clock precisely (*le quart d'heure de politesse* didn't exist in Brigid's language!) and it felt strange when she rang the bell rather than just letting herself in. I didn't make an issue of it, though. It was the sort of trivial point that could lead to a full-blown argument, and I wanted the evening to be as civilised as possible.

Opening the door to her, I enquired as to how the children were doing.

'Fine,' she informed me uninformatively as I took her coat and I hung it up under the stairs.

Brigid hadn't overdressed for the occasion — a denim skirt and a flattering, white blouse — and as I followed her into the kitchen, I could not help but notice how trim she was looking. Her gym classes were evidently paying dividends. Her bum had regained its former pertness, and as I remembered the sexy young thing I'd fallen for years earlier, I felt a twinge I'd not felt in a very long time.

But *easy little fella*!

I watched Brigid inspecting the kitchen, and despite the sour look she gave me, I could tell she was impressed (although to be honest, apart from watching television and fulfilling my own fitness regime, I had little else to do with my time other than clean and tidy).

I offered Brigid a glass of wine, which she initially declined, but she didn't take much persuading. Like a waiter, I poured her a drop to taste, and again I could see she was impressed.

'Are you not having one?' she asked, a little vindictively as I replenished her outstretched glass.

'I told you the other night, I don't drink anymore.'

'No harm in a little one,' she goaded, but I put her straight on the matter.

'For somebody like me, an alcoholic,' it felt good to *say* the word out loud, 'it's black and white. No grey. You either drink, or you don't.'

It is the only time I ever saw Brigid lost for words, and I felt she had a compliment on the tip of her tongue. But if she did, it was never paid, and an awkward silence ensued. Eventually, I realised Brigid was waiting for me to apologise.

'Look, I'm truly sorry about the other night...' I said, sincerely.

'It was despicable behaviour, Frank!'

'I know,' I whispered, hanging my head for effect. 'It will never happen again.'

'Huh!'

'Please, Brigid! I never laid a finger on you before Monday. It was...' I thought for a second. *What best to blame? The move to Ireland? Pressure? Inadequacy?* No, always easiest to blame, '...the drink.'

'No Frank. *You* are to blame. For the assault *and* for the drink-driving.'

I didn't respond, and instead, listened without interruption, as Brigid gave me her standpoint on our marriage. '...We've been drifting apart for over a year, Frank,' she insisted, 'and although you've been a good father, you stopped being a good husband *a long time ago.*

'Hitting me was the final straw, and I am not going to spend the rest of my life living in fear. I am genuinely pleased to see that you are trying to sort yourself out. But I'm afraid it's too little, too late as far as our marriage is concerned.'

Brigid had rehearsed these words, but she didn't sound totally convinced by them. She had not expected to find me, for want of a better word, 'recovering', and there was an unusually compassionate edge to her tone. All of a sudden, I felt peculiarly convinced that she hadn't quite given up on me.

'You can, *of course*, see the children,' she offered, changing tack, 'but only once you've proven that your intention to stay sober is genuine.'

'Where are they tonight?' I asked cautiously.

'My mother's taken them to her sister's in Derry for a sleepover,' she replied flatly.

I wondered where Brigid would be staying, and I also

wondered if she might not be considering a proper reconciliation later on.

But again: *easy little fella!*

'Well, shall we eat?' I asked good-naturedly, hoping she'd got it all off her chest.

'I won't change my mind, Frank.'

'Maybe not,' I nodded meekly, 'but at least hear me out.'

Brigid's intransigent position came as no surprise — moving out was the minimum 'sentence' I could expect for my 'crimes' — but I was ready to play ball.

'Whatever you... *we* decide, Brigid, I need to see the kids.'

'You've not been there for them in weeks. Months even.'

'I know,' I agreed contritely. 'But I'm here now. And I'm sober.'

'Huh!' she snorted.

'Even when I was arrested,' I began my own rehearsed speech with a penitent sigh, 'I was unable to admit that I had a serious problem, and it was only when I hit you that I could see that I had also hit rock bottom...'

I was heartened to see there had been no lasting damage following the assault. The only clue that I'd hit my wife was a small, red mark on her cheekbone.

'...But I've started the long process of dragging myself back up.

'Admission was step one. Step two will be to stay sober. And step three will be to prove to you that I am not a lost cause. Now, I know you must hate me right now, and you have the right to push for a *divorce*,' I paused intentionally, hoping to offend my wife's Catholic conscience with the *D-word*. 'But given time, you might change your mind.'

Brigid smiled; it was edgy and uncomfortable. She still looked hesitant, nervous even, but there was no longer fear in her eyes. Another tense silence ensued, which I broke by suggesting I serve the starter.

Over soup we discussed the children, and although Brigid made sounds about me packing my bags during the main course, she did not categorically ask me to leave, and by the time we were finishing off our dessert, we were chatting nostalgically about happier days — when we were in love; when life seemed like one big adventure.

We spoke about holidays in Egypt and the Maldives, trips to Prague, Budapest and New York, as well as our drunken youth when we partied in Edinburgh, Dublin and Amsterdam. And by the time we'd withdrawn to the sitting room for a coffee, Brigid was laughing heartily as I reminded her about one drunken night in our first flat.

Brigid refused a third glass of wine — 'We all know what can happen if you drink and drive!' she chided but only in jest — and as her mood softened, Brigid shuffled closer to me on the sofa. She even allowed my index finger to run sensuously up and down her thigh, but then she suddenly repelled my advances and pushed me away.

'Sorry,' I apologised. 'It was a bit previous.'

'It's not a question of being previous Frank. I just shouldn't have let it happen.'

'Not tonight maybe.'

'Not ever!' Brigid sobbed, as her eyes filled with tears.

'Come on Brigid. We're still man and wife.'

'No, Frank.' She took a moment to recompose herself. 'It's over.'

'You don't mean that.'

131

'Oh yes I do!' Brigid suddenly seemed just a little too sure of herself.

'I overstepped the mark just then, but we can both see there's still a spark. I know I'm going to have to move out, but the kids need their dad. I need you. And you need a husband.'

'No! That's where you're wrong, Frank. I came here tonight to end it. I want it to be amicable. But nevertheless, I've made my decision. *I* don't need *you* anymore, Frank.'

'You're not being very fair here Brigid!'

'And you're not making this easy, Frank.'

'Why? What?' I remember hesitating for a split second, then a light went on. 'You've been seeing someone else?'

'Yes,' she admitted sheepishly, and I felt my blood beginning to boil.

The bitch had made me feel guilty for giving her a slap, but now, with the full facts to hand, in my book, she got what she deserved. Inside, I was raging, but I managed to check my temper.

'Who?' It was all I could muster in protest.

'It doesn't matter.'

'It fucking well does!' Another hesitation and another light went on. 'Peter Flaherty?'

'He was there for me. You were not. Not since we moved back home.'

'*Home*? *Home*? This isn't *my home*. This isn't even Maeve or Joe's *home*. This is *your home*.'

'We moved for the children.'

'No. *I* moved here for them. You moved here for *you*. Anyway, don't deflect. How long have you and him been...?'

'A couple of months,' she swallowed hard; she was lying.

'You fucking slag!' I couldn't hide my disgust.

'There's the *real Frank*!' she laughed scornfully.

'You won't get me that easily!' I laughed back smugly. Very smugly. I now had the moral high ground. 'All of your *classes*. All of your *nights out*. Fool that I am, I never questioned you. Not once. Not even on that long weekend in Dublin. And that was way more than two months ago!'

Brigid didn't even have the decency to deny the accusation!

'...Perhaps, subconsciously, I knew what you were up to. Maybe that's why I started drinking so heavily. And maybe that's why I hit you.'

'Don't you blame your behaviour on me, Frank!' Brigid snapped back. 'You've been giving me dog's abuse for years! That smack was...'

'If I'd known what you were up to, I'd have hit you ten times harder!' I roared.

'Well, do it again then,' she goaded.

'Hah!' I laughed, regaining control, resisting temptation.

But I needed to calm down.

So, I excused myself and went to the bathroom.

Six

As I sat on the toilet the whole gamut of emotions coursed through my being: anger, sorrow, vengeance, self-pity, fear, loathing, anxiety, devastation.

No wonder sex had been the exception rather than the rule since I'd moved to Ireland. Brigid had been carrying on with Flaherty for... Well, as she'd said, what did it matter how long the affair had been going on?

But how had I not seen it coming?

The fact is, I never spotted the hidden agenda behind her *girls' nights out*, her *exercise classes* and most pertinently, her *political work* — which only goes to show how dumb I really am — but, in hindsight, it all made perfect sense.

To be honest, I hadn't shown Brigid any real affection in years, and on the odd occasion that it did happen, sex, for me, was nothing more than a chore. So maybe Brigid was right: maybe I had brought this all on myself: maybe *I* had driven her into the arms of another man.

Brigid had obviously come to dinner to insist upon a divorce (I'm not sure that she wanted to disclose the affair but sometimes a guilty conscience cannot help but speak) and a divorce was probably in my best interests too.

So, this was not the time to look back in anger; it was the time to negotiate.

'What next, then?' I enquired equably, as I walked back

into the living room. 'I mean, Peter has a wife to consider. And I doubt you can blame Collette as easily as you blame me.'

'We will have to take it one step at a time,' Brigid replied, dispassionately.

'*We*?'

'You and me!' she fired back, but I don't think that was what she meant.

'So, what do you suggest?' I asked, almost agreeably.

'Well, there's nothing to be gained from us blaming each other,' Brigid said neutrally, 'and if we're grown-up about this then there's no reason why we can't come to an amicable arrangement.'

Brigid took the opportunity to lay out what her version of an *amicable arrangement* entailed, and I left her to it, until she started carping on about the financial cost to *Pete* — he apparently stood to lose half of his business.

'What the fuck do I care about him!' I ranted, losing it for just a second. 'You're just rubbing salt into the wounds!'

'Sorry,' Brigid said mournfully; but she didn't really look as if she was. 'Anyway, *we* could buy you out...'

'*We*?' I interjected again, affronted.

'You know what I mean, Frank.' Brigid then paused. '*I* was thinking about £40,000?'

'I bet you were — we've got over £250,000 positive equity in this place alone!'

'Frank,' Brigid smiled falsely. 'Surely money is a secondary issue. Our main concern must be the children.'

In fairness, she sounded earnest when she went on to laud me for *making a real effort*, and she had a point when she asserted that she would be doing almost all of the providing for the children over the forthcoming years.

After that, though, I switched off and allowed my mind to wander: Flaherty, a knife, blood.

I re-joined the one-way conversation when Brigid pressed me about *my* plans, asking a little too keenly about *when* I was going to move back to England.

'I never said I was going back to England!' I contended.

'Well, you can't just continue drifting through life!' she insisted.

'Oh, for fuck's sake Brigid! Give me a chance. I need to get my head around this. And before I can plan to do anything else, I have to answer a drink-driving charge.'

What followed was, like many previous arguments, a constant round of gainsaying. This one essentially boiled down to *when* I was moving out and *where* I was going to live. In the end, Brigid agreed to let me stay in the house until the following weekend — it would give me time to find a place to rent.

The only stipulation I made was that Brigid did not allow Flaherty to move in until after our divorce had come through. She agreed — without hesitation. There were, I supposed, enough seedy hotels that they could use in the interim.

'So? Do you think you will stay in Ireland, Frank?'

'Yes!' I replied emphatically.

'But you're always going on about how much you hate it!' Brigid's irritation gave me something to smile about.

'Well, I want to be close to *my* children.' I insisted haughtily (although, to my shame, I hadn't actually given Maeve and Joe any real consideration thus far). 'I'm trusting you'll grant me regular access — without involving the courts.'

'We'll just have to play it by ear,' she shrugged.

'Maeve and Joe are all I have left!' I pleaded.

'Well, whose fault is that?'

'Oh, fuck off Brigid!'

She never let up!

'...*You* are the one who decided our marriage is over. *You* decided that I don't get a second chance, and we both know that, even if I'd never laid a finger on you, we'd still have been having this conversation. So, give me a break, Brigid! You can see I'm trying to change.'

'A few days off the drink does not constitute a change.'

'How long would then? A week? A month? A year? A lifetime? It's all arbitrary, because even if I did give up for the rest of my life then I'd have to start by giving up for a few days.'

'Sorry.' For once, my wife sounded genuine in her apology. 'I must admit I am surprised, amazed even, by the resolve you have shown this week. And I'm not asking that you stay sober forever, Frank. I don't think you need to go that far. You've just had a low period recently, that's all.

'We did have some wonderful times, Frank,' she smiled wistfully, 'and maybe I asked too much of you. Perhaps the move to Ireland was too much. Perhaps you found the transition too great. But we can't change what's been done. I'll always have a place for you in my heart, Frank, but there's no longer a place for you in my life.'

It was a nice sermon, and I wondered how long she had been working on it.

She was right about one thing, though: we couldn't change the past.

So, I tried to focus on what I could affect. The future — my future.

Whatever else happened, I would be staying in Northern Ireland until after the court hearing, and I would use the time to see if, free from the shackles of a loveless marriage, I could make a life of my own and so remain close to Maeve and Joe.

If it didn't work out then, with forty thousand in my pocket (maybe more if I pushed for it), I would go back to London. That would put considerable distance between me and my children, but the budget airlines would ensure that I got to see them on a regular basis.

'Are you listening to me?' Brigid was yelling. I had drifted off again.

'Yeah ... Well, no! I'm still in shock, Brigid.'

'But we're agreed on one thing: you'll be out of here by next Saturday?'

'I'll be gone,' I sighed, resignedly.

'Where will you go?' she asked, a little more diplomatically.

'What do you care, Brigid?' I growled.

And it all came out.

The hurt apparently went back a very long way. Years of pent-up anger about her dissatisfaction with our marriage and all of my many shortcomings poured forth, in a sustained and vitriolic outburst. And Brigid made sure her final blow was a low blow.

'...And now that I've got myself *a real man*,' she scoffed, 'I want for nothing!'

Charging forward, Brigid went to punch me, but I dodged her feeble effort, and as she went for a second shot, I grabbed her arm.

'Ha!' Brigid screamed manically. 'Why don't you hit me again, Frank? Make yourself feel big.'

She started to push me, but I wasn't rising to the bait. Then, as she lunged at me for a third time, she stumbled and fell onto the sofa and legs akimbo, I got an eyeful of her stockings and suspender belt and the sexy, lace underwear.

Suddenly, a crazed fury welled up inside me — she'd never dressed like that *for me!* — and if I'm brutally honest (which I'm about to be), I was on the point of forcibly taking her. It would have been rape.

I'd not had sex in ages, and fully aroused, I was intent on having my wicked way, but Brigid managed to struggle from my grasp, and it was only as I turned to grab her a second time, that I saw the men in balaclavas.

How long they'd been in the doorway I don't know, but the reason for Brigid's sudden and unwarranted provocation now became perfectly clear. When the verbal assault hadn't brought about a backlash, she had allowed her skirt to ride up to get to a more primitive reaction — and it had worked.

Now, in anticipation of what was to come, I gritted my teeth, trying to show no fear — Brigid wasn't going to get the pleasure of watching me wince and squirm!

And as the masked interlopers took hold of my arms, I smiled menacingly at my wife — *she would pay for this.*

Seven

I hadn't heard *our visitors* entering the house; they just seemed to appear. I guessed Brigid had told them that the back door would be left unlocked, and any noise they may have made would have been covered up by my wife's histrionics.

For a moment, time seemed to freeze, and I tried to take it all in.

There was a look of embarrassment on Brigid's face as she primped herself in front of *her friends*. Then she remembered herself, but her terror was just too phoney — it could have come straight from a silent movie. The only thing missing was the word 'Gasp!'.

The short, skinny one crossed over to Brigid and shoved her down onto the sofa while the taller, sinewy man walked up to me and pushed his face into mine. I glared hard at him in an effort to see if I recognised the eyes behind the masks.

I didn't.

He definitely wasn't one of Brigid's brothers, nor was his accomplice — he was much too small — and it was only as the man walked away from me that I was struck by the troubling thought that these were probably Flaherty's hoods.

I glowered at Brigid, but she would not look up, and with the two men pacing the room like caged animals, I was considering a counterattack when, without warning, I was punched on the side of the face. I could taste blood; it felt like half of my teeth had been loosened, and I readied myself to take my punishment.

I suppose everybody has been told at one time or another by a judicious parent that *what goes around comes around* — well, for me, it had just come around.

There can be no mitigating circumstances when a man strikes a woman, but when my assailant produced a gun from behind his back, my stomach lurched.

Surely, I wasn't going to be killed for one slap?

Then logic kicked in.

Alive — I was a worthless husband.

Dead — I had a life insurance value of over £350,000.

Brigid was about to cash in on her biggest asset, and I had made it easy for her.

I could simply *go missing*.

It might take years for the insurance company to pay out, but eventually they would, and once the dust had settled, she could waltz off into night with her lover. I was wondering if something similar was happening to Collette, when suddenly the butt of the gun connected with the back of my head.

And I was out cold.

Part III
October 2015

One

I don't know how long I was unconscious for, but when I came to, I was sitting face-to-face with my wife in the kitchen. Each of us tied to a chair, each of us gagged.

Brigid's eyes were full of tears and her lip was quivering uncontrollably, her fear was real.

As ever, I had misjudged the situation.

From the moment I had learned who the Carrolls were, I had known that something like this was possible. I had played out the scene countless times in my head, but alas, I did not make any contingency plans — the lazy belief that they weren't smart enough to figure out what I had done.

How *these people* had connected me to Liam's murder was anybody's guess.

And *these people* didn't need the police to eke out their own kind of justice.

I was a dead man walking.

Or rather, a dead man sitting.

Brigid may not have known what this was about, but having grown up in Northern Ireland, she knew full-well that *men in balaclavas* generally baulked at nothing to get what they wanted, and with the taller intruder holding a gun to her temple, my wife knew she was in mortal danger.

As Brigid strained at her shackles, the man was fixing me another steely stare, and dropping the gun to his side, he circled the room and at last, he spoke.

'Who paid you to set my brother up?' he asked directly, as he ungagged me.

'What?' I tried to sound desperate (which wasn't too difficult). 'What the fuck are you talking about?'

Again, without warning, I was punched in the side of my face.

'Let me re-phrase,' he snarled, pressing his nose up against mine, eyeball to eyeball. '*How and why* were you involved in my brother's murder?'

'Honestly mate, I don't have a clue what you're talking about,' I insisted through clenched teeth. Every word was causing me pain, excruciating pain, and as the man, Liam's brother apparently, looked over at his cohort, I began to sob.

To this day, I cannot say if my tears were genuine, or simply for effect, but after another interminable silence, he recommenced.

'Now, let me put it this way: *I know* you were involved in my brother's murder. I can't prove it but *I know* it.' He paused again. 'Now rest assured, *you will be dead* before the night is out. But if you want it to be painless, and you want me to spare your wife, then I advise you to come clean right now.'

'This is bullshit mate!' I decided the best form of defence was attack. 'I don't even know who you are. And what makes you think *I* would be involved in your brother's murder?'

'It's taken me some time to work it all out,' he replied, without answering my question. 'Tracking you down has not been straightforward, and while you might have thought moving over here was a smart idea, that only added to my suspicions.'

He picked me up by the throat then shoved me back down, the chair almost toppling. I was resigned to my fate, but before I did the honourable thing — before I confessed — I wanted to hear *the proof* of my culpability. Surely, he only *suspected*?

'This is no joke, Kelly,' my tormentor growled, using my name as a means of intimidation.

'Do you see me laughing?' I countered, looking him directly in the eyes.

'Two-and-a-half years ago,' he continued, his tone turning solemn, 'my brother was found dead in a lock-up...'

That was when the mask came off.

But if Patsy was expecting a reaction, he didn't get one. The newspaper article had forewarned me that Liam had an identical twin (it went a long way to explaining my sightings of *him* in the months after the murder).

'Liam telephoned me on the last night of his life. To be precise, he left me a message...'

His brother then proceeded to play it back for me:

'Patsy. It's me.

'I'm just in from Dublin, and I thought I might bump into someone in Cricklewood, but there was nobody about. And there's nobody in Kilburn either.

'I guess you're in Liverpool for the match.

'Anyway. I bumped into some bloke who knows our Maire and to cut a long story short, he has a job on — at the British Library of all places.

'He's a librarian or something and he says that there's a rare Charles Dickens' first edition in the library's store-rooms. He says that it's there for the taking and he reckons it's worth ten grand a-piece.

147

'Anyway. I'm just off the phone to him and I'm meeting him at 1.30 tomorr...'

At that moment a band started up in the bar.

'Give me a second...'

I listened as Liam walked outside.

'Right. Where was I? Oh yeah...

'Well, this Francis has a plan of the library for me to check out, but I'm going equipped — just in case he's mugging me off!

'I'll call you tomorrow afternoon to let you know how it goes, and hopefully, I'll see you on Sunday with a few shillings in me pocket...'

'But Liam never called back,' Patsy sighed. 'And the next time I saw him was at the morgue...'

As Patsy put his phone away, I took a moment to reflect.

It appeared I had made two mistakes — one in calling myself Francis (I should've used a completely different alias) and two, in telling Liam where I worked (but I'd had to mention the library to help convince him) — and although the message hardly proved my guilt, it did point a tenuous finger in my direction.

'...Now if someone had wanted *me* dead — or maybe even my sister — then I might have understood. But not Liam. He never really played any part in the family business. He was the only one of us Carrolls with brains. He could have made something of himself. Should've made something of himself,' Patsy mused ruefully. 'But Liam was too fond of the drink.'

'Look. Why don't we just call the police?' I suggested manfully, in an effort to convince Patsy of my innocence.

But Patsy shook his head.

'They had their chance, but they were obsessed with pinning Liam's murder on an associate of ours. They called in the Gards and made an arrest. But, as I told them, it was the wrong man. And although my brother's murder remains a *live* investigation, I don't think the police on either side of the Irish Sea are devoting too much time to it anymore.

'But *I* won't rest easy until I get to the bottom of who killed Liam and why.

'I paid a private investigator to retrace my brother's movements on the night before his murder. There was footage of Liam travelling on the train from Luton to Cricklewood. We also obtained images of him leaving McGowans in Cricklewood and later that night, leaving the pub on Kilburn High Street — making that call to me.

'Unfortunately, Liam's body was not discovered for more than a month, and none of the other pubs which he might have frequented on the Thursday in question had retained their CCTV footage — most places tend to wipe it after a week or two.

'It's a shame because CCTV might have put a face to *this Francis*.

'The police did follow up at the British Library, but every one of the library's Charles Dickens' first editions was accounted for.

'Then they told me what I already knew — my brother had almost certainly been set up.

'We have no idea how Liam got to the lock-up on the Friday afternoon — from the time he left the pub in Kilburn he seems to have vanished into thin air...'

Patsy had so nearly pieced the puzzle together.

His one crucial mistake was to assume that Liam's

meeting with *Francis* was at 1.30 *pm*. This meant I could now *prove* that I didn't kill Liam — I would be alibied by work. But before I shared the *good news*, I still wanted Patsy to outline precisely why he deemed me to be the prime suspect.

'…Then my sister mentioned you in conversation: *'Frank: an old neighbour.'* And I remembered you. You went mad at me one Friday night about a bit of music…'

Another of my many mistakes!

'Anyway, I asked Maire if she thought you might be *Francis*. My sister laughed in my face — insisted you were a family man. She told me how she'd tried to chat you up one time, put it on a plate for you, but you declined the offer…'

I looked at Brigid, and I'm sure I saw guilt in her eyes. Whatever else I may have been as a husband, I had always been faithful. Still, this was no time for points-scoring.

'Maire also said you 'worked for a newspaper or something' and so I instantly dismissed you as a possible suspect.'

'Look,' I groaned, again through gritted teeth. 'I think I can prove to you that I didn't kill your…'

'Ha! Ha! Ha!' Patsy laughed dismissively. 'I know *someone like you* didn't kill my brother! You were simply paid to set him up with some bullshit story about a valuable book. What I want to know is: who put you up to it?'

I was stunned into silence — my 'get out of jail free card' had just been rescinded.

There was now nothing I could now say to *disprove* Patsy's theory.

'You might have actually gotten away with it if I hadn't been listening to a feature on Radio Four the other week about the British Library and the digitisation of its newspaper collection.

'My ears pricked up when *Colindale* was mentioned — and it turns out that British Library Newspapers had been located not half-a-mile from where my brother's body was discovered.

'Francis and Frank. Working for a newspaper and a newspaper library. And you having been Maire's neighbour at one time. There were just too many coincidences for my liking, and I don't believe in coincidence.

'So, I got Maire to go back to where you used to live, and lo and behold, you'd moved — to Ireland, the new owner told my sister.

'He did give Maire a forwarding address — in Armagh — but you'd moved from there too. Mind you, it didn't take me long to find out where you now live!'

Patsy slapped me hard across the face, but I was numb to the pain.

'Now,' he snarled, once again grabbing me by the throat, 'I want you to fill in the blanks for me. And you're going to start by telling me who put you up to it.'

'Huh!' I snorted, frightened to speak — one slip of the tongue and I might give myself up.

'Don't make me kill your wife, Kelly!' Patsy screamed. 'Because I will!'

'What can I tell you?' I cried, playing for time.

Brigid's face was etched with fear. Her life was in my hands — literally — but unable, or maybe unwilling, to do the decent thing, I persisted with my denial.

'…I lived next door to Maire. So what? This is ludicrous. I've done nothing wrong. Your brother's murder quite obviously has nothing to do with me. You've just put two and two together and made five…'

'Don't insult my intelligence!' Patsy roared into my face. 'This is your last chance! Now, who the fuck paid you to set up my brother?'

'I haven't got a clue…'

Whack!

'Don't treat me like a cunt!' he raged. 'Now, we all know you're a dead man, Kelly. It's an eye for an eye, that's all. You for Liam. But if you don't tell me *the who* and *the why* then your wife goes to an early grave too.'

'You'll kill her anyway.'

It was a minor slip that partially betrayed my position of innocence. Thankfully, Patsy didn't pick up on it. Brigid hadn't missed it, though. Staring coldly at me, she *knew* I was guilty as charged.

'On my life,' Patsy persisted, 'if you don't start talking, then your two children will be orphans within the hour.'

He paused, waiting for a response, and as we eyeballed one another, something popped into my head. I don't know if I'd read it in a book, or heard mention of it in a documentary, but what I categorically remember is that it came from the mouth of a high-ranking *Mafiosi* who, recounting the executions he'd overseen, said that, the target of a hit would be dead before he had the chance to realise what was happening.

It convinced me that Patsy was only fishing, and that if I stuck to my guns, then Brigid and I would come out of this parlous situation with our lives. It would mean a death threat hanging over us forever. But it would never amount to anything more than a threat, because we would never go to the police. Or if we did, we did so in the knowledge that the

Carrolls knew who we were and who our children were too.

Then Brigid started frantically fidgeting in her seat. Evidently, she had something to say. And Patsy must have felt it was something worth listening to, because he immediately ungagged her and let her speak.

I often wonder how things might have panned out had my wife just kept her gob shut.

'Tell him the truth, Frank!' Brigid wailed. 'For pity's sake. These people are serious.'

'Tell him, what?' I demanded to know.

The fucking bitch! Informing on me from an uninformed position! Grassing me up!

'Listen to your wife Frank,' Patsy began softly. Then he exploded. 'Now tell me who the fuck set my brother up!'

Patsy signalled to his accomplice, and the other man came across and pointed his gun at Brigid's temple. My wife squirmed in her chair; her body taut in anticipation of a bullet. But I remained silent, looking impassively from Patsy to Brigid to the gunman.

I held sway here: *I* was controlling the situation.

Brigid would only be executed if I confessed, and when *Patsy's number two* shook his head and dropped the gun to his side, my certainty hardened. This man was not a mindless assassin, and he wasn't going to sully his hands with the blood of an innocent mother-of-two, based on the flimsy evidence presented: evidence which amounted to little more than an ambiguous message from Liam and Patsy's overwhelming sense of suspicion.

These people only ever killed *legitimate targets*.

Patsy's accomplice beckoned to him, and the pair stepped outside to talk, leaving Brigid and me to stare at one another.

'What the fuck have you done Frank?' she sobbed.

Her eyes were full of hatred; mine must have been full of guilt.

I didn't respond — how could I?

Instead, I reflected on the good times we'd had together, and in truth, despite our recent troubles, over the years, the good had outweighed the bad.

I recalled our first date — when I was so nervous about what to wear. It didn't matter in the end, though, because Brigid was so drunk when she turned up that she just wanted to take me back to hers to get my clothes off!

I remembered our wedding day in Barbados. Just the two of us, no family, no friends. The only people who we had to keep sweet were ourselves — the happy couple — because that's who a wedding day is really about.

Of course, I thought of Maeve and Joe too, and although my life would soon be moving in a new direction, I would make sure I stayed around to be there for them as they grew up.

Given what I'd just allowed Brigid to go through — having a gun pointed at her head because of something I'd done — I decided I would let her get on with her life; allow her to be happy with Peter.

Their affair had effectively been the final nail in the coffin of our ailing marriage, but I knew the marriage had become unhinged because of me. I had changed. Not Brigid. And she, not unlike Liam, was a victim of what I had done.

The two men came back into the room and I was sure that our torture was nearing its end, because although his face was still rigid with fury, Patsy's tone was softer.

'Why did you set my brother up?' he sighed.

'Even your mate can see that this is all in your head!'

'This is your last chance, Kelly. Just tell me why.'

I needed Patsy Carroll to realise that, if he was fed up with this game of contradiction, then the feeling was mutual. I remember staring at him and laughing contemptuously; the laugh of someone so exasperated by the situation that he didn't care what happened next, and I guess that was the spark, because in the instant it took me to begin and end my snigger, a shot had rung out, and Brigid was dead.

I may not have pulled the trigger, but *I* was responsible for my wife's murder, and as I stared at the gaping hole in the centre of Brigid's forehead, I slumped forward.

My hands were still tied to the chair, and as my heart pounded inside me like a balloon about to burst, I did something I don't care to admit to — I wet myself.

In the next moment, all I could think of was how embarrassing it was for me to have pissed myself in front of *these people*. But then Patsy put his gun to *my* head, and I steeled myself for the same fate as my wife.

It was a nightmare-come-true.

I really don't think I cared whether or not Patsy pulled the trigger — truly, I don't. All I had left was to deny him the truth: let him spend the rest of his days wondering. But before he put me out of my misery, his sidekick interceded.

'You fucking prick, Patsy! I told you it wasn't him!'

Maire didn't need to remove the balaclava for me to realise it was her.

'Well, I'll have to kill him now, won't I?'

Again, I steeled myself, but then Maire cut my hands free. I collapsed in a heap on the floor, and after just a second to gather myself, I got to my feet and spat straight into Patsy's face, taking him unawares. If I'd been more alive to the situation, I would have tried to wrest the gun from his grasp, but I hesitated, and the chance was lost.

Another moment of regret, in a life full of them.

Patsy pushed me back to the ground then put his boot into the back of my head. Automatically, I feigned unconsciousness. Even when he kicked me in the stomach, I managed not to flinch; I didn't groan either. I guess it was enough to convince him that I was out for the count.

Lying motionless on the floor, I contemplated the cruel irony of the situation, because if Patsy and Maire had turned up earlier, I wouldn't have known about the affair, and I might well have done the honourable thing; later, and Brigid wouldn't have been there to kill.

But I suppose every event, tragic or not, can be viewed in such a way, because everything that happens in life is, in one way or another, preventable.

If, for example, on your way to work today, you didn't have the money for a newspaper you might not have stopped off at the newsagents. Therefore, you would have been eighty yards further up the road, oblivious to the fact that the driver of the approaching vehicle had been out with friends the previous evening and had chosen to get behind the wheel even though he knew he was over the limit. With his reactions marginally slower, the driver might not have noticed the Belisha beacons until it was too late and because you were already halfway across the zebra crossing, you might now be dead. Or maybe just hospitalised. Or just badly shaken because you have quick reactions. Or perhaps you avoided the incident altogether because you had money for your newspaper.

Similarly, if Liam hadn't been *connected*, if Brigid had

not been having an affair (or even if she'd just not told me about it), if I'd not hit my wife, if I'd not lost my job (or if I hadn't driven while over the limit), if we'd not moved to Ireland, if I'd not killed Liam (or even if I'd just not seen him going into The Crown), or if I had simply confessed to his murder, then Brigid would probably still be alive.

And it seemed that there was no way for me to escape an equally brutal end.

The drawn-out silence was ended by Maire who sounded calm when she spoke.

'Not here!' she asserted.

'Where then?' Patsy asked.

I heard a lighter spark.

'Put that fucking fag out!' his sister hissed. 'This is obviously a no-smoking house.'

Patsy must have complied, and there was another lengthy silence as his sister thought it through.

'Look!' Maire sounded unnecessarily buoyant. 'We'll throw him in the boot of the car and kill him over at O'Keefe's. Christie will help us bury the body out in the bog.'

'We should just kill him here,' Patsy contended.

'No!' Maire took a moment to think before she elaborated on her plan. 'If we tidy this place up: make it look like a domestic, then we can make it appear as if *this* was down to *him*.'

I couldn't help thinking Maire's was a good plan — but only if I didn't escape — and as I listened to them rooting through the cupboards in search of cleaning products, I tried desperately to come up with a strategy of my own.

I heard them both snap on a pair of rubber gloves (I'd have done the same) then Patsy announced that there was 'a pair of *his and her* trainers over by the back door'. As they changed footwear, Maire suggested they move me before cleaning up, and I played deadweight as they picked me up off the floor.

I knew I needed to make my move before we reached O'Keefe's, and it crossed my mind that this might be my best opportunity — I would catch them off guard — but as they struggled to carry me out of the house, I could feel Patsy's gun in his hand, and I decided it was far too risky.

I was unceremoniously dumped in the boot of the 4x4, face first, then as I listened to their footsteps heading back to the house, I decided I must act.

Beneath my prone body was a holdall. I unzipped it and slipped my hand inside, groping about in the hope of finding a weapon. In a toiletries bag, amongst the shampoos and aerosols I hit upon a pair of scissors, which gave me a chance.

Granted, a very slim chance.

I'd have less than a minute to make it from the car to the safety of the fields beside the house where the dark would hopefully shield me as I made my escape, but as I got onto my knees, I banged my head on the parcel shelf above, and no sooner had I let out a stifled yelp, than the boot sprang open.

'I *feckin* knew you were playing possum!' Patsy raged and again cracked me hard on the back of my head. As I slumped back down, I let go of the scissors, and for a second time, I lost consciousness.

Two

I was still in the boot of the car when I came to, my hands tied behind my back with what felt like a scarf. The engine was working hard, though, which allowed me to scrabble about for the scissors I'd been holding, and once I had them back in my hands, I manoeuvred myself onto my side and manipulated them in such a way, that I was able to snip at the material binding my wrists.

Despite my constricted position, I made short work of my shackles, and I was just starting to flex my fingers when Maire spoke.

'Do you think he'll wake up before we get there, Patsy?' she sounded tense.

'Pull over and I'll whack him now if you want.'

I shuddered, as the opening scene from *Goodfellas* sprang to mind — a kicking body in the boot of a car; still conscious as Joe Pesci's character takes ungodly delight as, time and again, he stabs the man — and as we sped along the back roads of rural Ireland towards a Connemara bog-side, where the Four Horsemen of Connacht awaited my arrival, I knew I had to act fast if I was to avoid a similarly grim end.

I didn't feel afraid, though.

Perhaps because this was not the first time I had come face-to-face with *Death*.

He had, of course, been staring at me down the barrel of a gun just a few hours earlier, as *He* had done on the night Liam dragged me into the lock-up. But in the moment, I was thinking of another close call I'd had with *Him* back when I was a teenager…

We were on holiday in Clacton — mum, dad, Tommy and me, that is — and we'd spent the day on the beach. It was late afternoon; mum was away playing bingo while dad was dozing in a deckchair after one too many Tetleys. So, Tommy and I, without a thought for our safety, took our small, inflatable dinghy on its maiden voyage.

We rowed hard and soon the sandy coastline became our distant horizon, and as we stopped for a breather, lying back in the flimsy vessel, soaking up the early-evening sun, a vast shoal of fish passed by our 'boat' (well it may not have been vast, it may not even have been unusual, but to a young land-lubber like myself, it seemed phenomenal). I was mesmerised as the daredevil fish leapt out of the water, and I was in fits of laughter when one landed in our boat, and my older brother started squealing like a baby.

Calmly, I picked up the sprat, then — and I don't know why — I bit it in two.

Holding the flapping body in my hand, I crunched hard on the dying creature's head, tasting its blood in the back of my throat, and only as I spat the remnants away, did I remember I was not alone.

Tommy looked horrified, but mercifully, my discomfit was short-lived as the distant sound of sirens diverted his attention back to land — and simultaneously we thought of dad.

The people on the beach were now just tiny specks, and

there was no telling which speck was our father, but convinced something bad had happened to him, we began rowing as hard as we could.

A couple of minutes later, two police bikes and an ambulance arrived on the scene, and when we finally clambered out of the water, we scanned the beach for dad, but there was no sign.

The next thing I knew, a policeman was grabbing my arm — I thought he was going to tell me my dad was dead.

'Did the current take you boys out there, son?' he asked, anxiously.

It seemed like such a peculiar question.

'No. We just rowed out there,' I shrugged, sending a second policeman ballistic.

Only then did I realise that the Emergency Services had been called out on our behalf, and as the second officer ranted on about wasting public time and money, his colleague offered Tommy and me a few friendly words of advice.

Then he asked where our parents were.

Naturally, we lied: we told him we'd come to the beach on our own.

His colleague muttered something about them *being in the pub*, but as the lead officer was taking down the details of where we were staying, mum appeared, and she was given a friendly ticking off by the kindly policeman before we were allowed to go on our way.

'No harm done,' PC Fletcher smiled, and he bid us all a good afternoon.

It was another few minutes before we packed up and headed for the pier where dad was waiting. Dad had managed to drift away into the crowd when the police arrived, and he had sent mum down to the beach to take the rap.

As Tommy went with mum to get an ice-cream, dad pulled me to one side to tell me how proud he was. For keeping *schtum*, I supposed. But whatever the reason, it was the one and only time he told me that.

But I digress.

My point here is simply that, later in the afternoon, a riptide dragged two experienced surfers to a watery end — that's how close I was to Death — and ever since, I've always had the peculiar sense that God looks out for me...

So, crouching in the boot of that car, still and silent, I felt Him beside me, keeping an eye on me. But if I was to survive the ordeal *I* would have to create 'an opening' — because the next time the boot opened, a gun would be pointing directly at me.

With Death my certain fate if I did nothing, I unzipped the holdall and rummaged around. In a side-pocket, I found a lighter, and it gave me an idea. The odds were still stacked against me, but I felt hopeful.

At least, I did until Patsy spoke.

'We should just kill him!' he said, apropos nothing, and my heart skipped a beat.

'We stick to the plan, Patsy,' Maire overruled. 'We did a good job back at the house, so when the police start hunting for the killer, they'll be hunting for Kelly.'

Patsy and Maire must have cleaned every inch of the house they'd set foot in (time would prove they had left nothing incriminating behind) and with me safely stowed in the boot, they had every reason to assume their plan would work.

'Well, let's phone Christie,' Patsy suggested, after another interminable silence.

'No!' Maire was adamant. 'We don't phone anyone until we're close to Leenaun. Christie can meet us at the petrol station — he'll have somewhere for us to bury the body. Then, when the gun used to murder that woman surfaces in a few weeks' time — with Kelly's prints all over it — the husband goes from being the prime suspect to being the only suspect... It will be the perfect crime.'

The perfect crime: now where had I heard that before?

'I wanna *do* that smarmy fucker, myself!' Patsy insisted, venomously.

'Patsy. You always let your feelings cloud your judgement,' Maire sighed. 'There really was no need for all this. You read far too much into that phone-message. You saw evidence in coincidence.

'It doesn't matter who *Francis* was — it was probably just a made-up name. Whoever he was, he was sent by the Taggerts. We both know they're responsible for Liam's murder. That poor man in the boot had nothing to do with it.

'And you should never have killed his wife. You said you were just going to talk to him.'

'I was. Truly. But his fucking attitude sent me over the edge!' Patsy raged unapologetically. 'He was too cocksure. And I genuinely didn't mean to kill his wife.'

'Well, you did!' Maire yelled back. 'And once again, it's down to me to clean up your mess.'

Patsy didn't respond to that, well not verbally; and the car again fell silent.

The dimension of time had become meaningless, but it was obviously the early hours of Sunday morning. I hadn't a clue where we were, but I did know we were heading towards

163

Mayo, and when we reached our destination, I had to be ready to spring into action.

On my haunches, in a position of cat-like readiness, with a canister of deodorant in my right hand, and the lighter in my left, I would be ready to make a pre-emptive strike. I couldn't be sure that the lighter was working — it would be a bonus if it was — so I had to assume that the aerosol was my only 'weapon'.

Then suddenly, it dawned on me that I would have a better chance of escape if I could get the car to stop before we reached Leenaun. The Carrolls would be mob-handed in Mayo; at the moment there were just the two of them. And no sooner had the thought popped into my head, than Maire presented me with an opportunity.

'I'm dying for a wee Patsy,' she whined; she sounded as if she'd been dozing.

'For fuck sake!' her brother shouted. 'We're nearly there aren't we?'

'We've another fifty miles to go,' she complained, 'and if we don't stop soon, I'm gonna piss meself!'

'Well, you'll have to go in the bog!' Patsy laughed loudly, as the car came to an abrupt stop.

I listened as Maire opened the passenger door.

'Here. Take one of the loo rolls with ya!' Patsy said, a little more sympathetically. 'And hurry up!' he called after her as she slammed the car-door shut.

Then I started to count. At thirty, I reckoned Maire had had enough time to get settled, and so I started to groan. Feebly but audibly. My chances would be further improved if I only had one of them to take on.

'Oh shite!' Patsy gurned, unhappy at having to get out of

the warm car. 'He's fucking stirring Maire!' he shouted into the night, as he unlocked his door.

I guessed Patsy had his gun.

I had a canister of Sure.

At best, I would get one 'shot'.

The boot clicked, and my *cell-door* sprang open.

With the rear lights shining on him, I could see Patsy clearly — he was face-on with his weapon at his side. I seemed to have plenty of time to think about what to do next, and before Patsy had levelled the gun at me, I rose from my prone position, pressed down hard on the deodorant and simultaneously flicked the lighter — and it worked like a dream.

A huge flame billowed into Patsy's face, and before he could get a shot off, I had kicked him to the floor. With the higher ground, I had been able to leap out of the car and, leading with my right foot, I had landed a firm blow right in the heart of Patsy's chest. As I came down on top of him, I instinctively went for his right arm, biting it hard until he relinquished his hold on the gun.

I got to my feet first, kicked the gun into the ditch, and Patsy made a big mistake in going for it, because with the keys in the ignition and the engine still running, I went for the driver's seat.

There was a rustling in a nearby bush, and I could just about make out Maire who was hurriedly pulling her knickers up — they were white, almost fluorescent in the dark; and I remember feeling a definite *twinge*.

'You're a dead man, Kelly!' she screamed, as she raced me to the steering wheel.

But she was nowhere near quick enough and I was off.

Not in a flash — I was afraid of stalling — but fast enough for the Carrolls to soon become distant figures in the wing mirror, and they had disappeared out of sight before they'd found the gun.

I made random lefts and rights on the dark, lonely, rural roads until, after about ten minutes, I felt it was safe to pull over. In the small lay-by, I tried to gather my thoughts — I didn't know where I was, nor where I was going — and my first thought was to go to the police.

But out of pure self-interest, I never did.

If I grassed up the Carrolls for Brigid, then they'd simply return the favour and give me up for Liam. If convicted, 'life' would probably have amounted to no more than fifteen years. But it would have been a long stretch. The Carrolls would know people on the inside who could *sort me out properly* and I would have had to spend every second of every day looking over my shoulder; and it was in that moment, as I sat gripping the steering wheel, that I resigned myself to the life of a fugitive.

I set off on the road again — on the lookout for a signpost with a familiar place-name — and very soon, I had a choice to make: *right for Boyle or left for Tulsk?*

I'd never heard of Tulsk, so I chose right, and now with a vague sense of where I was, the next part of my plan was to find somewhere to lie low. It would buy me time and allow me to get a line on how the police were thinking.

I was hoping that I might yet engineer a solution to my predicament — a plausible explanation that would implicate Patsy for Brigid's murder and excuse me for Liam's. But all these years later, I am still thinking on it.

The back of my head was sticky with blood and my body

was aching all over. It felt as if one or two of my ribs might be broken and my left cheek too was painful to the touch. I had limited movement in my jaw, but all in all, it could have been worse; much worse.

As I drove, I groped in my pockets and I suddenly realised I had left my wallet back in Keady — on the bed with my suitcase, my passport and my keys. That meant the only money I had on me was the forty pounds I'd found in my trousers when I was getting dressed for dinner.

Instinctively, I scrabbled about in the driver's side-pocket and found a pile of loose change. There must have been twenty or thirty euros, all told — not that I could spend it just yet, but it meant one less thing to worry about.

At 4.56 (if the clock in the car was to be trusted) I happened upon a small town: Gurteen.

I decided Gurteen might just be the sort of rural spot which offered up a place for me to hide — and I needed to find somewhere fast, because very soon the sun would be rising, and someone was bound to notice the *northern plates*.

Given the hour, the town was deserted, and I stopped at the crossroads, hoping for divine intervention. None was forthcoming, so I chose right. After a couple more miles, I reached yet another crossroads. This time I went left, continuing along a narrow, winding road until an ancient-looking sign announced my arrival in County Mayo.

As I headed deeper into Mayo's bog-land, I sensed the surrounding landscape becoming just that bit more desolate and barren, and after about another half-mile, as I was driving past a small lake on my right, I spotted what appeared to be an abandoned cottage on my left.

Set back from the road in an overgrown field, it was at

least a quarter-of-a-mile from its nearest neighbour, and although, in the dark of night, it was impossible to be absolutely certain that it was deserted, I had to take a chance.

I pulled the car onto a grass verge about a hundred yards further on up the road, and having cut the engine, I got out and wandered back to the rusted entrance gate. The gate was secured with a twisted coat-hanger, which didn't take much to disentangle, and having opened it wide, I walked up the rutted lane. It soon became clear that this place had not been lived in for years — probably decades — so I doubled-back on myself and reversed the car into the yard behind the cottage.

Despite its state of disrepair, this was still somebody's property, so I knew I would have to stay on my mettle, and while I still had darkness as an ally, I walked down to the lake on the opposite side of the road to clean myself up.

Leaning over the water's edge, I cupped my hands and tentatively splashed my face; it was absolutely freezing. I could feel the open wound on the back of my head continuing to ooze blood, and I was sure it could have done with a stitch or two — unfortunately, I couldn't pop into A & E for a professional opinion.

Afraid that the lake water might cause it to become infected, I decided to leave well alone — there were a few bottles of Evian and some toilet roll on the back seat of the car which I would try to clean it up with — then after *a quick slash*, I walked back to the house.

I didn't re-secure the gate, though — just in case I needed to make a quick getaway — but I did pull it across to give the impression that it had never been opened. Then, back inside the car, using the water and a tube of antiseptic cream I found in Maire's toiletries bag, I cleaned the cut as best I could

Curling up on the back seat, I tried to find sleep, and although a million and one thoughts were racing round my head — foremost amongst them, *when would Brigid's murder hit the headlines?* — I dropped off fairly quickly.

It was the sound of a distant tractor that woke me up.

My eyes were stinging like mad — I had forgotten to remove my contact lenses — and I thanked the Lord when I found solution and a case — again in Maire's toiletries bag. I emptied Maire's lenses out of the receptacle and refilled it with the saline, then I took out my own lenses and was granted respite.

I only fell half asleep this time, drifting in and out of forgotten dreams, and it was near ten o'clock when I decided to get up. I said another 'thank you' when I remembered the glasses in my trouser pocket, and I put them on before examining my injuries.

My left cheek had a noticeable depression, confirming my unprofessional diagnosis of a fracture or a break. My ribs were probably just bruised, maybe cracked, and although painful, my jaw was tractable. The cut on my head had started to scab and was no longer seeping, but given what had happened to my wife, I realised I had got off lightly.

The morning was a wet and dreary one, and with the dim daylight barely able to break through the thick, dense greenery which shielded the rear of the property, it felt like winter. But despite the freezing cold, I didn't dare switch the engine on.

Instead, to get the blood circulating, I decided to stretch my legs, wandering around the dark, grey-stone cottage, which had once played home to a family of six, or maybe more. I couldn't help but feel mournful that such a fine property had been let go to ruin. In London's green belt, or more pertinently in Dublin's affluent outskirts, a building with so much character would have fetched the best part of a million. But here in *deepest, darkest Mayo* the house, like so many others, stood derelict — deserted by former inhabitants who, unable to scrape a living from the land, were forced to travel the world in search of work and wealth.

Over the coming days though, for me, this particular cottage would prove priceless.

I dared to climb the rotten, wooden staircase up to the first floor where I found a mouldy armchair and a coffee table, that once upon a time, had been home to woodworm. The chair retained its form and didn't collapse under my weight when I sat in it, and having moved the chair and table over to one of the upper windows, I settled down with my feet up, peering through the grime, waiting to see if anybody was out and about on this rainy Sabbath morning.

Nobody appeared, and as I picked at a couple of threads on my trousers, I smiled — because given the ordeal they'd been through, they looked remarkably clean. The trousers would have to last me a while — weeks or maybe months — and although they were damp at the crotch and must have stank of piss, happily, I couldn't detect my own stench.

As I continued sitting there, waiting for time to pass, freezing half to death, I wondered if the Carrolls had anything to donate to *this charitable cause*, and with nothing better to do, I went back 'downstairs' to sift through their holdalls.

Maire's bag contained just a pair of plain white cotton knickers, a change of socks and a navy hoodie. Of more use would be her toothbrush and toothpaste, her moisturiser and the tube of antiseptic cream.

Patsy, on the other hand, had 'left me' some nice bits: a

pair of jeans, two pairs of clean briefs, two pairs of socks, a grey hooded Gap sweatshirt, a Lacoste t-shirt, a pair of suede Nike trainers and a pack-a-mac.

Patsy's clothes were all medium and were certain to be a tight fit; a very tight fit (I was an extra-large the last time I bought anything new), but as I'd be *living rough* for the foreseeable future, how I looked was a minor detail on my list of concerns.

Despite the state of my own clothes, and even though I was absolutely foundered, I decided against wearing anything of Patsy's until the time to move on came, and as I continued rooting through his holdall, I was heartened to find a thick bath towel and his toiletries bag crammed full of shampoos, shower gels, disposable razor blades, shaving gel, nail scissors and a comb.

All I needed now was a bath!

At midday, I switched on the radio, but there was no mention of Brigid's murder on the RTE news. This left me in something of a quandary. I needed to eat, but could I chance going back into Gurteen?

I had water, which if rationed, would last a few days, and so, feeling safe, I decided not to take any risks.

While I waited to see what was reported in the next bulletin, I went through the rest of the car to see what else Patsy and Maire had brought.

There were the two toilet rolls and five bottles of Evian on the backseat, and I found some bleach in the boot. But no food. Then, as I rooted about in the glove compartment, my heart leapt as, hidden beneath a road map and a pair of faux-leather driving gloves, I found €640 — hardly a king's ransom, but it would buy me some time.

At one o'clock, Brigid's murder finally hit the RTE headlines:

'Lead story this hour: Sinn Fein council candidate, Brigid Kelly has been found dead at her home in Keady, County Armagh. Police are looking for her estranged husband, Frank Kel...'

Unable to listen, I switched off the radio and went back upstairs where I sat in 'my chair' to consider what I'd done. Appallingly, only now did I spare a thought for my children — two lives ruined before they'd begun — and although I like to believe the tears I shed as I sat in that cold and unwelcoming room were for Maeve and Joe — and their mother too — deep down, I know they were mostly tears of self-pity.

Only a need to go to the toilet got me out of my seat, and using an old shovel that I found in the yard — more rust than metal — I dug a small trench in a tract of rain-sodden ground which would serve as a 'latrine' until I moved on; and having done *the necessary*, I lay down in the back of the car, listening to the rain.

Delirious with hunger, I couldn't turn over, and so I got up and went back 'into the house', back on sentry duty. From my post, for hour upon mind-numbing hour, I watched the road in front of the field — my eyes fixed on it like a hawk's — waiting for the Gards to show.

But nobody ever came; nothing ever happened.

Just four cars passed by on that miserable Sunday afternoon, and by nightfall, I realised I would probably be able to shelter in this derelict, isolated property for as long as I wanted — or, at least, until hunger got the better of me.

At seven o'clock, I decided I must listen to the news report in full — I had to know if police fingers were pointing in just one direction, or maybe, just maybe, Patsy and Maire had left something incriminating behind at the house; something that might put me in the clear:

'Top story at seven continues to be the police hunt for thirty-five-year-old Frank Kelly following the discovery of the body of his estranged wife at lunchtime today.

'Thirty-three-year-old Brigid Kelly, a prospective Sinn Fein councillor, was found at the family home with a single gunshot wound to the head...'

I didn't turn off the radio, but I didn't take in another word, and as the newsreader moved on through the other headlines, I went outside to think — mainly about the Carrolls who I could only assume, for reasons similar to mine, had not gone to the police.

With nothing else to do, using Maire's bag as a makeshift pillow, I lay back down in the car and tried to sleep, but again, despite feeling desperately tired, I just couldn't drop off.

I was numb with the cold and aching all over. The pain in my ribs was making breathing difficult; my head was throbbing (as much from the stuff going on inside it as the cut to the back of it); and after hours spent tossing and turning, unable to take any more, I got up.

It was the middle of the night, but the rain had relented, so under the cloak of the early morning dark, I ventured out into the field — *my field* — and watched the world around me waking up.

The only house-light I could discern was a very remote one, and the only sound was the distant lowing of cattle, so I decided to risk switching on the car engine. I turned the heater up — full-blast — and when I could feel the blood in my hands, I went back upstairs to watch the world go by and ponder my next move.

It didn't feel anywhere near as cold on the Monday — the weather suddenly felt unseasonably mild — and once again, not much happened in this forgotten Mayo outpost.

I finally found sleep, and although it was only for two or three hours, I woke feeling refreshed (well, relatively speaking). I went back down to the car and drank a whole bottle of Evian, but this only added edge to my hunger, and knowing I would not be able to eat again until I came out of hiding (which wasn't going to happen until *my* story was no longer headline news), I went in a search of food — a Mars bar, an apple, absolutely anything would have done.

As I went through the side-pockets of Patsy's holdall, although I didn't find anything to eat, I did find a deck of playing cards (one of life's greatest invention; the internet of a bygone era) which would help pass the time, and then, as I took out the bath towel, something dropped out: a freezer bag.

And sealed inside was a gun.

I'd seen enough movies to know it was a semi-automatic of some description, and I quickly worked out how to unload the magazine from the handle, and then how to empty the bullets from the magazine. There were six in all, and having reloaded, I took aim at the trees.

With my trembling finger, I squeezed the trigger.

But nothing happened.

It took me a few more minutes to work out that a round had to be chambered before a shot could be fired, but prudently, I chose to leave my first shot for another day, and after removing the magazine from the handle, I stashed the two parts of the gun under the driver's seat before switching on the radio to listen to the news.

My story was already the third item — your fifteen minutes of fame doesn't last long! — and the tone of report had softened slightly with the police releasing news that my wallet, my passport, my mobile phone and my car all remained at the house.

Doubt seemed to be shrouding my whereabouts as I evolved from 'a suspect' to 'a person of interest'. However, there was no mention of a third party at the house — Patsy and Maire must have been extremely thorough — and although the police would eventually declare me a murder victim too, by the time that happened I had long since moved on.

Three

But for Patsy's deck of cards, I would probably have gone stir-crazy in that forgotten house — hand after hand I played: patience, poker, pontoon, gin rummy and cribbage; for imaginary stakes against imaginary opponents.

And still I cheated!

But it helped pass the time.

Nothing of note happened in the six days and nights I was holed up there — trapped in time — and I survived on a twice daily ration of water as I waited for Brigid's murder to slip from the public consciousness.

By the Wednesday, the story did not receive a single mention on any of the radio stations I tuned into — local or national — and weak as I was, I decided to hang it out until Friday night before I dared break cover.

The plan was to head for Dublin where I hoped I could 'lose myself' in amongst the city's unfortunates, and although I had the option of driving straight there, my plan was to go via Westport — a quaint holiday town I'd visited three or four times in the past — and dump the car on the outskirts.

I would then take the train to Dublin — I'd used the direct service from Westport once before — and although travelling by public transport was a definite risk, I felt it was a risk worth taking.

If I made it to Dublin, I would have to live as an itinerant for weeks, possibly months — the longer I could hack it the better — but once I'd served my time on the streets, I would check into a boarding house, clean myself up and then try to find some cash-in-hand work.

I wouldn't need to earn much — just enough for board and lodgings and maybe a little extra to pay me into the cinema or the swimming pool. With time, I hoped I might be able to re-build some sort of life for myself on the peripheries of normal society.

But I was getting ahead of myself.

As the evening drew in, I laid out the clothes I would be wearing to Dublin: Patsy's jeans, a crew neck t-shirt, his hooded sweatshirt, his trainers, his pants and a pair of his socks. A fortnight previously these items would have been far too small for me, but with circumstance forcing me to lose so much weight, I was hoping I might be able to squeeze into them.

Mind you, I would be changing back into my own filthy rags as soon as I reached Dublin. Patsy's clothes I intended to keep clean and dry until the time came for me to check into that boarding house.

I gathered up anything I wouldn't be taking, and dumped it all in the latrine, and one last time, I sniffed Maire's big knickers (it's hardly my biggest crime but her faint womanly scent had kept me going) and *when I was done*, I placed them on the passenger seat for later.

I had one last wee (I hadn't produced anything solid in days) then filled the hole in, and although a little obvious, it was doubtful that anybody would come by and notice it before nature had abetted me in the cover-up.

For the next few hours, I dozed on the back seat, listening to the radio, until at midnight, I took off the clothes I was wearing, folded them into Maire's holdall and prepared for what was going to be the hardest part of my night.

Naked as the day I was born — save the trainers on my feet — with a bottle of Maire's expensive-looking shampoo in one hand, and Patsy's towel in the other, I made my way down the stony track to the bottom of the lane, opened the gate and darted out across the road.

Having kicked off my trainers, I tentatively dipped a toe in the water. It stung like hell, but I had absolutely no intention of dragging the torture out, and leaving the towel on the roadside, I dived into *my bath*.

The intensity of that moment diminished all my other aches and pains — the throbbing at the back of my head, the discomfit in my ribs and the soreness on the left of my face — and after I'd *taken the plunge*, I don't think things ever seemed quite so bad.

I gave my body time to acclimatise, then forced myself to swim for a full two minutes — until I'd counted to one hundred and twenty. I returned to the shallows, and once I'd got a firm footing in the silt, standing knee-deep in the water, I washed myself methodically from top to bottom — hair, face, arms, back, torso, nether regions, legs and finally feet.

I ducked back under to rinse off then scrambled out of the lake and dried myself at the water's edge. Shivering violently, I struggled to slip my trainers back on, but having done so, I scurried back across the road, and leaving the gate wide open, I sprinted back to the car.

Before getting dressed, I sat down behind the wheel, turned the engine over and put the heater on until the warm had returned to my body. Then I put my clothes — or rather Patsy's — on which, if anything, felt a little loose.

Next, using the last of the bottled water and the last of Maire's toothpaste, I cleaned my teeth, and after spraying myself with some of Patsy's deodorant, for the first time since I'd left Keady, I got some proper sleep.

I woke with a start: 4.47.

Almost time to go.

I reached under the seat for the gun parts, which I reassembled and wrapped in the damp towel. I hid it at the bottom of Maire's holdall beneath my dirty clothes, and then I put Maire's holdall inside Patsy's larger one.

Finally, I took the faux-leather gloves from the glove-compartment — I would not remove them until after I'd dumped the car — and I 'bleached' the interior using Maire's knickers and the bottle of Parozone I'd found in the boot earlier in the week; the exterior would be wiped clean when I reached Westport.

In the dark, I took one last walk round *the old place* and listened to the night air: silence.

I got back into the car, manoeuvred it from its hiding place, and using just the sidelights, I reached the road. I hurried out, and having re-secured the gate with a twist of the wire hanger, I was set to go.

I drove slowly for a few hundred yards before turning on the headlights, and then I snaked along the deserted back roads, on the lookout for a signpost. Castlebar was the first town name I recognised, and about an hour after I'd set off, I was closing in on Westport.

With two or three kilometres to go, I turned off the main road and headed up a small, country lane. In the dark, it was impossible to know if there were houses nearby, but even if there were, I had no choice but to assume that nobody would be awake to see me dump the car.

I parked up at a point where the road widened — at the gate of a field — trusting to luck that the farmer didn't report it before I was on the train to Dublin. I gave the interior one final wipe down then turned my attention to the exterior, concentrating on the handles and the boot.

I threw the bleach and Maire's knickers into Patsy's holdall, which I zipped up and slung over my shoulder, I then locked the car, put the keys in my pocket, and with my hood up and my head down, I walked at a steady pace back towards the main road and on into town.

Each time a car flew past, I held out a half-hearted thumb, but only three or four passed me on the road, and thankfully none stopped. By the time I reached Westport, it was still dark, but with the town beginning to stir, I had to be on my guard.

I had chosen Westport because I was vaguely familiar with the town's layout and because I was hoping that another transient tourist boarding the train to Dublin, would pass through unnoticed and unrecognised, and although I was relying on memory to get me to the station, happily, as I passed the Castle Court Hotel, it all came back to me. I took the next left, and at just before seven, I entered the station where I was delighted to find the ticket-office already open.

Before I paid my fare, though, I paid a visit to the 'gents' where I took the opportunity to examine my reflection in the mirror, and I have to admit that I didn't *look myself.*

I had lost a fierce weight, and the damage to my cheek and jaw gave the left side of my face a sunken look; my beard had thickened out nicely, and peppered with a sprinkling of grey, it definitely made me look older; my 'disguise' was further helped by those awful glasses that I'd not worn in years; and to add to the subterfuge, I was also going to make sure that I didn't *sound myself* either.

So, having made *himself* presentable, it was my *South African* alter-ego who came out of the toilets, and having crossed the station foyer, *he* looked the vendor straight in the eye as *he* purchased 'a single to Dublin' using one of Patsy's fifties.

And the accent must have been passable, because the cashier didn't bat an eyelid.

I was starving — literally! — but *the South African* had to content himself with two cups of coffee from a vending machine — one of life's overlooked luxuries, a hot drink on a cold morning — and although the growing number of passengers milling about on the platform were making him self-conscious, *the South African* held his nerve, and he felt a huge surge of relief when, finally, he was able to board the train.

Now he could pretend to sleep.

The South African was obliged to look up when the inspector asked to see his ticket, and the pretence continued all the way to Athlone without further intrusion; but there, a portly, middle-aged woman chose to sit beside him, and she proceeded to read her broadsheet as if he was invisible. But as he lay his head back down, *the South African* realised this was actually a blessing, and the lady's newspaper provided him with 'cover' for the rest of his journey to Heuston.

The train arrived in Dublin at just after eleven, and the city streets were already starting to get busy. Necessity compelled *the South African* to join the Saturday hordes, and he ventured into a 'One Euro' store just off O'Connell Street, where he bought a sleeping bag for ten Euros, a roll mat for six, a digital watch for three and a pen-torch for the advertised price.

The cashier — 'Tara' according to her name-badge — looked as if she'd had a heavy night, and without a word and without looking up, she scanned each item — 'Beep! Beep! Beep! Beep!' — at something of a snail's pace.

'Twenty Euro,' she eventually informed *the South African* who handed her another of Patsy's notes, and having run her pen over it, she gave him his receipt, again without looking up.

From the 'One Euro' store, *the South African* went to the tourist information office where, this time, the lady behind the counter looked him straight in the eye.

'*Thinks!*' *the South African* nodded sheepishly, as she handed over a rudimentary but fairly concise map of the city, but he held her stare and again there was no challenge.

After studying the map in a bus-shelter, I decided that, later on, I would head out along one of the canals in search of somewhere to shelter, but before I sought refuge for the night, I needed to make my first foray into the world of the beggar.

I used a public toilet as a changing room, and having folded Patsy's clean clothes into a carrier bag which I put inside his holdall, I re-emerged through the automatic door, dressed in my own filthy jumper, hoodie, combat trousers and trainers, ready to do battle

I only knew Dublin as a tourist — Temple Bar, Grafton Street, pubs and clubs, shops and restaurants — and for the next few weeks, these popular city centre spots were going to be my *place of work*.

On that first Saturday afternoon, I huddled down in a doorway just off Henry Street, crossed legged with a discarded paper cup at my feet. With plenty of passers-by, it seemed like a good spot, but in the two long hours I sat there, I didn't make four Euros.

Still, I was grateful for every penny.

Begging may have felt demeaning and soul-destroying, but it paid for my dinner that evening — sandwiches bought from the 'reduced items' chiller in a small Centra. I also bought two days' worth of supplies — beans, bananas, yoghurts, toothbrush and toothpaste, toilet rolls, milk and water — and with my groceries loaded, I traipsed off towards the Royal Canal in search of somewhere to sleep.

I walked for a mile or so before I spotted a portacabin within the grounds of disused business premises that looked vacant. There was an 'under offer' notice fixed to the surrounding fence and I guessed it wouldn't be long before everything was razed to make way for more apartment blocks. For now, though, it remained empty.

I glanced up and down the towpath — nobody — and I was up and over the fence in a matter of seconds. The door to the portacabin was, as expected, padlocked. Peering in through a side-window, I could see it had served as an office of sorts in the past, but the place had been left in a mess. After another quick 'shuftie', I lobbed a brick through the window and waited in the shadows for the night watchman to make an appearance.

I gave it a good half-hour, but nobody came, so in the end, I clambered in, and once I'd rolled out my mat on the carpeted floor, I settled down to eat for the first time in a week.

My jaw still didn't feel quite right, so I began with a litre of milk. Next, I opened a tin of beans which I *gulped* straight from the can, and only then did I try eating the sandwiches —

which I just about managed. After a 'dessert' of yoghurt and banana, I washed it all down with a few glugs of water, and hunger curbed, I sat down to let my food digest.

Before I turned in for the night, I brushed my teeth, and having stripped to my underwear, I 'climbed into' the sleeping-bag and lay down on the floor, using the holdall as a pillow.

I soon found sleep, but at 03.34 — I checked on my new watch — I was woken from my slumber by a gentle pitter-patter on my sleeping bag. I thought there must be a leak somewhere; but it wasn't rain coming in through the roof, it was the sound of tiny feet: rats!

I let out an involuntary squeal and sat bolt upright as the vermin darted for cover. Given the hour, I had no real choice but to stay put, but I didn't sleep another wink. For the rest of the night, I gripped the top of my sleeping bag in balled up fists, praying (literally) that if I let *them* be, then *they* would return the favour.

When morning came, I searched in every nook and cranny, but mercifully I seemed to have scared the rats off. I couldn't go back to sleep though, and with nothing else to do, I spent the whole day playing cards, once again waiting for time to pass.

I set the alarm on my watch for six on Monday morning — I was worried that someone might appear; that I might be arrested — and after a day spent skulking the streets and hunkering down in a shop doorway, I made just enough to pay for my dinner, which was again purchased from the 'reduced items' chiller in Centra.

With nowhere else to go, I decided to return to the lock-up, praying that my furry friends did not make a re-appearance. And my prayers were answered. My Tuesday,

Wednesday and Thursday followed an almost identical pattern. However, on Friday, even before I had climbed in through the portacabin window, I could hear *them* — lots of *them*.

As it was dry, I decided to carry on further along the canal in search of somewhere more inviting, and it was past closing time before I eventually found an accommodating spot — in an alleyway behind a pub.

I rolled out my mat, and using some discarded plastic sheeting to shield me from the elements, I settled in behind a tall stack of empty beer crates, not expecting to be disturbed until the morning.

But just as I was nodding off a 'courting couple' arrived.

'…Just stick it in me,' she was saying, on the other side of the crates.

There followed a prolonged bout of grunting and groaning before her lover made one final elongated moan and I guessed it was all over — for him anyway. The pair sauntered off, back up the alleyway, but unable to re-settle, I was soon following in their wake.

I wandered back into town along the Liffey and ended up in Fairview Park, where there seemed to be plenty of other waifs and strays hanging about — members of Dublin's underclass: men and women down on their luck — drunks, drug addicts, people with mental health issues, and maybe even the odd fugitive like me.

I was just glad I had Patsy's gun.

I followed the footpath around to the opposite side of the park where I found a sheltered spot, in behind some bushes, close to a private gym. It wasn't the Gresham but it was dry. So, I rolled out my mat, and with the gun in my hand and the safety on, I settled down for the night.

Nobody bothered me, though.

Not on that first night, nor on any of the subsequent thirty that I dossed down there.

During that time, my days were spent squatting down on the pavement, relying on the generosity of strangers to pay for my dinner, while my nights were spent in the bushes; but after more than a month of rough sleeping, I decided it was time to try moving back into the real world.

Close to Mountjoy, I had spotted a hostel that appeared to be used exclusively by foreign nationals. It seemed like the sort of place *the South African* might avail of, and at just after nine on his sixth Monday morning in Dublin, my alter-ego walked up the impressive, whitewashed entrance steps and pressed the bell.

Over the intercom a voice asked him the nature of his business.

'I was wondering if you had a room available?' *the South African* enquired politely.

Without further ado *he* was buzzed in.

With rising damp on the walls and a pungent aroma of sweat, mould and fried food lingering in the air, the house was not quite so impressive on the inside. But the landlady, Eleanor, seemed pleasant enough.

'All rooms are single,' she informed *the South African*. 'One night: €28. One week: €175.'

Proffering €175, *the South African* signed in under the name Graeme Smith, and having shown him to his room, Eleanor handed him the key and she told him — in no uncertain terms — the house rules.

Guests were not permitted 'under any circumstance', ditto alcohol; boarders had to vacate the building by nine-thirty every morning and were not permitted to return until six in the evening; and the front door was locked at 'ten-thirty sharp' every night.

Despite the fact that I had not washed in a month — I hadn't even changed my clothes — Eleanor was too polite to comment, but she did point out that there was a communal bathroom on each floor, and that *the South African* still had half-an-hour before he needed to leave the premises.

I took the hint.

As soon as I closed the door behind me, I stripped and headed straight for the bathroom with Patsy's shampoo and shower gel in hand. It felt like heaven to stand under the powerful stream of hot water — another of life's overlooked luxuries — and I might have stayed there all day had I not been up against the clock.

Back in my room, I dried myself quickly then arranged my toiletries (or rather Patsy's) in the cabinet beneath the sink in the farthest corner of the room. I sprayed myself with deodorant and dressed in the clothes I'd worn on the train journey from Westport to Dublin, and having gathered up my dirty clothes and trainers, I fired the lot into Maire's holdall.

I then took a long, hard look around the room but could see nowhere to stash the gun, so I decided to carry it around with me, and having counted the money in my pocket — €540 in notes, €54 in change, plus £40 sterling — I double-checked *the safety*, tucked the gun down the front of my jeans and walked out into the dank corridor where I could hear Eleanor vacuuming.

The surprise in Eleanor's eyes as her 'cleaned up' tenant bid her a good morning, was patently obvious, and as he left to do his laundry, *the South African* could not contain a mirthful smile.

There was a launderette just around the corner from the hostel, and having dumped everything — bag and all — into one of the large machines, I paid for a cupful of detergent, and once the cycle was in progress, I headed for Penneys.

Working off a vague mental list, I had everything ticked off in less than ten minutes: a pair of walking shoes, eight pairs of thick woollen socks, two pairs of chinos, a fleece, a raincoat, a pack of five polo shirts, two jumpers, gloves and a woolly hat, underpants, thermal vests and a pair of long johns.

Everything was selected on grounds of practicality and price (fashion and style did not enter the equation), and although I knew the weight had been dropping off me for weeks, I was still shocked to find I was now just a thirty-two inch waist (the last pair of trousers I'd bought — for my brother-in-law's birthday — had been a size forty-two inch) while jumpers, t-shirts and underwear were now all a loose-fitting medium rather than a snug-fitting extra-large.

I was doing my best to act naturally as I headed to the checkout, but the more I tried, the more conspicuous I felt. As I queued, I could feel the eyes of the world on me, and I could do nothing to prevent myself from constantly staring at the floor.

A nudge in the back hurried me along.

'Till eight is free there,' the lady behind me tutted.

'S-sorry,' *the South African* stammered, and without looking up, he shuffled to the designated till where the young cashier gave an audible sigh with each item she scanned and bagged. It made for a disconcertingly prolonged and public wait, but *the South African's* purgatory was finally brought to an end when she demanded payment.

'158.60!'

The South African proffered three fifties and a ten, and once the cashier had handed him his change, he began to breathe a whole lot easier.

However, just inside the main door, a burly security guard blocked his path.

'Excuse me sir,' the guard said, menacingly.

'Yis?' *the South African* replied calmly.

Eye-contact was unavoidable and everyone within earshot turned and stared.

'Have you a receipt for *all* of the goods in your bag?'

'Er, yis,' *the South African* nodded and produced said docket.

'Mmm…'

The lumbering prick took an age to scan the receipt, leaving *the South African* in full public gaze, grinning inanely, thinking about the loaded gun tucked down the front of his pants.

'Very good,' the security guard smiled, giving everyone a glimpse of his tar-stained teeth and *the South African* a whiff of his smoker's breath. 'Are you working here or just visiting?'.

'Working,' *the South African* politely lied.

'What part of Oz are you from, mate?' the guard enquired chummily.

Was my accent that bad!

'Pretoria!' *the South African* smiled as he went on his way.

'Oh, right!' the guard nodded.

The dimwit!

It was a very scary moment, but I reflected that, while half-a-dozen people, maybe more, had witnessed the incident (and every onlooker had had ample opportunity to scrutinise my face as I answered the security guard's charge) nobody had recognised *me*, and I walked back to the launderette, with my head held a little higher.

After drying my clothes, I headed into town, and *the South African* went to a city centre bookmaker, where a few small bets paid to keep him warm through the afternoon *and* returned a €25.60 profit!

I spent most of the winnings in a charity shop — on a set of screwdrivers, a lambswool jumper and a copy of John Boyne's *Mutiny on the Bounty* — and I arrived back in the hostel at half-past-six precisely.

Once in the privacy of my own room, I took the gun from the front of my pants, removed the magazine from the handle and unloaded the bullets. I then moved the bed away from the wall and got down on my knees to examine the skirting.

Using a Phillips screwdriver, I detached one of the boards and, as I had hoped, there was enough space between the floor and the plasterboard wall into which I could secrete the gun parts and the bullets.

I reaffixed the board to the wall and manoeuvred the bed back into position, confident that the gun's hiding place would never be discovered, and at long last, I could lie down on the bed and allow fatigue to kick in.

I was up at eight the next morning, and on my way back to my room from the shower, I noticed a discarded hearing aid in a bin on the corridor, which sparked another little brainwave. It was an old model — pink and large, not one of the inconspicuous modern equivalents, and I guessed one of my fellow boarders must have recently upgraded — and having retrieved it from the bin, I took the hearing aid back to my room and put it in amongst my toiletries.

In accordance with the rules, *the South African* was out of the front door at just before nine-thirty, and he spent the first part of his day walking from one betting shop to the next — studying the form and keeping himself warm.

After lunch — a couple of plain hamburgers and a cup of coffee from McDonalds — *the South African* went into the public library in Phibsboro. A pamphlet in the entrance hall told him that he couldn't join (not without ID), but nobody asked any questions as he wandered around. *The South African* was even left in peace to leaf through the daily papers, and so was able to spend his entire afternoon there, reading every column inch.

I left the library just before five, when it closed, and having bought myself a cup of soup, a sandwich and a bag of marshmallows on my way back to the hostel, I ate my *three-course meal* in the comfort of my room. Then, having finished my book, I brushed my teeth and went to bed — I had an early start the next day.

My alarm woke me at 5.45. Almost on autopilot, I got up and got dressed — thermal long johns, the lambswool jumper, my old hoodie and combat trousers, two pairs of socks and my old trainers — which were starting to fall apart. I then dabbed my beard and hair with Vaseline — I needed to look the part — and in my mendacious garb, I snuck out of the hostel and headed down to Connolly Station.

Over the two previous days, I had earmarked five 'pitches' that I intended to use, in rotation each weekday morning, and so, huddled in a blanket, with a polystyrene cup at my feet, I sat at the foot of the sloping, stone walkway leading up into the station concourse, hanging my head in shame as the feet rushed past, praying that the early bird might just catch a bigger worm.

It had been an educated guess that, with less competition, mornings would be the best time for a beggar to 'graft', and as hoped, the hearing aid, which I wore conspicuously, seemed to elicit a little more charity from the passers-by.

The hearing aid would also serve as an effective deterrent to any would-be do-gooder who might otherwise have tried to engage me in conversation, and although, once or twice in the years to come, people did insist on speaking to me, shamefully when this happened, I pretended to have a speech disability too, responding to any questions with a series of incoherent grunts.

I can only thank God that nobody ever engaged me in sign language!

From the outset, it was apparent that the change to my 'working hours' was going to pay dividends, and at every given opportunity — when there were no approaching footsteps — I would empty the shrapnel from my cup and into a carrier bag which I had hidden beneath my blanket.

At a quarter-to nine, I gathered up my belongings and hurried back to the hostel where I counted the morning's 'take' — €53.61, a living wage if you don't have a habit to feed — and hopped into the shower.

I would discover that begging was a very demeaning way to survive — it isn't, as some believe, 'easy work', but simply a means to an end. Still, I cannot deny that I did all right out of it.

I guess I averaged about €50 a day, and come Saturday, I would trade my coins for notes at one of the 'exchange machines' dotted around town. I begrudged paying the commission, but that was the price of anonymity.

Then, every Sunday evening, I would pay my €175 at reception, before going up to my room and getting ready for the week ahead.

And very quickly, my life fell into predictable routines.

Weekdays, my early morning was spent begging. Late mornings I could be found in one of Dublin's public libraries. Afternoons were frittered away in the bookies. I'd have dinner back in my room, sometimes take an early evening stroll and always do a little reading before I went to sleep. My alarm would wake me before six, and another day in purgatory would begin.

Every Friday afternoon, I would call into one of Dublin's many charity shops — to buy a *new* book and sometimes a *new* item of clothing. I also acquired other second-hand knick-knacks that made my life a little more bearable — cutlery, crockery and best of all, a digital radio alarm clock.

With very little to waste my money on, I gradually built up a *tidy stash* and I hid it inside a fake canister of Lynx — picked up on a market stall — that I kept 'hidden' in amongst my other toiletries in the cabinet under the sink. Over time, I would have to buy a second.

I did my laundry every other Tuesday, I visited free museums and art galleries at weekends, I occasionally went to the cinema, and I managed to stay fit because I walked absolutely everywhere.

I became almost invisible, which had been my primary objective when I arrived into Dublin, but now that I no longer worried about being recognised (I didn't even flinch the morning that a policeman told me to move on. I just lied my way out of the situation), I yearned for the company that ordinary people take for granted.

Once upon a time in my life, I craved *time alone* — those ten minutes in the shower, the walk to the newsagents, the drive to work. Those few precious moments away from other people and other people's problems — but in a pariah's world, *time alone* is an unavoidable constant.

By now, *the South African* recognised a few of the faces in the hostel, but he could never engage anybody in anything more than general conversation, and although I could rise above the melancholy most of the time, one afternoon, stood in the bookies, I noticed the date on the newspaper — 24th April — Maeve's birthday — and I started to cry.

Right there — in the middle of Paddy Power.

With no photographs, all I had left of my children were the fast-fading memories in my head *and* the residual guilt in my heart, and it was that guilt which brought me back through the chapel doors.

On bended knee, I said a decade of the Rosary for the repose of their mother's immortal soul, and I beseeched Brigid to look out for our two little babies, and although I didn't seek forgiveness for my sins (God knows I don't feel any remorse), I actually found the experience quite liberating, and very soon, Mass had become another facet of my weekly routine.

I had been going to Mass for seven months or thereabouts when, having popped into Starbucks on my way home from St Brendan's, my world was brought to yet another grinding standstill by yet another newspaper report.

I was cursorily flicking through a supplement from the Sunday Independent, when suddenly, I found myself staring at a photograph of Brigid. In it, she was standing beneath a Sinn

Fein banner, and as I pushed my coffee and my pastry to one side, I thought I was going to be sick.

It is now two years since...

Two years!

Two lost years!

I got no further than those first few words.

Automatically, I turned the page and was confronted by three more photographs of my wife — one as a young girl, the second of Brigid at her graduation and the third as a loving mother (with Maeve and Joe's faces pixelated).

Also included in the story was a shot of me — the one from Brigid's bedside cabinet: the one of me, drunk, at my brother-in-law's fortieth — and in something of a daze, I closed the paper, stood and left the coffee shop.

I ended up in Fairview Park where I sat on a bench and replayed the events of that fateful Saturday night in Keady over and over in my head. Patsy had given me countless opportunities, but even though a confession might well have spared Brigid, I didn't have the decency to own up to what I'd done.

My steadfast denial was an unforgiveable act of cowardice — and for what? So that I could live in solitary confinement, in this prison of my own making.

I remained in the park until the dark had set in, and as I made my way back to the hostel, I purchased my own copy of the Sunday Independent. Then, back in my room, I read the story in full:

THE NEW DISAPPEARED

It is now two years since a gruesome discovery was made at a

195

house in the border town of Keady...

At 11.57 on the morning of Sunday 25ᵗʰ October 2015 the PSNI found Brigid Kelly, dead from a fatal gunshot wound to the head...

The thirty-three-year-old mother-of-two was the outspoken Sinn Fein council candidate...

Describing the murder as 'brutal and cold-blooded', police immediately named thirty-five-year-old Frank Kelly, the victim's estranged husband, as their prime suspect...

The couple had recently separated, and it appeared that Mr Kelly had taken things in a tragic direction...

The alarm had been raised by Mrs Kelly's mother when her daughter did not arrive to collect her children...

With both cars still at the family home, along with the prime suspect's wallet, his bank cards, his driving licence and his passport, it was presumed that Frank Kelly was hiding out locally...

Extensive searches on both sides of the border produced nothing...

There had not been a single witness report of Mr Kelly...

Then, nine days later, in the boot of a stolen car — found dumped just outside Westport, County Mayo — Gardai discovered traces of blood. The blood matched samples found at the home in Keady: the blood was Frank Kelly's ...

Was Mr Kelly a victim too?

Had the perpetrator, or perpetrators, tried to frame him for his wife's murder?

Forces on both sides of the border have since been treating the case as a double murder, linking the motive to Brigid Kelly's budding political career. The Sinn Fein council candidate had been particularly vocal about paramilitary groups operating in her prospective ward ...

Nobody has ever claimed responsibility, but it is widely assumed that for speaking out against and standing up to this scourge of decent society, Mrs Kelly and her husband paid with their lives ...

While his wife has been laid to rest, the whereabouts of Mr Kelly's remains is still unknown, and with the recent 'disappearance' of John-Paul McGann from Lurgan, of Sean Cunningham from Strabane, of Joe Trainor from Newry, of Austin Sherry from Crumlin and of Liam Grimley from Cookstown, there is a dreadful sense that an abhorrent facet of our past may be about to infiltrate the present.

Are these five men 'the new disappeared'?

The article went on to give accounts of what had happened to the four other men, but my interest ended there.

    With Frank Kelly dead, presumed murdered, the world

had stopped looking for *me*.

But the Carrolls *knew* I was alive, and if they were reading the same article, then what would they be thinking?

Before going to bed, I took the newspaper across to the mirror, and when I compared the man looking back at me to the picture of the shaven-headed thug in the Sunday Independent from little more than three years previous, I came to the conclusion that a plastic surgeon could not have done a better job.

I had Patsy to thank for the sunken side of my face; this probably made the real difference. The weight loss had played a big part too; as had the long hair, the beard and the glasses.

All that remained was the badness inside.

The only real downside to be gleaned from Emer McDade's article was that my DNA is now forever on two national databases, so, if I ever come into conflict with the law — on either side of the Irish Sea — then a simple cross-reference will have me found out for who I really am and almost certainly, for what I have done.

The next morning, as I cowered down beneath my blanket close to Connolly Station, I couldn't get those pixelated images out of my head, though. Where were Maeve and Joe? Were they still in Armagh with my in-laws?

Probably, I concluded.

I knew the only way I could ever be reunited with my children would be with a prison warder at my side, but if I visited Armagh, then there was a chance that our paths might cross — a chance that I might, at least, *see them* again.

And so, I started making plans to take the train north.

But an unexpected turn of events resulted in my travel plans being put on the back burner.

Four

Just two days after I'd seen my picture in the paper, as I was coming 'off shift', I was mugged.

There were two of them — drug addicts by the look — and while one held the blade to my throat, the other frisked me and helped himself to the money in my carrier bag. Cuffing me round the back of the head, the knifeman advised me to *stay the fuck away from Connolly*, and despite my deep sense of injustice, I took heed of the warning and switched my time and place of work.

Afternoons meant longer hours for less money, and the greater competition meant I was challenged for a pitch on more than one occasion. But I never argued; and thankfully, I was never threatened again.

I had to modify my daily routine accordingly — up at nine, beg all day, dinner, shower, read, sleep — but in essence, life carried on much as it had done before. The only real difference was that I could now only patronise the launderette, the library and the bookmakers at weekends.

Christmas was on the near horizon when, late one afternoon, a note dropped into my cup. Like most people, the woman smiled piteously, looking at my hearing aid rather than me, and conscience assuaged, she hurried on her way.

Catching a whiff of her perfume — Gucci Bamboo; Brigid's favourite — I did something I rarely did and looked up. I was fixating on the woman's legs — they were 'dressed' in sheer black nylon, and something was stirring within me — when she glanced back with a benevolent smile, and there was no mistaking *her*: Maire.

I gave it a few seconds before getting up, and following at a safe distance, I was racking my brain for a way to propose a deal — I'd say that we'd both lost loved ones, and that the only way forward was to leave the past behind.

But how could I get her attention?

Maire ended up outside a pub in Temple Bar, Fitzsimons, where she met up with an attractive blonde, and after flirting briefly with the bouncers, the pair sauntered on in.

I realised if I was to get inside too, then I would have to change out of my *work clothes*, and although I knew it would take at least an hour to get to Mountjoy and back (and Maire might have moved on by the time I returned), I had little choice in the matter.

Back in my room, after a very quick shower, I threw on clean underwear, two pairs of woollen socks and my best 'charity shop threads', and it was just after eight when I arrived back at the pub.

'Ticket only,' one of the *faux friendly* bouncers informed me, as he blocked my path with a gloved hand.

'Sorry mate,' *the South African* chirruped. 'I just thought I saw a friend of mine go in there.'

'Not without a ticket he didn't,' a second Behemoth piped up.

'Look, I'm not trying to gate-crash the party... It's just that, I, er, go back to Jo'burg in the morning...'

'You still can't come in,' *number two* informed *the South African*.

But *number one* must have been feeling the Christmas spirit.

'Go in for two minutes. You can't buy a drink and you can't stay. If you find your friend, bring him outside. But fuck me about and you'll be in trouble...'

'Cheers mate!' *the South African* smiled gratefully. 'I'll be back out in two!'

Within twenty seconds I had clocked Maire — she was with a group of about a dozen, at a table coming down with drinks, and I felt it safe to assume she was ensconced for the night.

For the sake of appearances, *the South African* continued to scan the place in search of his fictitious friend, and when he returned back outside, he apologised to the doormen — *he'd been mistaken.*

'What time does the party finished?' he asked, by way of parting shot. 'Just in case he comes here late on?'

'Last orders are at midnight,' *number one* informed him helpfully.

I'd aim to be back around then.

The South African now needed a word with Eleanor.

'I have a favour to ask,' he informed her sheepishly, when she appeared at the door of her basement flat.

'Favour?' Eleanor enquired, with an unusually cynical tone.

'It's just an old friend of mine is in town,' he told her edgily, 'and I might be late.'

'How late is 'late'?'

'One; maybe half-past,' he grimaced, then as an afterthought added, 'we won't be drinking — I don't.'

The rules of the hostel were rigid — the doors were locked

at half-past-ten — but I was hoping Eleanor would make an exception for one of her long-standing tenants.

'Knock my door when you come back,' she said flatly; she must have been feeling a little of the festive spirit too. 'I'll let you in. Just this once... But no later than one.'

With time to kill, I went to the Savoy Cinema on O'Connell Street, but I was back in Temple Bar before midnight, milling around in amongst the Christmas crowd, keeping a beady eye on the door to Fitzsimons.

At half-past the hour, *numbers one and two* (along with *three, four and five*) were escorting what appeared to be the last of the revellers from the premises, and I guessed Maire and her friends must have already moved on.

Then, just as I was about to head back to the hostel, she appeared at the door with her entourage, and as they ambled off down the street, chatting animatedly, I followed — again at a safe distance.

As I was passing Supermacs, my eyes were drawn to a raucous hen party on the opposite side of the pedestrianised street, and although I only glanced away for a matter of seconds, by the time I 're-focussed', Maire and her friends had vanished.

I panicked for a few seconds, but then realised the group must have turned left, down a side-street, and thank God I hadn't dallied any longer, because as I turned the corner, Maire was opening the door to an upmarket-looking apartment block, chaperoning her friends inside.

Making a mental note of the street name — Cows Lane — I ran all the way back to the hostel, arriving at the door to Eleanor's basement flat at one o'clock precisely, and all of a sudden, I was feeling strangely nervous.

I was certain that there had been a glint in Eleanor's eye earlier when she told me to *knock the door*, and although Eleanor was older than me — by ten years, maybe more — she was a handsome woman; and when she answered the door to me with a most becoming smile, I could feel the butterflies rising in the pit of my stomach.

As Eleanor stepped forward, I leant in — thrilled by the thought of kissing a woman again — but Eleanor strode straight past and up to the main door at ground level. By the time I came to my senses, she was swiping the master key-card over the security scanner, and having let me in, she bid me a polite 'good night', oblivious to the notion I'd taken.

Eleanor went back down to her own 'private space' and me up to mine, and I felt both amused and annoyed, but once I'd managed to get her *out of my system*, I turned my attention to that other lady in my life — Maire.

It was highly unlikely that Maire would simply acquiesce to my request for a truce — I would need to *persuade* her — and having spent the night mulling it over, I was up early the next morning to check out a few things.

First, I headed for the Royal Canal, and I was pleasantly amazed to find the portacabin I had briefly called home still standing. More astonishing, was the fact, that in the interim, nothing had changed — even the smashed window hadn't been repaired. I could only speculate, that either the sale had fallen through, or there was a problem with developing the land — not that I cared — but whatever the reason, it would save me the trouble of finding somewhere to stash Patsy's holdall.

Maire's holdall was always going to be hidden at my other former Dublin residence, and having double-checked that all was as it had been in Fairview Park, I headed into town to do a bit of Christmas shopping.

I picked up two identical sets of bright yellow waterproofs from an army surplus store, two padded shirts — one large, one extra-large — from Penneys and an extra-extra-large black hooded tracksuit from a market trader in St Stephen's Green.

Then, later on, back at the hostel, I packed the holdalls — into Patsy's went the tracksuit and shirts as well as a scarf, gloves, a belt and an old pillow, while into Maire's went one set of waterproofs.

On Sunday morning, after retracing my previous day's footsteps, I threw Patsy's holdall in through the broken window of the portacabin and Maire's into the bushes where I'd slept rough for almost a month, and at midday Mass, I prayed that nobody happened upon either.

Then, on Monday morning, for the first time since I'd been *mugged off my pitch*, I showed up at Connolly Station wearing the second set of bright yellow waterproofs, and with no sign of my assailants, I got to work; and thank goodness I did, because I made over €100.

With the festive spirit lingering well into the New Year, I continued to turn over a very healthy profit as my life quickly reverted back to its previous format. But on a miserable Tuesday evening in late January, despite knowing that the applecart could be irreversibly upset, I put my plan into action.

I began by taking the gun from behind the skirting board, and having assembled it, I loaded it, put the safety on and tucked it into the front of my pants. Then, for the first time in more than three years, I popped in my contact lenses, but as it was imperative that *the South African* 'look himself' when he left the hostel, I had to wear my glasses too.

My vision was a complete blur, but I could have found my

way to the portacabin blindfolded, and as soon as I was inside, I removed the glasses, and sight restored, I got changed.

To begin with: shirt, pillow, shirt.

I was hoping the outfit would make me appear far heavier than I was, and having secured the pillow with the belt, I put on the tracksuit. Although uncomfortable to wear, the ensemble did not impinge upon my movements, and after pulling on the gloves, I slipped the gun and my glasses into the leg pockets of the tracksuit and, with the scarf up round my face and the hood tight around my head, I clambered out through the window and back over the fence.

I took a circuitous route to Temple Bar and, on the off-chance I might catch her returning home after a midweek drink, I walked between Fitzsimmons and Maire's flat. But with no sign of *my prey*, I returned to the portacabin and changed back into my *civvies*.

I re-packed the holdall — which I left in the portacabin for next time — and once again sporting his glasses, *the South African* made his way back to the hostel, arriving home at just before curfew.

On the Thursday and again on the following Monday, I repeated the sequence, but to no avail. However, on the Wednesday — just nine days into a plan that I had been prepared to wait months on — who should be coming out of Supermacs?

It had been a calculated assumption that Maire would be a regular in the pub closest to her apartment, but I genuinely never expected our paths to cross at just the fourth time of asking — and when I tell you that Patsy was with her, you may sympathise a little with my crazy notion that God looks out for me.

With CCTV omnipresent in Temple Bar — hence the hood and the scarf and the need to operate on different days at slightly different times — I could 'feel' my every move being monitored as I hurried past the siblings.

My original plan had been to walk up to Maire in the hope we could broker a deal. I would have maintained my innocence — insisting that I'd not gone to the police because I knew that would make sitting ducks of my children. I was going to plead with her, telling her I just wanted to see Maeve and Joe again. I would say that I was prepared to forgo any vengeance for Brigid, and I would guarantee neither she nor her brother were ever implicated in my wife's murder... *if* I got a new identity.

The Carrolls would surely know people who could arrange for that to happen.

It was supposed to be a civil conversation — the gun was simply insurance — and I'd run every potential scenario through my head, trying to spot the pitfalls, trying to pre-empt her reaction, trying to cover every base.

But in every one of those scenarios Maire was on her own.

Patsy being there changed things.

Still, this was likely to be the best chance, perhaps the only chance, I would ever get.

So, I had to make the most of it.

Having scuttled down Cows Lane, I ducked between two cars parked right outside Maire's apartment block and I started my stopwatch. As the seconds ticked by, I steeled myself for the confrontation, trying to envisage what might happen next:

'Could you spare me some change?' was going to be my opening gambit.

I would get up and stagger towards them while they did

their best to ignore me.

Maire would be fumbling in her bag for the key.

But I couldn't let them get inside.

'Could you spare any change?' I would shout more vociferously.

'Fuck off mister!' Patsy would lash out.

I'd ham it up, teetering backwards as he caught me a glancing blow.

'Hold on,' Maire would have a heart, and this time she'd be fumbling in her bag for some change.

'Fuck him, Maire!' Patsy would be less benevolent.

'Kindness costs nothing,' she'd insist.

He'd go to cuff me again but his sister would intercede on my behalf.

'Leave him Patsy. He's done no harm.'

I'd remain silent as she held out a few coins to me.

Then, in a flash, I'd produce the gun — their gun — from behind my back.

Suddenly, they'd realise I had them penned in.

'Get down on your knees,' I'd instruct calmly, holding the gun against Patsy's temple.

I'd watch them watching me.

Neither would have a clue who I was, nor why I was there.

'What do you want?' Patsy would enquire, suddenly diplomatic.

With a wave of the gun, I would direct them up against the entrance door. Hands shaking, I would pat Patsy up and down. Then Maire. I would let my hand rest on her breasts and then on her crotch longer than was reasonable, before taking a backward step to glance up and down the lane; all the while keeping the Carrolls in my line of fire.

Still no-one.

After a pregnant pause, I'd demand an apology, and the look of bemusement on Patsy's face would be priceless. Maire would be concentrating, though — trying to remember. She'd only have my eyes to work with, but the penny would eventually drop.

'Frank Kelly?' she would state questioningly, simultaneously letting her brother know what this was about.

He would look up at me. Long and hard. Disbelievingly.

'We need to come to an agreement...' I would suggest positively, before changing my tone and glaring at Patsy. 'But first, you need to apologise for killing my wife.'

'You apologise first!' He would have a defiant look, there would be no fear in his eyes, a madman on the wrong end of a gun. 'After all, this began when you killed my twin!'

'Yeah, sorry for that!' I would laugh mockingly: confessing would be such a release.

'Well, your wife simply makes us quits,' he would retort casually.

'Quits?' I would say meaningfully. 'Well, if that's the case, then we can all move forward!'

'Fuck you!' Patsy would remain defiant.

'No Patsy!' Maire would intercede. 'We can sort this out!'

'Shut up Maire!' Patsy and I would shout in unison.

'Somebody will come,' he would warn.

'Shut the fuck up!' I'd scream.

'You haven't got the balls to kill us, Kelly,' Patsy would goad.

'Oh, Patsy dear! How wrong you are!' I would respond manfully. 'I too used to think I didn't have it in me. But just ask Liam... I got such a rush when I cracked his empty skull with

208

my hammer and snuffed the life out of him!'

Patsy would tense up, but I'd afford him a quick, hard kick to the shin.

'Don't even think about it,' I'd grin, menacingly.

'Fuck you!'

I'd press the gun hard against his temple.

'Go on then, big man!'

I'd have more to get off my chest, though.

'Don't you want to know why I killed Liam?' I'd tease.

'Fuck you!' Patsy would be a coiled spring.

'Yes!' Maire would try to distract me.

Patsy would make a desperate grab for the gun, but I would be alive to it.

And bang!

Maire would scream as her brother's lifeless body collapsed beside her. I would move back from the doorway, making sure his blood didn't sully my footwear.

'It didn't have to come to this Maire,' I would insist, solemnly. 'There was a compromise out there. I wouldn't have gone to the police. But alas, Patsy couldn't bring himself to apologise.'

'So, why did you kill Liam?' She would be extraordinarily composed, given what she'd just witnessed.

But I'd guess it was a ruse.

Still, I'd want to explain; I'd need to explain

'I killed Liam because of that night you had your party. I mean, what decent people would have their music blaring at three o'clock in the morning, when they knew a little girl and a pregnant woman were living next door?'

'That's absurd,' she would contend, instantly recalling the night in question. 'Liam wasn't even there.'

A crucial blunder on my part, but one that Patsy had already flagged that up for me, on the night he killed Brigid.

'Well, I suppose I got the right twin in the end!' I would laugh — viciously.

'So, you're telling me that three people are dead just because of some loud music?'

'No, Maire...' I would look down at her cradling her brother, covered in his blood. 'Four are.'

And bang!

At long last, Patsy and Maire turned into the cul-de-sac.

I waited until they were at the door to the apartment block before I appeared, and as I stepped from between the two cars, head down, I glanced at my stopwatch: *fifty-eight seconds.*

It felt like so much longer.

It took a moment for Maire and Patsy to register my presence. They seemed to freeze as I walked up to them. There was no conversation and head still down, I produced the gun from behind my back. One bullet a-piece — Patsy first, then his sister.

Even I couldn't fail at such close range.

Had Patsy not been with her, I might not have killed Maire (although I probably would have; after all, she had been prepared to kill me then frame me for my wife's murder) but her brother's presence effectively forced my hand: Patsy would never have agreed to a truce, Patsy would have wanted me dead.

So, as I lay in wait, I decided I had to get my retaliation in first.

As I walked away from the apartment block, I took care not to break into a run; but I did move briskly. In no time at all, I had passed Supermacs, then Fitzsimons, and soon I was crossing the Liffey at Annesley Bridge.

I had kept the scarf up and my head down *at all times* — even when I'd fired the fatal shots — and although there was bound to be CCTV footage of me travelling to and from the immediate crime scene, I was sure that nobody had actually witnessed the double-murder (although people must have heard the gunshots).

I have no idea how many 'potential witnesses' I passed on my way to Fairview Park, but I hadn't heard a siren by the time I entered it, and with no obvious cameras in or around any of the entrances (naturally, I had checked) my hope was that the Garda would assume the murderer had made good his escape along the railway tracks that ran immediately beside the park, or by exiting at the far end and disappearing into one of the side-streets off the Clontarf Road.

A glance at my stopwatch told me I had already put the best part of an hour between myself and the shooting, and just so long as the police didn't start their manhunt immediately, I felt I had a good chance of getting away with it.

Then, after finding Maire's holdall exactly where I'd left it, I discarded my contact lenses and lay down on the cold wet ground and waited to see which came first — the police or the morning.

Five

I realised that if I was found hiding in a bush with the murder weapon on my person, then I was done for, and I was resigned to being apprehended. But I no longer cared. I had Brigid's revenge.

All night I lay, ears cocked, listening for any sign of activity in the park, but nobody came, and as soon as day broke — and before anybody did appear — I took off the tracksuit and one of the shirts, unbelted the pillow, and put on the yellow weatherproofs from Maire's holdall.

I just about managed to squeeze everything I'd worn the night before into the small holdall, and having emerged from the bushes, carrying it over my shoulder, I exited the park by the entrance I'd used six or seven hours earlier, hoping that I looked like a different man.

The next part of my plan had always been to follow my daily routines, and after taking a roundabout route 'to work' — up through Marino and past Croke Park — I set up, as usual, near Connolly Station at just after 6.30.

I was back in the hostel at just after nine for my morning shower, and after depositing the bullets and component gun-parts back behind the skirting board, I took the pillow out of the holdall and left it on the bed.

Then I got dressed and, with my bag of 'dirty washing', I headed for the launderette, and a couple of hours later, I was donating the *pristine* shirts and tracksuit to the SVP shop on Dorset Street.

Now, it was a matter of waiting to see what transpired.

I spent the rest of my day, as ever, between the bookies and the public library, and with news of the double-murder plastered across the front pages of the evening edition, I picked up a copy of The Herald on my way home, to read in my room.

And one phrase stood out: *gangland killings.*

The double-murder, I supposed, could not have been planned and for want of a better expression, *executed* more professionally. It was already being connected to the murder of a man named Desmond Taggert who had been shot dead at point-blank range, outside his home in Coolock just six days earlier. According to the report, both murders were 'more needless *gangland killings* in an ongoing feud that is afflicting the capital'.

At the weekend, the *gangland killings* were revisited in a six-page feature that included photographs of 'a man police wished to speak to'. There were no close-ups, just grainy images picked up on the street CCTV and the cameras inside Maire's apartment block, and with only my eyes and forehead visible beneath my disguise, detectives were going to struggle to identify me, unless they had something else.

I had done quite a good job of making myself appear 'bulky', and thankfully, there were no eyewitnesses — my main concern — and now, with the murders being linked to Dublin's shady underworld, the likelihood of somebody coming forward and embroiling him or herself in a high-profile court case seemed, at best, remote.

There was no mention of 'evidence' either, and although I would have loved to go online to investigate — and maybe even find out what had been reported about the murders of Liam and Brigid — I was afraid to.

Common sense dictates that television's portrayal of a sophisticated Secret Service — with the power to scrutinise every individual's 'virtual life' — must be more fiction than fact, but I have yet to pluck up the courage to put my theory to the test.

All I know is what I read in the newspapers: that the prime suspect was 'dressed in black' (*correct*)... 'approximately six feet in height' (*correct*)... 'of heavy build' (*incorrect*)... 'last seen entering Fairview Park' (*correct*)...'

And, best of all: 'Detectives would like to speak to the driver of a dark grey or black Toyota Auris seen driving at speed along the Clontarf Road close to Fairview Park, at approximately midnight on Wednesday...'

The inference being that *the man in black* had an accomplice, a getaway driver.

Just in case things went wrong, I had taken the same basic precautions I had taken prior to murdering Liam — making myself unidentifiable and planning my route both to and from the crime-scene — but it was only as I lay in wait, wondering how I should offer the proverbial olive branch, that I realised that this was my chance to kill my wife's murderer (Maire was merely collateral damage), and in that minute, I decided that my best chance of getting away with it would be to make it look like an execution.

With the media aiding and abetting my strategy, and with the time-gap between the murders and the present continuing to grow, so my conviction that I had, once again, got away with the ultimate crime hardened.

Another week on and the Sunday Independent ran a story

under the banner 'Drug Barons Battle for Territory', which included cursory mention of the Carrolls and linked the three sibling murders directly to Dublin's wider drug problem. After that, I never heard another word, and the long and the short of it was that, *the unfortunate soul* who could be found begging in and around Connolly Station, was never implicated.

The one outstanding issue was the gun, but I felt I needed to bide my time, and it was a Saturday morning, five or six weeks after the murder, before I decided the time was right to get rid of it.

I was up unusually early, and sporting a pair of pink Marigolds, I retrieved the component parts from behind the skirting, filled the sink with bleach, and meticulously scrubbed the magazine, the handle and the four remaining bullets with a green scourer.

When I was satisfied that everything was 'clean', I wrapped it all in a towel, snapped off the rubber gloves and got dressed. Before handling the gun parts again, I put on a pair of woollen gloves, slipped the bullets into one pocket of my raincoat, while the magazine and handle went into the other. Then, I headed for the city centre.

Crossing the Liffey at the Sean O'Casey Bridge, I stopped halfway to admire my surroundings, and with so few people out and about, it was easy for me to surreptitiously take a single bullet from my pocket and drop into the water below. I then walked slowly to Butt Bridge where I crossed back over the river, again stopping halfway and again, as I took in the view, there was another small splash. Next, I shuffled on to the Rosie Hackett Bridge and made yet another brief stop in the middle and lastly, I re-crossed at the Halfpenny Bridge, and having dumped the fourth bullet into the grimy Dublin river, I lingered for just a moment, before I made my way up towards Croke Park.

I followed the familiar towpath along the Royal Canal, past the lock-up (where I hoped Patsy's holdall was still sitting), and I had almost reached Broombridge Station before I had a quiet moment to myself.

Picking up a stone from the ground beside me, I edged forward and tried to skim it off the water. But to no avail. I tried twice more, then after one last look round, I produced *another stone* from my coat pocket and watched it sink with the others — hopefully without a trace.

I continued along the towpath for another half-mile or so, stopping under a road bridge, and this time I didn't bother with the pretence of *duck and drakes* and, without further ado, I flung the magazine into the water.

I then double-backed on myself and made my way to the portacabin, and after climbing in through the broken window empty-handed, I re-appeared with Patsy's hold-all over my shoulder — not that it contained anything incriminating, just my clothes, but better safe than sorry.

It was only later in the evening, back at the hostel as I stood in the shower, that I became agitated — anybody could have seen me tossing the gun into the water and I wasn't wearing a disguise — and although the thought troubled me for days, it really shouldn't have done, because, to the best of my knowledge, neither bullets nor gun-parts have ever resurfaced.

Six

It was just after Easter when something else happened to steer my life on a different course.

I was working one of my regular pitches, just around the corner from *Connolly*, when a gentleman, on his way to catch a train, stopped beside me and took out his wallet. I sneaked an upward peek, and from the corner of my eye, I could see he was about to drop *a note* into my cup — it looked like a twenty!

Then, out of nowhere, a hooded youth appeared and snatched the wallet out of his hand.

Instinctively, I kicked out a leg, tripping the young thief, and as he stumbled to the ground, I forgot myself. Holding him down, calling him all the names under the sun, *the South African* pulled the wallet from his grasp.

I allowed the would-be mugger to wriggle free, though — or rather, *the South African* did (neither of *us* wanted the police called!) — and as the lad scarpered off, the wallet was handed back to its rightful owner.

'So? You don't need a hearing aid then!' the man remarked insightfully. He had a harsh Dublin accent, not the well-educated enunciation I'd been expecting.

'No,' *the South African* replied ashamedly.

'So, why do you live the life of a beggar?' he asked derisively, as he took out a fifty.

'I won't bore you with the details,' *the South African* sighed.

Then he did just that.

'I followed my heart to Ireland but that didn't work out…'

I'd always planned to say this to Eleanor if ever she asked, and I'm not sure why I felt the need to tell my tall tale to a complete stranger, but I did

'Don't look so frightened,' the man smiled kindly, placing a warm hand on my cold one. 'I'm not looking for an explanation. But why don't you just go back to South Africa?' he probed suspiciously, although his tone was tinged with sympathy.

'Well…' my South African alter-ego hesitated before he explained that his family had 'exiled' him. He told the man that the girl he'd fallen in love with had been his brother's fiancée.

'…They'd met in Cape Town in 2013,' he expounded, 'and she was living in our family home. And while my brother was planning his wedding, I was *doing the dirt* on him. But I loved Catherine. And when she ran back home to Ireland I followed.

'I was only here for four weeks when she dumped me, and although I picked up work here and there — cash in hand — bad has gone to worse for me. And I've been living like this for more than two years.'

There was a long, drawn-out silence, and I waited with bated breath for his response.

Without a word, the man handed me a card, a business card, his business card:

Damian McCarron: Financial Adviser
224b Dolphins Barn
Dublin 8.

'I owe you,' Mr McCarron said, as he went on his way. 'And I don't say that to very many people.'

A couple of days later, I visited Mr McCarron's office. It was located in an anonymous block on the south side of the city — an hour's walk from the bedsit — and my hand was shaking as I pressed the button beside his name.

'Yes?' a hoarse Dublin accent enquired over the intercom; I couldn't tell if it was him.

'I'm here to see Mr Damian McCarron,' *the South African* said vaguely.

'You'd better come up then,' McCarron laughed, and he buzzed me in.

I ascended to the fifth floor, and McCarron met me at the door. His office was like something out of an old, black-and-white, private-eye movie — the frosted glass in the door, embossed with his name, bookcases replete with leather-bound volumes, a huge wooden desk with a plush reclining chair for Mr McCarron and two smaller, but equally comfortable armchairs for his clients.

'Big D...' That's how McCarron introduced himself, as he held out a massive, right paw.

It was hard to believe that this was the same shambling figure I'd helped out at Connolly Station. I hadn't noticed how tall and broad Big D was and although he must have been well into his sixties — with more greying-ginger hair coming out of his nostrils than was left on his head — he carried plenty of menace. He had the tiniest, blue eyes, deep-set behind an enormous red beak, and he wore dentures that seemed to constantly give him trouble.

'Graeme,' *the South African* chuckled inwardly, as he took

a seat.

'So? Are you looking for work then, Graeme?' Big D enquired matter-of-factly.

'No,' *the South African* shook his head. 'I need to get to London.'

'You'll be needing a travel agent then!' the other laughed.

'I can't travel using my real name,' *the South African* told him straight.

Big D raised his bushy eyebrows.

'You know,' he said charily, 'you are the only white South African who has ever knocked on my door. Back in the day, it was the blacks and Asians. Then it was the Eastern Europeans. These days it's mainly Roma or refugees, fleeing one conflict or another … Or criminals,' he added, meaningfully.

Suddenly I had a dreadful feeling that he knew who I was.

'I've done some things of which I'm not very proud,' *the South African* said contritely, hanging his head to avoid the other's steely gaze.

'As I told you before, I don't need an explanation,' Big D interrupted. 'If you can get me the money then I'll do as you ask — regardless of what you've done. Now, I won't charge to send you across the Irish Sea — that's in return for your kindness the other morning. But a new identity will cost.'

I had only been looking for Big D to transport me over to England, but interest piqued, *the South African* cut straight to the chase.

'How much?' he enquired directly.

'Twelve thousand if you want authentic documentation,' Big D was more upfront than I'd expected. 'And I promise you, that's a massively discounted rate.'

'Can I have some time to think about it?'

'Take as long as you like. I'll still be here *when* you next call. But a word of advice, my Boer friend,' Big D was grinning darkly, and he let the ensuing silence exacerbate my unease. 'If I receive any unwanted calls from those in authority, I *will* find you and show you my nasty side.'

'It won't come to that.'

'I'm sure it won't,' he nodded. 'But be warned...'

That night I totted up my savings: €4,527.

It would take me another decade to cobble together the twelve thousand that Big D was asking — and I didn't have that sort of time — but if he managed to stow me across in the back of a lorry, with over £4,000 in my pocket, I could travel to London and try to get back in touch with my brother.

I couldn't sleep that night, though, for thinking about the 'authentic documentation'.

With a new identity I might be able to build a life for myself: a proper life.

But before I did something I might repent at leisure, I needed to *see* my children one last time. It was a long shot — a very long shot — but while I was still on the same island, I had to visit Armagh in the vain hope our paths might cross.

Seven

As I headed north from Connolly Station, my mind flashed back to my last train journey — how times had changed! — and it was just before noon when the Translink train arrived in to Portadown.

I walked from the station across to the High Street and I didn't have to wait too long for a bus to Armagh, but after two hours playing the tourist, traipsing every inch of *the Cathedral City*, visiting the Armagh Museum, the Planetarium, the restaurant quarter and of course, both cathedrals, I realised I had sent myself on something of a fool's errand.

This had always been the likeliest outcome — because, if Maeve and Joe were with my in-laws, then they'd be living in the country, making a chance sighting highly unlikely — nevertheless, I felt crushed.

I was still feeling despondent as I climbed the stairs to my room back in Dublin, but in the corridor, I found a scratch-card and I wondered if my luck was about to change. Just as I was scratching off the last of the foil though, a door opened, and instinctively, I slipped the card into my back pocket.

The South African bid the man who appeared a nervy 'good evening', but the man didn't respond, and as *the South African* turned the key in his door, he glanced back down the corridor to see the man searching for something.

With the card almost scratched, *the South African* could

hardly own up to having found it, though, and as he closed the door behind him, the guilt was gnawing away at him.

Sitting down on my bed, I was taken completely unawares when I broke down, and that night, in the knowledge that I was highly unlikely to see my children again, I cried myself to sleep.

My melancholy didn't last long, though, as, during Mass the following morning, I had come up with a way to raise the money for those authentic documents — a 5/1 shot would do it! But the following afternoon, when *the right horse* was running, I bottled it.

And thank God I did, because the bay mare trailed in last of the seven runners.

My only option now was for Big D to get me back across the water, and when he did, I would call on the only person I could trust with the truth: my brother. And, with luck, Tommy would be my conduit back to Maeve and Joe.

So, on Tuesday morning, with the time for dithering over, *the South African* decided he would ask Big D to get him on a ferry. But before he called in to see the world's most dubious 'financial adviser', he had to do his laundry.

In the laundrette, as I was going through my pockets, I found that poor Lithuanian guy's scratch-card in my jeans, and as I scratched away the last of the foil, I sensed that it was going to be a winner.

And I was right — €25,000 right!

The irony of the situation was not lost on me, however, because, given the winning sum, the scratch-card could only be 'cashed in' through official channels — it was worthless to somebody like me!

Or was it?

After all, I was off to see a man who might just be interested in buying it off me — for a price, of course.

When *the South African* showed Big D the scratch-card, from the glint in the man's eye, he knew that he was about to be made an offer he couldn't refuse.

'Okay,' Big D mused. 'In exchange for the scratch-card you will get genuine identifications — a birth certificate, a passport and a driving licence, a one-way plane ticket to London, plus five thousand sterling.'

'Eight,' *the South African* haggled.

'You're not on Dragon's Den, my Boer friend. My position is non-negotiable!'

'Right,' *the South African* sighed, 'how long will it take?'

'How long is a piece of string?' Big D smiled enigmatically. 'I'll be in touch.'

'A week? A fortnight? A month?' *the South African* pressed.

'These things take time — *months*,' he stressed as he perused the scratch-card one last time before handing it back to me. 'You'll be sorted before the end of the year, I promise...'

(Later on, I would check the card and discover it had to be cashed in by *31.12.2018*).

'...Now, I need some specifics if I'm to find a suitable match.'

'Okay,' *the South African* nodded.

'Now, what age are you?'

'Thirty-seven,' *the South African* replied plainly.

'Thirty-seven!' McCarron sounded incredulous.

There followed a long silence as he waited for a more credible specification. But *the South African* didn't give him one.

'Okay,' he shrugged. 'You're the boss.'

'So, how do you get hold of *bona fide* documents?' *The South African* was as curious as he was suspicious.

'I'll tell you no more than the fact that I *acquire* a dead man's birth certificate. The only sticking point is that you'll become Irish, so you'll need to practice the accent.

'Now, I need to find someone born at around the same time as you. So, before you leave, I need to confirm that you want me to seek out documentation pertaining to a man born in the early 1980s?'

The South African nodded and stood.

'Uh! Uh! Uh!' *Big D* wagged a meaty digit. 'I want €2,000 — in cash — by way of a deposit before I set the ball rolling.'

The South African hesitated — Big D's cash offer was now effectively £3,000.

'If you're fucking me about,' he snarled savagely, 'then you'll be paying me in more than money!'

'I'm not!' *the South African* protested. 'I swear... I just haven't got the cash on me.'

'You've got until midday tomorrow!' Big D asserted, unyieldingly.

The South African was back the next morning with the deposit.

'Good lad,' Big D grinned, as he counted it out. 'Next — I need a contact number.'

'I don't have a phone,' *the South African* explained.

'What century are you living in?' he asked angrily. 'Well, where do you live then?'

The South African gave Big D the address of the hostel.

'Well, you'll need to stay put until you hear from me,' he

advised, by way of parting shot, and as I re-emerged on the street below, I realised I had put my trust — not to mention €2,000 — in the hands of a transparently crooked man.

Now, it was just a matter of hoping that my trust was repaid.

Spring turned to summer; autumn followed; and as winter started to creep in, I began to think I had handed over my €2,000 in exchange for the proverbial magic beans. But on a dreary Thursday evening in mid-November, just as I was going to offer the scratch-card to Eleanor, there was a knock at my door.

And there *he* was.

'Be at my office tomorrow morning at eleven with eight signed passport photos of yourself *and* the scratch-card. Your new name is John Doherty. D-O-H-E-R-T-Y.'

That was all he said. Then he was gone.

For three years, I had been tying my hair back in a greasy ponytail using a thick, rubber band; it had not been cut properly since Brigid died, but the next morning, I was first in line at the barber shop, four doors up from the hostel.

I had the back and sides cropped to grade four, but I kept some length on top, and although still flecked with a little grey, my natural chestnut colour returned almost miraculously. I had my beard trimmed and shaped into a neat little goatee too, and I barely recognised the man in the photographs I had taken in a chemist on my way to Dolphin Barns.

'You're lucky I didn't trust my instincts!' Big D mused, as he regarded *the new me*. 'I was inclined to look for the birth cert of a male born in the 1960s!' he laughed, viciously.

'You've obviously been hiding from someone...' he added saliently, but I didn't respond.

Then it was down to business.

'Now sign the back of your photos and sign these too,' he said, handing *the South African* two application forms. 'And don't forget it's John Doherty.'

John had been practising his new signature and signed where instructed.

'Now, give me the scratch-card.' Big D held out a mighty paw.

The South African (or was it, *John?*) complied.

'Okay,' Big D nodded, as he inspected it. 'I'll give you another knock in about two weeks ... *John.*'

'I thought...'

'Well, you know what thought did?'

'No.'

'Put a feather in the ground, thought he'd grow a chicken!'

'What?'

'Don't worry about it!' he laughed, handing me back the scratch-card. 'Your passport and licence will take another couple of weeks to put together. These photos have to be verified by people of social standing before they can be sent to *my friends* at the passport office and the RSA. You'll not be getting fakes.'

'Who was...?'

'John Doherty? Born Dundalk — 27th July 1981, died Belfast before he was two. The different jurisdictions help us a bit. My contacts do the rest. Now, I'll need you to show a modicum more patience while we get this sorted.'

'I understand,' *the South African* nodded.

'And you'll want to work on the accent,' McCarron counselled as he showed *the South African* out.

As I left, two men came in — shady looking characters; heavies — and I wondered what else went on behind the closed doors of Big D's office.

More than the procurement of illegitimate documents, I supposed.

On the last Saturday in November, the knock on the door came.

It was one of the heavies.

'Be in Mr McCarron's office tomorrow morning: *ten a.m.* sharp!' he growled. 'And make sure you have his money.'

It was as straightforward as that.

'Scratch-card?' Big D demanded the moment *the South African* was back through his office door.

'May I see the IDs?' *John* asked, in his best generic Irish accent.

'Not bad!' Big D chuckled, as he produced a brown A4 envelope. 'Inside are one *authentic* birth certificate, one *official* Irish driving licence, and one *bona fide* Irish passport.'

Then he handed over a much smaller envelope, stuffed with notes, which *the South African* proceeded to count out.

'What's this?' *the South African* asked calmly, but *he* was raging inside.

There was only £4000.

I'd always known Big D would do something like this.

'Hold the head!' Big D said, neutrally. 'If you're going to live in England, you'll be better off with a UK licence. So, once you're settled, you send your new address — along with four more passport photographs and your Irish driving licence

— to the Dublin PO Box that I've written on the back of your plane ticket. There's a contact number too – emergencies only. The extra grand will ensure that John Doherty gets a *genuine* UK driving licence without having to jump through any official hoops.'

'But…' *the South African* protested.

'You're not really in a position to argue, are you *John*?'

I shook my head.

'As I've told you,' Big D continued, 'the three documents I've given you are, if not legitimate, genuine, and although there are no guarantees in this life, you should be able to go a long way with them.

'But,' he said advisedly, standing, 'if you try to be clever, or you do something to make authorities look your way…' Suddenly he leant across the desk and grabbed me under my arms, so tightly that tears came to my eyes, '…Then you'd better hope that no cunt ever comes knocking on my door!'

'That won't happen,' I wheezed.

'Well, for your sake, I hope not…' Big D gave me one of his knowing smiles and relinquished his vice-like grip, 'because I have your face on camera, and I have *contacts* everywhere.'

For the first time, I noticed the CCTV behind him, pointing directly at the chair I was sitting in.

'Now, here's your plane ticket,' he said, producing an A4 sheet from a drawer to his left. 'You're checked in on Ryanair's 8.15 flight to London Luton on Monday morning; one small suitcase for the cabin. And don't forget that PO Box number is on the back, so don't just throw it in the bin when you land.'

As I went to take the print-out, he pulled it back.

'Scratch-card!' Big D demanded for a second time, and this time I gave it to him. 'Hughie!' he then bellowed.

Hughie appeared and took the card back out with him. When he left, the door locked, and I tensed up.

'If this is a set-up,' Big D grinned ominously, 'then I wouldn't want to be in your shoes.'

'It isn't,' I said fearfully.

But what if the scratch-card was fake?

I'd heard of such things before.

As I mulled over the consequences, Big D tap-tapped his computer keyboard without uttering another word, and when Hughie returned and whispered in his boss's ear, Big D glared at me.

Then he burst out laughing.

'Well, it's been nice doing business with you *Mr Doherty*!' he smiled, and when he stood, so did I. 'If you don't send me a new address by the end of next year, then there will be no UK licence.'

I nodded.

'And whatever else happens, I never want to see you in Dublin again.'

'You won't,' *the South African* told him, and this time, Big D asked Hughie to escort me off the premises.

After attending midday mass, *the South African* went down to Eleanor's basement flat to inform her that he would be leaving very early the following morning. It was the first time they'd seen one another in weeks, and Eleanor was visibly taken aback by the new look.

'It appears we had a very handsome man hidden beneath that scruffy exterior!' she joked, before allowing *the South African* to go upstairs to pack.

In my room, I bagged up the clothes and any other belongings that I couldn't take with me to England. I then gathered up every piece of loose change I could find, and after dropping three black bags on the doorstep of the SVP, I spent the next hour swapping my remaining coins for notes at one of the supermarket 'exchange machines' I'd used over the years.

I spent my afternoon exchanging my euros for sterling at a number of bureaux de change — £2,735 to add to the Big D's £4,000 — and after one last walk around the city-centre — for old time's sake — I treated myself to a roast beef dinner at Bewleys.

Late in the afternoon, *the South African* returned to the hostel with a bunch of flowers, a box of chocolates and a bottle of Rosé Champagne for Eleanor — 'a thank you for your kindness over the past three years!' — and she seemed genuinely touched.

Then, after a long, hot shower, I retired to my room for the very last time, and as I lay down on the bed, I knew that I wouldn't be able to sleep for worrying.

Could *John Doherty's* documents really be genuine?

One way or the other, I supposed, I would find out at the airport.

Part IV
November 2018

One

I will forever love Dublin, and I will never tire of saying so — because *she* brought me Patsy; *she* allowed me to avenge my wife's murder.

And I will forever love *her* people, because without their unmitigated generosity, I would have been in the gutter — they paid for the roof over my head, they ensured I never went hungry, they allowed me to put by a few euros aside for that rainy day, and they bestowed upon my miserable life, a modicum of normality.

Perhaps if I'd arrived in the capital during the dark days of the recession, then I might not have been so lucky, but while the rest of the Emerald Isle continues in its struggle to shake off the shackles of austerity, Dublin has risen like a phoenix from the flames, and once again, *she* prospers.

And I, for one, say, "Good luck to *her*!"

How things escalated from my neighbours playing loud music to me, single-handedly, killing three members of the same family *and* playing a crucial role in the murder of my wife, I'll never know.

But while four people were dead and my children orphaned as a consequence of my actions, I was about to embark upon a new beginning.

As I got off the bus and made my way towards 'departures', I could have done with a stiff vodka. I was well-aware that, like all my fellow passengers, my behaviour was being monitored. So, as I approached the automatic gates with my 'ticket', outwardly, for the cameras, I was doing my best to appear relaxed.

I scanned the barcode, and after a momentary pause, the gates opened. Then, like the rest of the herd, I made my way to baggage control. I calmly removed my belt and my shoes and put them in the grey, plastic tray with my suitcase.

As I walked through the body-scanner, though, I was having palpitations.

In the greater scheme of things, I don't know if £6,725 in cash is considered that much anymore, and *John* had his story prepared — he was moving to London and so had changed up all of his savings into sterling — but thankfully, he wasn't asked to account for the money.

I passed by the airport shopping 'mall' and walked on down to the departure gates, where I paced the shiny, marble airport floor, looking out at the aeroplanes coming and going, until finally, *Flight FR332 to London Luton* was called.

I was feeling sick to my core as I joined the queue to board the plane. At the gate, I handed my passport along with my boarding pass to a member of the Ryanair ground crew. I smiled nervously as the pretty, young stewardess checked both. She scanned the ticket and looked long and hard from my passport to my face. Then, with a cursory smile, she sent me on my way.

Why an alarm bell hadn't rung is anybody's guess — a simple cross-reference between two official databases (the death register and the passport office) would surely have been enough to trigger a very loud one — but presumably, to avoid adding needless red tape to the mountains that already exist, interaction between these discrete administrative offices is kept to a minimum.

During the flight, *John* drew up a mental list of what he needed to do if he was to integrate into normal society. He would have to find a home, he would have to find work, set up a bank account, get a National Insurance Number, obtain a medical card. *John* would have to gauge the risks posed at every juncture and work his way around them.

There was no 'big welcome home' at Luton for this prodigal son, and an hour after passing through airport security, I was disembarking the Easybus at Hendon Central, and a one-stop journey on the Underground took me to Colindale.

From the station, I headed straight to my brother's flat.

I would have to be a tad economical with the truth if I was to persuade Tommy that *I* hadn't killed Brigid, and again, I had a story prepared: I would tell Tommy that Brigid had been killed by the Carrolls (truth), that the Carrolls believed she had touted to the police (lie), I would tell him that I escaped (truth), that I lived rough in Dublin (truth) and that I had bided my time to take revenge (truth), and I would insist I had gone into hiding and acquired a new identity because I was a marked man (half-truth).

Of course, the glaring omission would be the murder that instigated the other three: Liam's.

My return to NW9 was a massive risk — this was, after all, the place where I'd grown up — and it was a distinct possibility that someone I passed on the street would recognise *me*.

The South African was ready to tell anybody who may

have challenged him that they were mistaken. But would it be enough?

The walk to my brother's apartment block took me directly past the scene of Liam's murder, and as I hurried by the lane down which I'd taken a leak, down which I'd found the empty lock-up, guiltily, I glanced left.

It was readily apparent that the lock ups had been razed — no doubt, a result of the gruesome find made there five years earlier — but as a chill ran down my spine, I wondered if a lost soul still lingered.

Being honest, at 11.40 on a Monday morning in late November, I was not expecting my brother to be in — as a teacher, Tommy should have been at work. Still, the sweat was running down my back as I pressed the bell to his flat. Then, when he buzzed me in without speaking over the intercom, my chest began to tighten. I hesitated momentarily before pushing open the security door, and as I made the slow ascent to his second-floor flat, I tried to focus.

Like everyone else, Tommy must have believed one of two things: either I was a dead, or I was a wife-killer — I'd have to explain that I'm neither. There was a lead weight in my stomach as I turned the final corner of the stairwell and saw his door — number fifty-seven — and at the sound of a key in the Chubb lock, I froze.

As the white door slowly opened, I thought I was going to faint, but to my amazement (and, I must admit, relief) I was faced by a complete stranger. Dressed only in his briefs, I guessed the man had been expecting someone else too.

I was standing there, wondering if Tommy had moved to Dubai like he had been threatening to, when I was rudely brought out of my reverie.

'Who the fuck are you?' the man demanded to know. He was of Mediterranean extraction, but he had a broad London accent, and he glared at me through forebodingly dark eyes, as he waited for a response.

'I'm sorry,' *the South African* apologised. 'I'm looking for an old friend. He lived here a few years ago…'

It was all I could muster.

'What's his name?' the man asked warily, his tone sceptical.

'Thomas Kelly.'

'Never heard of him,' he shrugged. 'I bought this gaff about a year ago — off some high-ranking police officer. A Chief-Superintendent. But his name was Singh. He was a…'

The man deliberated for a long moment, but he never finished the sentence and a decidedly uncomfortable silence ensued.

'Look I'll get you that copper's details for you if you want,' the man said irritably, as I mulled over what to say next (the art of conversation would have to be re-learned). 'I've got them here somewhere.'

Not a good idea!

'It's all right, mate,' *the South African* remembered himself. 'I've a couple of other places I can check out first.'

This was yet another lie. I now had but one option, and it was a long shot, because I didn't even have an address for my parents, just the name of the town they'd moved to: Walton-on-the-Naze.

Back outside, my thoughts turned to a rumbling stomach, and I headed towards the High Street where little seemed to have changed in my years away — different pub names and more takeaways, Romanian food stores to go with the Polish ones, and more bookies and charity shops perhaps.

One long-standing symbol of Colindale life remained open for business, though.

The Café Anglais might sound like an upmarket bistro, but in truth, it is little more than a 'greasy spoon'. But as 'greasy spoons' go, it is top drawer — a place where *the suits* and *the hoi polloi* are happy to eat under the one roof.

Condensation fogged the glass-fronted premises and conversations were raging as I entered. I ordered a coffee and a *Full English,* then took one of the few available seats, opposite an old man who was engrossed in his morning newspaper.

While I waited for my breakfast to arrive, I could not stop myself from glancing around the café. There were several faces dotted around the place that I thought I recognised, not friends, not even acquaintances, just faces with a certain familiarity.

But none of them seemed to be paying me any heed.

Soon, the waitress appeared with my breakfast, and with hunger superseding anxiety, I tore into my food. I was mopping up the last of my egg when the old man got up and left, and as he hobbled out the door, a *subbie* named Sean Rice sauntered in.

Sean Rice had been two years above me at secondary school, and we'd never got on. 'Ricey' was too full of himself for my liking — a braggart who liked to tell *the world and his wife* how well he was doing. He was the type who tried to buy other peoples' favour with his largesse at the bar and right up until the time I moved to Ireland, I'd bumped into him on a fairly regular basis in the pubs around Colindale — never once, had there been *a double* for me, though.

My former nemesis was the sort of man who would call it as he saw it, and if he recognised *me*, he would probably glory in it. *The South African* was ready to argue the case for mistaken identity, but it was doubtful that he would convince Sean Rice, and in such a public arena, one or two others might just back him up.

As Ricey scanned the café for an empty seat, I stared down into the remnants of my congealing egg. I could *feel* him homing in on the seat opposite me, though, and as his cement-covered boots shuffled up to the table, I was trying to tell myself that this situation might yet work in my favour — it was reminiscent of being challenged by that security guard in Penneys; a similarly fraught moment which persuaded me that I could walk Dublin's streets without fear of being recognised.

'You saving this seat for someone special?' The old, sarcastic tone was still in evidence.

'Er, no,' *the South African* shook his head, automatically looking up.

'Well, someone special's sitting here now!' Ricey laughed out loud, and as he looked at me, he seemed to hesitate, but he didn't say anything else and crossed to the counter to place his order.

Like so much around me in my 'home-town', Sean Rice was different but just the same — greyer and fatter maybe, but there was no mistaking the broad grin, the carefree manner and the mischievous look in his eye.

I had recognised Sean instantly and while he queued, I was certain that he was trying to work out who I was. I could *hear* the cogs in his head working overtime. Had he heard about what had happened to my family? About what had happened to me — the kid he used to bully at school?

I could have got up and left. But I needed *to know*. So, I stayed put.

As he waited to be served, Sean constantly glanced back over at the table and when he caught me gawking, I forced myself to hold his stare — I had to front it out.

'Is that yours?' he asked matter-of-factly when he returned, pointing at the copy of The Sun that the old man had left behind. It seemed like a loaded question, and I felt myself tense up.

'No,' *the South African* replied, again holding Sean's stare.

'Good stuff!' he smiled insincerely, as he sat down, and as he turned straight to the racing pages, I realised, that when he'd been looking back across the café, Sean had been eyeing up the discarded newspaper *and not* me.

'Ricey!' a booming vice roared. It was one of the nameless regulars from the Colindale pub scene. 'Get your arse over here! I need a favour.'

'You always need a fucking favour, Ray!' Sean sighed wearily as he got up and trudged across the café, and this time, he didn't look back.

Maybe in the recesses of his mind, Sean Rice had identified something in the drawn and sunken face in front of him. But he hadn't recognised Frank Kelly. Nobody had. I had lived within spitting distance of the Café Anglais for more than thirty years, but now I was a stranger in my own back yard.

Perhaps in the days and weeks following Brigid's murder, rumours about me abounded. Or did the news even make it back to London? I flatter myself to think that, from time to time, my name cropped up in conversations in Erin's Hope and The Moon Under Water. But did it?

In the greater scheme of things, my fifteen minutes of fame (or infamy) had long since passed, and rather than wasting time gossiping about Frank Kelly, the good people of Colindale would be concentrating on their own lives and their own problems.

Will I be able to afford the mortgage repayments if interest rates rise? Who will win the Premier League this year? Do I have enough money put aside for Christmas? Is my new neighbour a paedophile? How will Brexit impact upon my business? What happened to the war in the Ukraine? Where will I buy my new sofa from? Is China the new Soviet Union? Is my son on drugs? Is another bomb on the London Underground imminent? Should I wear the brown suit or the navy one for my nephew's christening? Am I saving enough for my retirement? Is India the new China? Is my daughter pregnant? Whatever happened to the kidnapped schoolgirls in Nigeria? Do I prefer Eastenders or Coronation Street? How many lines will I do on the Lottery tonight? How many lines of 'charlie' will I do tonight? Am I gay? Do I have cancer? Where the fuck is Gary Glitter these days?

Like the *once King of Glam Rock*, Frank Kelly is yesterday's news.

After finishing my breakfast, I wandered along the Edgware Road to the Premier Inn where I booked in for two nights.

I was unable to check into my room before four, though, so leaving my case in reception, I took a walk to Specsavers where *John* made himself an appointment for the following morning.

I also popped into ASDA and bought a pay-as-you go smartphone, and the second I was outside the store, I dialled the only number I had left to dial — my dad's.

How or why the number stuck in the memory, I do not know, it just did, and although *the South African* had a 'wrong number spiel' rehearsed, he needn't have bothered, because the line went dead.

I could have cried.

I spent my afternoon in the bookies and was back at the Premier Inn at four o'clock on the dot. In my room, I wrote down that list of the things that needed to be sorted out if *John Doherty* was to establish himself as a real person. Priority would go to a new home, a GP, a job, and a bank account.

Then, for the first time in years, I watched the television.

After Newsnight, I climbed beneath the duvet, and as I dropped off, I hypothesised as to how the cards would fall: the stakes were high and *John* would have to play his hand wisely, and while he would have to do plenty of bluffing, he would need to stay calm at all times, because just one bad call, and *John's* chance of a new life would be lost.

Two

The next morning, *John* returned to Specsavers, and by midday, he had his new prescription (which was only marginally worse than Frank's had been back in 2012).

John selected two pairs of frames and took the optician up on the offer of a free pair of monthly disposable contact lenses, and 'Alison' informed *Mr Doherty* that he would receive a text when everything was ready.

From Specsavers *John* headed for the library in Burnt Oak where, as a non-member, he had to pay to use the internet. *John* willingly paid the two-pound charge, and once the young library assistant had logged him onto one of the public terminals, he set about establishing himself in the online world.

After creating Hotmail and Facebook accounts, *John* visited a number of property websites. The nicest studio flat that he could find within budget was advertised by a private landlord on Gumtree, and having made an appointment for an immediate viewing, *John* walked from the library to Montrose Court — a shabby 1920s apartment block, which overlooked an even shabbier shared lawn.

The landlord, Mr Tailor, struggled with the key to the lock of the solid, metal, entrance door, and *John's* first impressions weren't overly positive.

Then, having led *John* up the communal stairwell to flat

number eight, Mr Tailor opened the bright, red front door, and the pair stepped into a dark and claustrophobic entrance hall with no natural light.

Faced by three doors, Mr Tailor opened the one to the left — to show *John* the immersion heater and the heating thermostat. The door straight ahead opened into a bathroom that consisted of a toilet, a walk-in shower and a sink — above which hung a plain, oval mirror. The fixtures and fittings were dated, and the single, low-wattage light bulb did nothing to lift the gloom, but it was serviceable, and everything appeared to be in working order.

The third door to the right opened up into the main living area where a large, double-glazed window let the daylight flood in. The room comprised a tartan-clothed, sofa-bed, a free-standing MDF wardrobe and a matching chest of drawers. Set out by the window was a small pine dining table and two chairs, and the annexed kitchenette (which, like the bathroom, had been fitted in another era, with doors and work surfaces in a rainbow of greys), had everything a tenant would require, and it appeared functional and clean.

Mr Tailor explained that the initial lease on the flat would run for six months, that the council tax and water rates were included in the monthly rent, and with the heating running off Economy Seven, the only bill *John* needed to change into his name was the electric — which Mr Tailor could arrange.

Two month's rent — one month as deposit — was required to secure the property, and happy enough with what he saw, *John* shook Mr Tailor's hand and the pair drove back to Mr Tailor's office, where the relevant paperwork was filled out.

In his best Dublin accent, *John* explained he had only just arrived from Ireland.

'... So, I'll have to pay with readies,' he said, almost apologetically.

'Cash is king!' Mr Tailor informed my new alter ego.

'I'll set up a UK bank account as soon as I can,' *John* said, as he handed over £1,200, 'and I'll sort out a direct debit.'

'It needs to be set up by the twentieth, Mr Doherty,' Mr Tailor said, as he counted out the money. 'But, as I say, cash is perfectly fine.'

I watched nervously as Mr Tailor tested the notes — first with a pen and then under a fluorescent light. If any 'failed' *John* was going to laugh it off by saying he'd changed his euros in a Dublin pub before coming across to England. But, in the event, they all 'passed'.

Then, while Mr Tailor disappeared into a back room to make photocopies of *John's* passport and driver's licence and to put the money in the safe, I nabbed his 'magic pen' and slipped it in my pocket — it would mean I could test all of Big D's notes later on in the hotel.

'Mr Doherty,' Mr Tailor sounded serious when he returned into the room, and I shifted uncomfortably in my seat. 'Don't look so worried,' he smiled, 'I was just going to say that although the lease is not due to commence until the first day of December, if you wish, you can move into the flat today — a few days early.'

Mr Doherty signed the tenancy agreement and Mr Tailor handed him a copy — along with the keys to his new home — and after giving Mr Tailor his mobile number, *John* left the office and headed back to the hotel.

Although keen to move in, I wanted to make the most of the comparative luxury of the Premier Inn, and back in my

247

room, I settled down for another evening in front of the box with a bag of Kettle Chips, a king-size bar of mint Aero and a two-litre bottle of diet coke.

I checked out at noon the next day, and having walked two miles north along the Edgware Road, like Mr Tailor, I struggled with the key in the lock of the entrance door (I would eventually discover the knack was not to push it in fully before turning). Then, after hanging up my few clothes in the wardrobe and re-setting the DAB clock-radio, I looked round the flat and made another list — this time, 'things' that I needed.

Back at ASDA, I picked up a 32" flat-screen TV in the pre-Christmas sales, a half-price quilt and the cheapest towels and bed linen I could find. I also bought new cutlery and a George Foreman grill — there were pots, crockery, a kettle and a toaster back at the flat — as well as a week's worth of groceries and a few odds and sods in *the George* clothes sale. I had to pay for a minicab to get me home, and once I'd put the groceries away, I set about making the flat feel like mine.

Once he had tuned the television, like all good citizens, *John* contacted the TV Licensing Agency. Without a bank account though, he had to go back out to pay for his licence at the post office, and although he begrudged parting with the money, it meant another 'official' proof of address would soon be arriving in the post.

Back in the flat, I put on the kettle, and as I waited for it to boil, I counted my money: £5052.65. I then tested each note with Mr Tailor's pen (every single one was 'good'), and having separated out £3,500, I wrapped it in cellophane and hid it inside a bag of sugar. This money was to cover the rent and electricity until the lease expired; it would also be used to open a current account.

That left me with about £1,550 which, given the exorbitant cost of living in the capital, wasn't going to last long, and sooner rather than later, *John* would have to find work.

On Friday afternoon therefore, *John* brought his passport, his Irish driver's licence, a letter from Southern Electricity and his tenancy agreement to the Job Centre in Hendon where he was interviewed by 'Julie'.

John gave Julie the waffle about having just moved to London from Dublin, and once he'd filled out the necessary paperwork, Julie informed *Mr Doherty* that, his National Insurance number would be generated and posted out to him forthwith.

From the Job Centre, *John* headed to Hendon library, and using the same IDs, he was able to join. *John* made immediate use of the free internet access to find his nearest GP, and after borrowing a Baldacci and a Billingham, he walked to the Woodcroft Medical Centre, back in Burnt Oak, where there were yet more forms to complete.

Soon though, *John Doherty* was registered as a patient with Dr Murkhani, which meant that, in the not-too-distant future, he would have a medical card to go with his NI number, and once he had received these official documents, *John* would cross that most daunting of thresholds: the bank's.

The next day, *John's* glasses and contact lenses were ready for collection, and after a moderately profitable afternoon in Ladbrokes, he treated himself to a Chinese takeaway.

Later, as I lay in bed, I could not help but think about how easy it had been for *John* to assimilate, and on Sunday, on bended knee at The Annunciation Church in Burnt Oak, I thanked God for this chance.

The rest of my day, however, was spent in sombre contemplation, depressing myself, thinking about all I had lost; and on more than one occasion, during that long, long afternoon, I had to 'quench my thirst'.

As I had discovered back in Keady, though, once my physical need had been addressed then my psychological compulsion was defeated too, and having just about managed to stave off *my demons*, that night, I went to sleep reminding myself that, if *John Doherty* was to build a future for himself, then I must remain sober.

Three

Just a week after arriving in England, *John Doherty* had a National Insurance number and a medical card — as well as all his other 'proofs' of identity and address — and he wasted no time in taking the final crucial step on the path to 'self-accreditation'.

John called into the Santander in Burnt Oak, first thing on Monday morning, and having made the earliest available appointment with the Customer Services Advisor, he returned on the Thursday, 'armed with' his Irish passport and driver's licence, his UK medical card and his National Insurance number, a letter from Southern Electricity, his letter from TV Licencing and the £3,500 he wished to deposit.

As *John* watched Gavin count and re-count the notes, he was again ready with his story about having cashed in his euros at a Dublin pub — just in case — but all appeared to be in order.

The falsely personable Customer Services Advisor entered *John's* particulars onto the computer system along with the details of his two direct debits — Southern Electricity and Tailor Properties — before giving *John* the patter about data protection and his rights as a Santander customer.

Then, after signing yet more paperwork, *John* was handed a copy of the bank's terms and conditions and informed he would receive a 'welcome pack' containing a paying-in book and a chequebook, early the following week.

'...Your new Visa Debit card and the pin code will arrive separately. And don't forget that you must phone the customer helpline to activate the card.'

Moments later, *John* was standing and shaking Gavin's hand.

Now he just had to wait and see what happened.

After his appointment with the bank, *John* went to the library and signed up with a couple of temping agencies. Without qualifications, *John's* options were limited, but there seemed to be plenty of seasonal work about, and having given vague details of his job history — as a labourer and as a warehouseman in Dublin — *John* was hopeful of getting a start somewhere.

Next, *John* logged into his Facebook account, only to discover that Tommy had de-activated his. Thinking around the problem, *John* sent a 'friend request' and an accompanying message to Mark, Tommy's best friend since primary school, about setting up a veterans' football team. Like Tommy, Mark loved his football, and only time would tell if he bought into the deceit.

Then, before leaving, *I* googled, 'Peter Flaherty + Armagh + councillor', and soon, I was clicking on a link to an article from the Armagh Observer that included a recent photograph of Flaherty standing outside the Sinn Fein office alongside Colette — *the respected councillor* had obviously re-built his marriage!

A little digging revealed that Flaherty was now running his own property company, and as I scrolled down the PF Properties website, I suddenly came up with a vague idea of how 'Pete' might breathe his last.

Step one was to set up a phoney e-mail account and bang off a general enquiry about a site that PF Properties had up for sale:

06/12/2018; 13.26
FAO: Peter Flaherty
Mr Flaherty,

I am contacting you with regards the site for sale on the Ballyhoy Road (ref: 45126CX).

I would like to arrange a viewing at your earliest convenience.

I look forward to hearing from you.

Sandip Patel.

By the next day Flaherty had replied:

07/12/2018, 08:42
Mr Patel,

The site is on for an asking price of £80,000, but I would expect it to fetch in excess of £100,000.

We will be pushing for the sale to go through by early spring.

I therefore propose a viewing in the New Year.

If you let me know a date that is convenient for you, I will clear my diary and work around it.

Kind regards.

Peter Flaherty.

Mr Patel would make a considered response.

There was further good news on the two other fronts.

Firstly, when *John* logged into his Facebook account, he

discovered that Mark had accepted the 'friend request'. Mark also asked for further details about the team, and *John* would apologise later — saying he'd got the wrong 'Mark Walters' — but not before he had taken the opportunity to trawl through Mark's 1648 friends.

It took almost an hour, but eventually, I found him — my brother, that is.

Tommy had a new profile — *Paul Thomas* (his first and middle names reversed) — and although *Paul* hadn't posted anything himself (or at least nothing that I could access), he had been tagged in four photographs.

The first was taken in the Dubai desert, a second was outside the Jumeirah Beach Hotel and a third was a picture of Tommy, posing on a jet-ski. They were from 2017, and in all three, Tommy appeared to be on holiday.

The fourth photograph, however, was a group-shot from January 2018 — with the strapline, "A night out with my teaching colleagues!" — and it was enough to convince me that my brother must be working in the mega-rich Arab state.

Whether it was of his own volition, or for his own safety, was a moot point, and although it wasn't much, I now had a window on my brother's world and a way to contact him.

All I needed now, was *a workable angle*.

John's other bit of good news was an e-mail from one of the temping agencies, inviting him to interview — ASAP — and with no time like the present, he went directly to the office on Burnt Oak Broadway.

Half-an-hour later, *John* was being offered a job — it was as a Packing Assistant on the night shift in a local retail warehouse, and although the contract only ran until the end of January, it came with an immediate start.

That same evening, *John* was clocking on for his first shift at Pritchard's where the work was largely autonomous. Each employee had to operate his own conveyor-belt, and with tough targets to meet, there was little or no time for conversation with colleagues; but *John* wasn't there to make friends.

As he clocked in for his Friday night shift, *John* was able to give Matty, the operations manager, his current account details. He had activated the account that same afternoon and had stopped off at a cash point on his way to work to 'test' his bank card — and a mini statement confirmed that *John's* £3,500 was safely 'pugged away', with the bank I'd grown up calling the Abbey National.

And so, life began to settle into new routines. *John* would get up at around midday, go for a walk or do any shopping that needed to be done, he would eat his main meal around four, leave for work around six, do his shift until two in the morning, walk the half-mile back home, have a little supper before going to bed and sleep through until midday.

And with plenty of extra hours to pick up at Pritchard's, and with *John* always keen, he worked fifteen straight nights before he finally took one off.

Only then did he return to the library — it was time for *Mr Patel* to respond to Flaherty.

22/12/2018, 12:02

Mr Flaherty,

Apologies for the delay in replying to your e-mail, but it is a very busy time of year for me.

Saturday February 10th is probably the date that suits me best.

255

I hope it suits you too.
Kind regards
Sandip Patel.

Unexpectedly, I received an instant reply. Flaherty must have been working:

22/12/2018, 12:08
Sandip,
Saturday 10th February would be perfect.
I suggest meeting in the morning.
Please let me know if this is convenient.
Kind regards
Pete.

Sandip now, eh Pete?

Before responding, I took a few minutes to check flight times and prices. Easyjet could fly *John* into Belfast on the Saturday morning, and with no delays, *Mr Patel* would be able to rendezvous with Flaherty by ten. *John* would then have plenty of time to make the 19.50 flight to Luton that same evening. Not that I revealed these plans to 'Pete':

22/12/2018, 12:18
Pete,
My plan is to take the afternoon flight from Liverpool to Dublin on Friday 9th February.
I can meet you at the site on Saturday at around eleven if that suits.
I will probably head straight there — with a satnav I should have no difficulty in finding it.
Any problems and I can always phone the office.

Once you have confirmed, I will get my secretary to book the flights.
Many thanks
Sandip.

Another instant reply:

22/12/2018, 12:19
Sandip.
All in the diary: 11am on Saturday 10th February.
Obviously, I will meet you at the site if that's what you wish.
Alternatively, you can call by the office, and I will drive you there myself.
I will, of course, keep you abreast of any other interest.
Kind regards
Pete.

John immediately booked the flights using his debit card; including car hire, the trip cost less than £100.

22/12/2018, 12:23
Pete,
Flights booked.
I look forward to meeting you.
I will be in touch again when I've arrived in Ireland.
Many thanks
Sandip.

I knew the site on the Ballyhoy Road — it was in an isolated spot — and my plan was to park up on a road running parallel. I would find my weapon of choice — probably a lump of rock

— as I crossed the farmer's field, and once I'd done the deed, I would simply retrace my steps back to my car.

All things being equal, *John Doherty* would be on his way back to Belfast International before noon, and he should be back home in Burnt Oak well before midnight.

Flaherty had effectively just signed his own death warrant!

Four

John's contract with Pritchard Packaging was not extended, so he returned to the Job Centre at the start of February and was pleasantly surprised to learn that he now qualified for Jobseekers Allowance *and* housing benefit.

John was all smiles for Julie as she told him this; and Julie was all smiles too.

Skinny with brightly painted fingernails, Julie's lank, mousey hair may have hung limply over her face, but she had nice teeth and unusually green eyes. While not exactly ugly, Julie was a little rough (Burnt Oak, I guessed), but as my date with destiny was just days away, *John* baulked at asking her out.

Mr Patel sent an e-mail to Flaherty on the Friday afternoon — to let *Pete* know he was in Dublin. He said he would meet him at the site, as arranged, and *Pete* messaged him back, almost instantly, to confirm.

On the Saturday morning, there were no nerves as *John* boarded his flight to Belfast, but when he reached the car hire desk, he suddenly remembered that this was the first time anybody had checked the licence.

As *John Doherty's* details went onto the Europcar computer system, I was certain it was going to trigger an alarm bell — but that simply didn't happen.

It was just after nine as I exited the car park in a nondescript black Ford Fiesta and with a clear road, I expected to be Armagh at around ten; this would give me plenty of time to park up, cross the field and be in position to *meet* Flaherty; but as I made my way south, I started to fret about what might go wrong.

CCTV cameras appeared to be covering every inch of the M1— and if the car was linked to the crime, it wouldn't be long before it was traced back to *John Doherty*.

Then, there were the other people in Flaherty's office who would surely know about the appointment with *Mr Patel* — and what if Flaherty was accompanied by one of them?

There was also a chance that a neighbour would notice the car parked up, or spot *the stranger* crossing the field.

It was, though, the 'virtual' paper trail that was giving me greatest cause for concern.

IT specialists could undoubtedly trace it back to a library in north-west London, and they would quickly discover the name of the library member logged on to the computer from which Mr Patel's e-mails were sent — and *John Doherty's* address was on the library database.

Any of these factors could see me apprehended, but as I left the motorway and passed by Portadown, although the fear was rising within me, I reminded myself that *I wanted to get caught for this one* — because I had a story prepared that might put a silver lining on my sorry existence.

If arrested, I was going to tell the police what had happened in the house in Keady on that fateful Saturday in October 2015, but I would transpose Flaherty for the Carrolls, alleging that he had turned up at the house when Brigid chose me over him.

I would contend that he was armed and that he had shot my wife, and that he planned to set me up for the murder. I would tell them that I had been bundled into the boot of a car and that I'd been tortured for days but that I managed to escape when Flaherty dumped the car in Westport.

I'd claim that Flaherty had been threatening to kill my children too — which was why I couldn't go to the police — and that I had lived in fear on Dublin's streets for years. I'd say I absconded to England in the back of a lorry in an attempt to find my family, but to no avail, and that in the end, I had returned to Northern Ireland, using a fake ID bought in London, to take my revenge.

Neither Flaherty, nor the Carrolls, could contradict my claims, and although I would get *life*, it would mean no more than twenty years (which might be halved for good behaviour) and when I was released, I could be reunited with my children who, I hoped, would see me as *an avenging angel*.

I was about three miles outside Armagh when an armoured police vehicle overtook me at high speed. Then another and another. A fourth sat on my tail for the next mile or so, and we were almost in town before a suitable gap in the traffic appeared for him to overtake.

Less than a mile from where I intended to stop, I saw yet another armoured vehicle (quite possibly one of those which had overtaken me) parked up in a layby on the Killylea Road, and I decided to abort — Flaherty would have to wait another day.

Shamefully, I must admit, that the armoured vehicles were probably the excuse I was looking for — I could never survive ten days, let alone ten years, in prison — and once again, I had put my liberty over the chance to see my children again.

My hands were shaking violently — I needed a drink — and at the next side-road, I turned the car around. I stopped off at the first petrol station I passed, and a bottle of Pepsi Max quenched my thirst.

As I put the plastic bottle in the forecourt bin, it dawned on me that, with a car to avail of for another few hours, I might yet be able to *see* my children who, I could only assume, were still living with my mother-in-law — and Teresa's house was just a few miles from where I sat.

I'd been to the house so often down the years that I had no difficulty in remembering the way, but as I drove past and peered in through the mature conifers which shielded the property from the road, I could see two unfamiliar cars on the drive and a stranger tidying around the garden. Having parked up at the gate, I walked casually up the drive, announcing my presence with a polite cough.

'Hello,' the man smiled.

'Hi!' *the South African* reciprocated. 'I'm looking for Teresa McGeown.'

'She hasn't lived here for a few years,' the man informed me. 'Can I help?'

'I was here to deliver some bad news. Teresa was a friend of my mother's, and my mother sadly passed away a few weeks ago. We couldn't get in touch by phone...'

'You probably never heard then...'

'What?' *the South African* looked bemused.

'It's just...' the man hesitated. 'Well, it's common knowledge, I suppose. But the family moved away after her daughter and son-in-law were murdered... By paramilitaries... Or so it's alleged,' he added, guardedly.

'Oh!' *the South African* shook his head and apologised for

taking up the man's time.

As I headed back to Aldergrove, I kept asking myself if the man had said 'the family moved away' or 'the family were moved away' — and to this day, I'm still not sure — but with the paramilitary link to Brigid's murder (and mine!) the latter was quite possible, and if my in-laws and my children had been moved for their own safety, I could not help but wonder if my brother had been moved on too.

The only way I could find out for sure would be to send *Paul Thomas* a message on Facebook. It would mean leaving another digital footprint that might bring the police to my door.

But what choice did I have?

Five

The next morning, after mass, I went to McDonalds for breakfast, and using my phone and their Wi-Fi, I set up yet another fake Facebook account — this time in the name of *Franchesca Lewis*.

I uploaded a cover pic (a Pulp Fiction banner; Tommy's favourite film) and a profile pic (a photo of an attractive female from Google Images), and once *Franchesca* had changed her settings to private, she sent *Paul Thomas* a friend request with a private message

'Hi Paul. Only just started working in Dubai. Your name came up as a suggested friend, and I was wondering if you were the same Paul Thomas, who used to be best friends with my brother, Trevor, at school? If so, it would be great to meet up — just for a coffee or something. It must be fifteen years since we last met, and although time changes us all, you do look like my Paul. And I must say you're looking well. Apologies if I have the wrong 'Paul Thomas' but I'm pretty sure I don't. ☺☺☺'

I was hoping that my brother's ego would get the better of him and that he would see this as an opportunity to date a pretty girl. But two days later, when *Franchesca* logged back into her Facebook account, she was to discover that *Paul Thomas* had deleted his.

That left me one flimsy straw to clutch at — Walton-on-the-Naze — and I was planning to go down there during the week, but the next day Pritchard's called, offering *John* a job.

It was a zero-hours contract, but with nothing else in his life, *John* was able to pick up shifts at the drop of a hat, and soon, he was getting almost as much work as he had been before Christmas.

Life became another round of sleep and work — with a little TV and a lot of thinking time thrown in — until, on the Wednesday of Easter Week, something happened to make *John's* sorry existence that little bit better.

John was in ASDA, picking up a few essentials, when he bumped into Julie. She was on her own and having exchanged smiles and a nod of recognition, *John* loitered in the next aisle, waiting for their paths to cross again.

This time he spoke — just a simple 'Hi!'

With her oversized plastic glasses, there was definitely something of the nerd about Julie, but she looked cute as she blushed at *John's* opening gambit. Julie's hair had been cut and coloured into a trendy, jet-black bob, she had good, clear skin and she smelt all sugar and spice, and *John* wasted no time in reminding Julie where he knew her from.

Predictably, Julie asked about work, and *John* told her he was back in gainful employment before giving her some *bulldust* about starting up his own business.

It was, of course, a complete lie, but it seemed to have the desired effect, and doubtful that the chance would present itself again, *John* changed tack completely.

'Do you fancy going out for a drink sometime?' he asked, uncertainly.

'Oh,' Julie sounded shocked.

'It's only a drink,' *John* shrugged.

It had not passed under my notice that Julie's fingers were ringless, but as soon as the question was out of my mouth, I realised she might be unavailable for all sorts of reasons — boyfriend, girlfriend, hair-wash.

'Why not?' She smiled. Then, 'I don't actually drink myself.'

'Nor do I,' *John* clarified. 'So, what about a coffee?'

'Sure,' she smiled again, this time more relaxed. 'I'm not working on Friday, so maybe we could meet over the road — at Costa? Say noon?'

And noon it was.

From Costa we walked to Colindale Station and caught the tube to Hampstead where we walked arm-in-arm across the Heath and down towards Parliament Hill. We had a bite of lunch in a quaint, little bistro before heading back up to the Underground and home along the Northern Line.

As we said goodbye at Burnt Oak station (my instincts had been right) Julie indulged *John* with a kiss, lip-to-lip, dry but lingering, and we arranged to meet up again on Easter Monday.

For our second 'date', we returned to Hampstead where we watched *Citizen Kane* at the Everyman, and on the Thursday, we took in a play at the Tricycle theatre in Kilburn.

By Friday night, Julie was at the flat, and after leaving the coffees unmade on the kitchen worktop, *I* was soon relieving *myself* of years of pent-up frustration on the sofa-bed.

Julie was not so innocent as I'd assumed. In fact, she was randy as hell. To be honest, she seemed willing to do anything — and I mean anything! — to please this prudish *missionary-man*.

Julie got off on having sex where she might get caught —

in the park, in her sister's marital bed, in the cinema, in the toilets at ASDA, in the car park at ASDA, even on a bus — and very soon, she was spending most nights at the flat where it was a struggle to keep up with her in bed.

John might have tried harder to satisfy Julie, he might have tolerated having his space invaded (she had already sequestered *her own drawer*), he might even have kept counsel about the dirty knickers she left all around the place, but when the nagging began — after little more than a week of cohabiting — he could read the writing on the wall.

'You need to find something better than the odd shift at a warehouse,' she complained pointedly one evening, adding officiously, 'you can't expect to have this place subsidised by the taxpayer forever!'

Julie was, of course, blatantly disregarding the fact that she was effectively living there rent-free, but she had a point, and when *John* saw a twelve-year-old Ford Transit that had been converted into a burger van for sale on Gumtree, he saw a way forward.

The van was kitted out with frying plates, hot rings, a deep fat fryer, a soup pot, a fridge, a hot water urn and a generator. It was 'taxed and MOT-ed' until December, and *John* managed to haggle the owner down to £2,350.

With just over a month left on the tenancy agreement on his flat in Burnt Oak, *John* didn't know how Julie would react when he told her that, come June, he would be moving to the Essex coast; her enthusiasm for the move took him completely aback.

Julie was eager to help where she could, and she guided *John* in filling out the relevant self-employment and tax forms. She also encouraged him to 'test the water', and having contacted Tendring council on *John's* behalf, she organised a weekend trading permit for the month of May. Then, on the May Day Bank Holiday weekend, having set up a monthly direct debit with Churchill Insurance, *John* was on his way to Clacton.

As well as being a business opportunity, this was, more importantly, an opportunity for me to try and find my parents; it was also an opportunity to get away from Julie and her sexual demands.

On the Bank Holiday Monday evening, with over £250 clear profit in his pocket, Julie was desperate to show *John* how impressed she was, but in the aftermath, as she lay beside him, patently unsatisfied, toying with him in an effort to get him going again, *John* broke the 'bad news'.

'I'm going to try and make a real go of this burger business over the summer,' he informed his lover optimistically. 'It will mean moving down to Walton at the end of the month. But,' his tone turned doleful, 'I'll be dossing down in the van for the foreseeable.'

John was hoping that Julie would get the message, but all of a sudden, she was talking about transferring to Clacton; about setting up home 'properly' and about how much she wanted children!

'Perhaps, we should take things one step at a time.' *John's* voice betrayed his reticence.

'You're just like the rest of them!' she screamed, getting out of the bed. 'You're a user!'

'Calm down, Julie!'

It was all *John* could think to say.

Julie did eventually calm down and climb back into bed, but things were never quite the same after that, and the following Sunday, when *John* returned to Burnt Oak — after a much less profitable weekend — it came as no surprise that Julie wasn't there to welcome him home.

Julie had taken *all* of her belongings from the flat, and although he felt a small tingling of disappointment, *John's* overriding emotion was one of relief, so when Julie phoned the following evening to suggest they take a break, *John* couldn't have agreed more.

Six

At the end of May, *John* signed off on the lease of the flat, and once Mr Tailor had inspected the property, he told *John* that the deposit would be re-paid into his bank account within ten working days.

Then, with all of my worldly possessions in the back of the van, I left London behind.

On the last day of May, *John* called into Tendring council offices where he paid for another monthly permit — this time in Walton-on-the-Naze itself, where he was given a pitch outside the leisure centre — and after a visit to the local 'cash and carry', he prepared his 'signature chilli con carne'.

As well as the standard 'chilli bowl', *John* transformed his staples into 'chilli dogs', 'chilli chips' and 'chilli burgers' — charging an extra pound for a dribble of the hot stuff — and it proved to be a relative success.

Trade in June was moderate, but with the van doubling up as my home, I managed to make a small profit. I quickly realised that the burger business was only ever going to be a short-term fix, and that longer term, *John* would have to go back to school and gain some qualifications.

I have to admit though, I liked working in Walton — probably because, with nobody in the town ever going to recognise *me*, I felt able to relax.

For the first time in years, I found I wasn't afraid to make polite conversation with strangers, and I didn't need to put on a ridiculous accent either.

In all but name, I could be myself.

So, before he made any drastic changes to his life, *John* would work through the summer and see how things went.

Another daily routine had now been established: alarm call at 7.45, brush teeth and splash face, coffee, visit the cash and carry, and open for business at ten. I would close up at six, swim for an hour, and after a walk, I would park up every night in a layby on the A133.

My evening walk took me around Walton in search of my parents' bungalow — I had never actually been to the property; but I had seen photographs, and I was certain I would know it if I passed by it. However, even in a town as small as Walton-on-the-Naze, there were just too many back roads, side-streets and dead-ends. And worse still, every bungalow seemed to be painted in the same, ubiquitous *seaside primrose*.

Then, out of the blue, fate brought my father to me.

It was late one afternoon when he walked past my van, and although I only caught a glimpse of him in profile, instinctively, I *knew*.

I was sorely tempted to call after him, but I needed to bide my time, and instead, having closed up early, I had to settle for following him along the seafront and onto the High Street.

Dad was looking older (well, of course, he was — what I mean is, he looked old) and as I watched him struggle up the hill to the edge of the town, I felt a pang of sadness. Dad, in particular, had been so excited about the children spending their summers in Walton.

But that never happened.

Eventually, Dad turned into a driveway that serviced three similar bungalows, and having watched him disappear into his, I withstood the temptation to knock and headed back to the leisure centre — I needed to have my story straight before I gave mum and dad the shock of their lives.

The main thing was that I'd found them.

It was about a week later when Dad walked past the van again — and this time, as he crossed over the main road to the seafront, he was met by my mum. My heart was already racing, but I thought it was going to explode when, from behind my mother's long, pleated skirt, appeared a pretty girl and her young brother.

I was frozen behind the counter as I watched the four of them disappear down the stone steps and onto the beach, and once again, I shut up early.

Having crossed the road, from a vantage point on the promenade, I looked down onto the beach where *my children* were running gleefully towards the sea.

I laughed inside as Joe dipped his toes into a receding wave, only to flee in the next instance as another broke on the shore, scrambling back up the golden sands to the safety of his grandmother's arms.

His older sister was more adventurous. At eight years old, Maeve was brave enough to paddle up to her knees, filling her bucket with water before pouring it into a hole her grandfather was digging on the beach.

As I wrestled with the idea of approaching them, I became conscious that, if anybody was watching me observe those two beautiful children playing innocently on the beach — oblivious to the dangers of the real world around them, oblivious to me — then they might have got the wrong idea.

Then, my dad looked up to where I was standing.

He waved and called out.

I didn't catch what he said, but the tone was definitely friendly, and I thought I was going to be sick. But as I gathered myself and prepared to join them down on the beach, a young woman, a redhead, passed by me on the promenade. Only then did I realise my dad had been waving at her. He hadn't actually noticed me.

Whoever the woman was, she knew my parents, and she was familiar with my children too, because Joe ran up to her, arms outstretched. The woman picked him up, and I could only stand and stare as she walked off with my mum, each of them holding one of Joe's hands.

Maeve called out to the woman and my mum, and they stopped and turned, waiting until dad and Maeve had caught up with them. Then as one, they wandered off towards the pier with Maeve and Joe continuing to frolic in the surf, the sea breeze carrying their squeals and yelps up to the promenade; up to me.

Tears were stinging my eyes, and although I was desperate to follow — desperate to see my children at close proximity, to speak to them, to pick them up myself — I had to let them walk away into the evening sunset, content in the knowledge that I knew where they were staying.

There was no sign of them next day, however. Nor the day after. Nor the day after that. And I was left to wonder if I should have approached them when I'd had the chance. But what would I have said? What could I have said?

I didn't sleep well for days, wondering if I would ever see my children again, but in the end, I came to the logical conclusion that Maeve and Joe must have been on holiday in England, visiting my parents, their grandparents.

The redhead might just have been somebody my parents knew, or she might have been a social worker there to collect them, to bring them back to Ireland where they presumably still lived — probably with my in-laws, probably under assumed names, probably in a new town — and although I realised it might be the following summer before Maeve and Joe returned to Walton, I had come to learn that patience was a virtue.

On the upside, I now had plenty of time to put together a credible explanation for my 'reappearance'.

Once July kicked in, business picked up, and *John* made hay while the sun shone. And he needed to, because come September, turnover would fall off the proverbial cliff-edge and *John* would almost certainly have to find alternative employment.

With jobs in Walton at a premium, and without qualifications, *John* knew he would have to take anything he could find, so when he saw a card in a newsagent's window — "Cleaner required for pier arcade. Early mornings." — he wasn't too proud to ring the number.

Within the hour, Mr Arnold was interviewing *John* for the position — two hours cleaning per day, seven days a week, for the remainder of the holiday season — and a few minutes later *John* had been offered the job.

Needless to say, he accepted.

The next morning, at half-past six, Mr Arnold was showing *John* the ropes, and by the following Friday *John Doherty* once again had a regular payment going through his

Santander account to top up on the erratic income from the burger van.

I was managing to stay clean with a daily shower at the leisure centre, but the weekly trip to the launderette was doing little to eliminate the smell of the fat from my clothes, which were, to put it politely, getting grubby. I'd not had a haircut since Dublin, and my beard and my hair — which I was again wearing in a ponytail — were starting to look a little wild. But I decided I would wait until the autumn, when *John* would be going back to school, before I tidied up my appearance.

John's academic journey began with a visit to Walton library where he read through the prospectus for Colchester Institute. *John* had a number of options open to him, and after an informal interview at the Adult Learning Centre in Frinton, he chose to sign up for GCSEs in English, French, History, Mathematics and Geography at the campus in Colchester — daytime classes, ten hours per week, starting mid-September — and, all things being equal, he would be re-sitting exams that *I* had already passed, shortly before Christmas.

The study schedule would exclude *John* from working full-time, but he had been saving scrupulously, so even if he didn't find any alternative part-time employment, he would be able to pay the rent on a flat in Walton for, at least, six months — time enough to get his five GCSEs.

John was planning to wait until the weather turned cold before he started looking for a flat, but change was forced upon him on the last Thursday in July by a nasty piece of work who entered the changing room, just as *John* was getting ready for his regular evening swim.

The man had an obvious scar on his right cheek, and just as obvious was the fact he didn't have any swimming gear.

John tried to ignore the man, but as he turned his back, a 'friendly' hand on the shoulder 'invited' *John* to sit and his heart started to race.

'Now, I don't want things to get unpleasant,' the man warned grimly, as he sat down on the bench beside *John*, 'but you're up gonna have to give up your pitch.'

'I have a trader's licence,' *John* protested.

'That keeps you right with the council,' the man snarled darkly. 'But from now on, if you wanna trade anywhere from Harwich to Clacton, you deal with me.'

'And you are?'

'Your worst nightmare,' the man growled, his voice echoing in the enclosed space.

'How much?' *John* enquired nervily.

'Two hundred-a-week.'

'What!' *John* was just about clearing £300.

'You've been fucking lucky!' the man insisted, giving me a dig in the ribs. 'I know that you've been operating *on my manor* since May — which, by my reckoning, means you owe me the best part of two grand.'

'I don't have…'

'Don't worry!' he laughed, hoarsely. 'I'm a fair man! I allowed you to operate 'cos I didn't need the pitch. Not until now. But a friend of mine's just come back from *a six-year vacation* and he's prepared to pay me the going rate.'

'But I'm giving you first refusal. So, either you pay me *two ton* right now and we shake on it… Or you can fuck off!'

I didn't feel as if I had any choice in the matter.

'Good man!' he smiled, his tone turning convivial. 'Now, make sure you phone the council first thing in the morning. Tell them you're giving up the pitch with immediate effect.

Kapiche?'

I nodded dumbly.

'Oh!' he pretended to remember something important. 'If you go to the *old bill* when you walk out of here, I'll make it my business to find you.'

'Don't worry,' I reassured him. 'I have no intention of going to the police.'

After the small-time hood had exited by the only door, I sat in shock for quite a while, but I decided to go for my swim anyway — to see if it calmed me down any. It did a little, although inevitably I spent the whole time thinking about what to do next.

I decided I would put the van up on Gumtree — it still had four months' tax and MOT, and I reckoned I would get back most of what I'd laid out for it. I also brought forward my plans to find a flat.

The very next morning, *John* visited an estate agent on the High Street, and by the afternoon, he was viewing a one-bedroom, second-floor apartment in a modern block, close to the seafront.

The flat was fully furnished — a double bed, a pair of two-seater sofas, a dining table and chairs, fitted wardrobes, and a fitted kitchen with brand new *white goods* including a dishwasher, a washing machine and a tumble dryer — and at £500 per month it was within *John's* price range.

John was impressed enough to go straight back to the office, and once he had paid an ambiguous, but nonetheless sizeable, 'letting agent's fee', Karl ran all the credit checks, and when nothing flagged up, *John* paid two month's rent and signed a six-month lease.

That evening, having parked the Transit in the communal

car park, I pulled on a pair of rubber gloves and scrubbed it from top to bottom. Bedding, towelling and every last item of clothing I owned (apart from those I stood in) went into the communal bin while the mattress I'd been sleeping on for months would be going to the municipal dump the next morning.

All I held onto were a change of underwear, my cleaner's uniform, my toiletries, the DAB clock-radio, the television I'd bought back in London and any food and condiments which were still in date; and after a long hot shower, I went to bed without eating.

The next morning, after my cleaning shift at the arcade, I dumped the mattress and headed for ASDA where, as well as groceries and toiletries, I bought an entire new wardrobe — two pairs of chinos (one navy, one tan), a pair of jeans, two jumpers, three polo shirts, three shirts, three crew neck t-shirts, a black tracksuit, a woollen jumper, a fleece, pyjamas, underwear and socks, a pair of brown loafers and a pair of black brogues, a new pair of Speedos and a pair of trainers — and back at the flat, I brought everything upstairs and hung it all up.

Once I'd put the groceries away, I changed out of my uniform and after another long, hot shower, I got dressed — navy chinos, a white polo shirt and brogues — and I felt like a new man.

After a coffee and a doughnut, I went downstairs and took a few photographs of the Transit van on my smartphone, and in under five minutes, *John* had it advertised on Gumtree for £2,500.

Next, *John* updated his home address via the TV Licensing website, and although still raging that he had allowed himself to be bullied off the pitch so easily, he still phoned Tendring Council.

What else could he do?

But perhaps the fates had decreed this change in circumstance, because, as luck would have it, just two days later, as *John* was finishing his cleaning shift, Mr Arnold asked for a quiet word. '… A vacancy has come up in the arcade, and I need somebody I can trust…'

Mr Arnold didn't say what had happened to Charlotte, but he could not stress enough how every member of staff was constantly monitored by CCTV.

'… Not that you'll be handling any cash,' he added, sternly.

'Well, I don't know what to say,' *John* faltered.

'*Yes*, would seem appropriate,' Mr Arnold smiled. 'And you can start this afternoon if it suits.'

'Thanks.'

'But do tidy yourself up, John,' he advised, father-like.

And so, *John* bought himself a pair of clippers and cropped his hair — a grade two all over — before shaving off his beard completely. Then, for the very first time, he popped in the monthly disposables he'd got free from Specsavers when he arrived in London, and when *John* turned up for his first shift as the arcade's 'Customer Service Attendant', he could tell Mr Arnold was as impressed as he was surprised.

As Mr Arnold outlined *John's* duties and responsibilities, he reminded *John* that the position, like his cleaning job, was temporary.

'…The contract will run week-to-week — probably until mid-September,' he added, almost apologetically.

John understood.

On Monday, *John* visited the Job Centre to inform them of his change in circumstances and was handed yet more paperwork to fill out. As he would no longer be self-employed, *Mr Doherty* was advised to complete the online self-assessment for HMRC in good time, and having kept meticulous handwritten accounts and *all* of his receipts over the past three months, *John* had no difficulty in completing the form, and he had sent it off by the end of the week.

John had a secondary reason for being in the Job Centre, though — to discover what benefits he might be entitled to come mid-September; and it appeared that he would be eligible for both JSA and housing benefit.

John's savings pot received another boost with the sale of the burger van — £2000 was considerably less than he wanted for it, but it was the price of a quick sale — and he now had almost £5,000 in his current account.

John also had another £630 in his Lynx canister — money he had been able to keep from the taxman, money that should allow him to put aside his weekly wage over the coming month — and once he started college in September, if *John* could survive on his JSA, then he would have more than enough to cover his rent and bills until the lease ran out on the flat at the end of January — by which time he should also have five GCSEs.

What happened after that would be entirely dependent on how things panned out with my parents.

To that end, I had written 'my story' down on paper, and for weeks, I had been practising what to say and how to say it, and as dusk fell one Friday evening, I finally mustered the courage to knock on the bungalow door. But I hadn't planned for what came next — because the gentleman who answered the door was *not* my dad.

There was a slight resemblance, but the man at the threshold was smaller and *much* older than my father. And not only had I convinced myself that he was my dad — and that his wife was my mum — but I had also been certain that the man's grandchildren were Maeve and Joe.

I guess I had seen what I wanted to see.

'Yes?' the man enquired sternly, holding very firm eye-contact.

'I'm looking for Mr Tony K-Kelly,' I faltered.

'Never heard of him!' he shouted, eyeing me suspiciously. Despite his age, the man had a distinct air of authority; he was definitely not the type to let a stranger run rings round him.

'I think he lived here a few years ago...'

'Did he indeed?' the old man sneered. 'Well, I'm quite sure I would have noticed the intrusion — because my wife and I have been living in this house since 2006!'

I stood agog.

'Now, if that's all!' he said, dismissively.

'I erm...'

'Get off my property before I call the police!' he raged, slamming the door in my face.

As I turned away, I could hear him saying, to his wife presumably, that, 'It was just some bloody cad!'

And he wasn't far wrong.

I had deluded myself into thinking that I had rediscovered my parents *and* my children, but with my one remaining hope shattered, back in the flat, I spent the night fighting my demons, drinking glass after glass of cold squash, knowing just one sip of something stronger and I would be back in the gutter.

After a night spent tossing and turning, I woke the next morning in a peculiarly positive mood, reminding myself that life could be a whole lot worse — after all, I'd settled into my new flat and I loved living by the sea, so perhaps Walton-on-the-Naze wasn't the worst place to be.

And once *John* had gained his GCSEs, his life would improve a little more.

If he failed, *John* did have another option, though. It was something I had been thinking about for months — ever since my nights parked up on the A133. But to become a lorry driver, *John* would require an HGV licence.

The first step in obtaining one was to exchange his Irish driving licence for a UK equivalent, and while *John* could and probably should, have sent the document off with a D1 form to the DVLA in Swansea, Big D had never let him down.

So, he decided to show a little more faith in the man — and if Big D was true to his word, then *John Doherty* could expect to have a 'genuine' UK driving licence within weeks, or maybe months, and then he could work towards obtaining that HGV licence.

Using the photo booth on the pier, *John* had four passport-sized photos taken, and he posted them along with his licence and his Walton address to the PO Box in Dublin that Big D had given him.

It seemed like a sensible thing to do.

At least, it did until the waiting began.

Seven

As the days passed, I became riddled with doubt: all the negative *what ifs*.

But what good was worrying?

I decided that, if Big D hadn't come through by the time *John* had got his GCSE results, then *John* would simply revert back to Plan A and look for 'office work' — maybe in Walton, maybe Colchester, maybe back in London, or maybe somewhere new. Then, through hard work and further study, he would endeavour to forge a 'proper' career for himself.

By mid-August, having evidently proven his trustworthiness to Mr Arnold, *John* was assigned cash-handling duties — just changing up notes for the holidaymakers — and on the last Friday of the month, a familiar face was at the counter looking to change up two *tenners*.

John watched as the man ambled over to the fruit machines, and a short time later, as *John* patrolled the arcade floor, he stopped to pick up some litter from beside the machine the man was playing.

As *John* stood, he glanced at the spinning reels and the man glowered — some punters just want privacy. The pair were eyeball to eyeball, and it was clear that the man didn't have a clue who *John* was.

Then *John's* phone buzzed.

John wasn't supposed to take calls when on duty, but he knew it was Mr Arnold — and he knew what his boss wanted. *John* snuck into the next aisle to answer the call, trying his best to be discreet.

'No Mr Arnold,' *John* argued animatedly. 'You need to be back here before two... We must get to the bank — *today*... We've not lodged since before the Bank Holiday — and there's more than twelve grand in the safe...'

Suddenly, *John* stopped speaking — the man was eavesdropping.

As *John* hurried back to the customer service desk, he wondered just how much of the conversation he had let slip, and later on, as he made his way home along the promenade, *John* realised it was more than Mr Arnold would have liked.

'I recognise you from somewhere,' the man had crept up behind *John*. He was slurring his words a little as he muttered in *John's* ear.

'Maybe,' *John* turned, looking him up and down. 'Weren't you in the arcade today?'

'Of course!' the man laughed and patted *John* on the shoulder, pointing at the uniform.

John smiled, still uncertain if the man also remembered him from the leisure centre.

'Do you wanna come for a drink?' the man asked ingratiatingly, but *John* must have looked at him strangely, so he got straight to the point. 'Look, I overheard you on the phone earlier...'

'Right,' *John* nodded, edgily.

'So how much money is in the safe?' the man enquired in a barely audible whisper, constantly looking around. But there was nobody close.

'I dunno,' *John* shrugged.

'I do believe you said *more than twelve grand*,' he prompted.

'Right,' *John* swallowed hard: an acknowledgement of his indiscretion.

'So?' Suddenly the man had his arm round *John's* shoulder. 'Can we get our hands on it?'

'The arcade's fully alarmed,' *John* explained, tentatively, 'and there's CCTV everywhere. But if...'

'Go on,' he said, eagerly.

'Look.' It was *John's* turn to glance round furtively. 'Call in tomorrow. My boss usually takes his lunch at one o'clock. Let me check out a few things. It might not be possible...'

'But it might be,' the man grinned.

'Maybe,' *John* reciprocated, and the man gave a conspiratorial wink.

We were in business.

The man appeared in the arcade the next day at precisely one o'clock, and *John* was again patrolling the floor. Mr Arnold was ensconced behind the desk, so it proved easy to engage the man in a very brief and very discreet conversation.

'So?' he enquired.

'It's possible.' *John* whispered excitedly. 'But I can't talk.' The man followed *John's* eyes to Mr Arnold. 'He's already had lunch...'

'So?'

'Make sure you're walking past the pier at just after eight tonight. I'll catch you up on the promenade and I'll tell you everything then.'

The man licked his lips greedily, and then he left.

Just as *John* came off shift, the man was passing by the arcade. He was on his own, heading along the seafront towards Frinton; and *John* gave it a couple of hundred yards before sidling up alongside him.

'Carry on walking.' *John* was whispering, even though there was nobody else within a hundred yards. 'It has to be tonight.'

'How much?'

'We'll get at least fourteen grand.'

'*At least*?' The man echoed, barely able to contain his glee. 'So? What's the plan?'

'Meet me later and I'll explain.'

'Where?'

'Under the pier.'

'Right … So, what time?'

'It's got to be late: after everything closes.'

'Pubs shut at midnight … Say one?'

'1.30,' *John* advised cautiously, 'just to be safe.'

'So? What's the coup?'

'If I tell you now, you might come down mob-handed and do the job yourself!' *John* laughed good-naturedly. 'I'll spill the beans at 1.30 — so long as you're on your own. And if you tell anyone about this, then the deal's off.'

'I dunno,' he looked at me doubtfully. 'It sounds a bit dodgy.'

'It is a bit dodgy. We're going to commit a serious crime, aren't we? Look, meet me later and I'll explain it all to you then. You'll also understand why it needs two pairs of hands.'

'Mmm,' the man was still unsure.

'Look, you can frisk me if you like,' *John* said flatly. 'I won't have anything on me apart from a torch. And anyway, what have you got to lose if we don't see it through? A night on the piss? You'll have saved yourself a few quid if nothing else!'

'Go on then,' the man said, nodding thoughtfully. 'But I'll give you more than a slap if this is some sort of piss-take.'

'I can't have anyone else involved,' *John* reminded him, ignoring the threat.

'Don't worry, I don't want to dilute my share of the profits any more than is necessary,' the man said, a little more loudly than I would have liked, then he shot right and darted up the steep, stone steps that snaked between the rows of brightly coloured beach huts, standing on the bank above the promenade.

'*Radix malorum est cupiditas!*' I whispered as I watched *my friend* disappear.

I'd done something like this before.

Eight

When I got home, I put my cleaner's uniform and shoes into an ASDA carrier bag, and then it was simply a matter of waiting.

At around ten-past-one, having checked the TV listings, I left the flat carrying the plastic bag, and having crossed the road in front of my block, I turned into a lane on the opposite side that led to the top of the steps, up which *my friend* had disappeared some five hours earlier.

Naturally, I had checked my route for CCTV — there was none that I could see.

About halfway down the steps, I crept in between two rows of beach huts and found a vantage point which gave me an unobstructed view of the promenade. It was a clear night — a full moon — and at 1.28 (by my watch) I glimpsed a movement below.

Like me, *my friend* was dressed in black with his hood pulled up over his head, and after a quick look round, he darted down onto the beach and out of sight. I gave it a couple of minutes to see if anybody else appeared, then, leaving the carrier bag beneath one of the huts, I came out of hiding and followed in his footsteps.

My friend was waiting under the pier, and he was holding his right arm down by his side, so I knew he was 'carrying' — I hadn't expected a gun, though.

'Over here,' he hissed digging me in the ribs with his weapon. He wasn't so friendly now. 'Whatever's in that safe, the split is gonna be eighty-twenty!'

'That's not fair!' I screeched, indignantly.

'Shut the fuck up!' he snarled, jamming the gun into my stomach. 'Otherwise, I'll just take the fucking lot!'

My friend quickly frisked me and found the torch in my pocket. He examined it cursorily, before handing it back to me, and only then did he notice the latex gloves.

'What the fuck are they for?' he demanded to know.

'I can't afford to leave prints,' I explained calmly. 'Mr Arnold never lets me near the safe. And he certainly doesn't know I've got a copy of the safe key. I need him to suspect one of his dopey nephews.'

My friend grinned and seemed to relax.

'So, what's the plan?'

'First, we need to locate a specific spot beneath the arcade — it's an old escape hatch. I can get into the arcade through it, without triggering the alarm,' I told him plainly.

'Well, lead the way then, Tonto!' *my friend* snorted, nudging me on with the barrel of his gun.

I came to a stop, close to one of the concrete pillars which formed the base of the pier and shone my torch upwards, lighting up the rusted, steel girder which rose up into the dark.

'The tide's gonna be in soon,' *my friend* observed, 'so we need to hurry. How long is this gonna take?'

'Here it is!' I said, excitedly.

'What?' *my friend* barked, giving me a curious look. 'I can't see anything.'

'Up there,' I persisted, and he moved in beside me.

My friend still had the gun levelled at me, but as he came in closer for a better look, raising his head and letting his eyes follow the torchlight, he let his arm drop limply to his side.

And then crack!

And then bang!

Nine

I had grabbed *my friend's* hair at the back, and with all my might, I had slammed his head against the pillar. In the same moment, a shot echoed under the pier. I had no idea how close I'd come to death, but obviously, I hadn't been hit.

My friend was out cold, and as he lay prone in the sand, I carefully plucked the gun from his grasp. Then, cupping my palms, I poured handful after handful of seawater into his mouth. He gagged once, but then the spluttering stopped.

From the moment *my friend* had threatened me in the changing room, I wanted to kill him, and although I never actually expected an opportunity to present itself, when he appeared in the arcade, the plan came to me in a trice.

The phone call to Mr Arnold was the bait.

Greed was the key — and *my friend* couldn't unlock the door quickly enough.

Our moonlight tryst had been arranged to coincide with a high tide, and now as the sea washed over the corpse, I walked away from the crime-scene along the beach, staying close to the edge of the surf, safe in the knowledge that the incoming waves would soon wash away my footprints and any evidence I may have inadvertently left beneath the pier.

About a half-mile along the shore, I made my way back up the beach to the promenade, and having climbed up onto the bank above, I disappeared into the *parish* of beach huts, hoping to locate the one beneath which I'd hidden the carrier bag and my uniform earlier in the piece.

As I sneaked through the regimented rows back towards the pier, I realised I couldn't differentiate between huts, so instead of hunting for my needle in the haystack, I crawled into a gap between two huts and waited for the sun to rise.

Lying there, I contentedly listened to the waves crashing against the sea wall, *doing their work*; and I must have dozed off, because when I awoke, the sun was already up.

It was 06.10, and I hurriedly dodged between beach huts until I reached the stone steps, and after retrieving the ASDA bag from its hiding place, I quickly changed into my cleaner's uniform and work shoes.

I put the clothes I'd been wearing into the plastic bag, but the gun, I kept about my person. Then, at precisely 06.25, I emerged from between the beach huts and casually walked down to the promenade. This formed part of my usual morning route, and when I bumped into a couple of familiar dog-walkers heading in the opposite direction along the seafront, I made sure we had a brief exchange of pleasantries.

John did his cleaning shift as normal, and after getting some well-earned rest, he was back on the pier at just before midday for his afternoon turn on the arcade floor, and although he was on red alert throughout the day, waiting for the police to cordon off the beach below, it would be Monday morning before the blue and white tape was in evidence.

The pier remained open, though, and *John* was on tenterhooks as the gossip abounded, but it didn't rise much above general speculation, and he went home, wondering just what line of inquiry the police were following.

Not that I panicked — after all, I had been in a similar situation twice before.

The next morning, after a bowl of porridge for breakfast, *John* arrived back at the arcade to do his cleaning, and Mr Arnold informed him that police had identified the dead man.

'He's been named — officially — as Ian Stirling…'

John gave his boss a blank look.

'… You'll know him when you see his picture,' he said, 'he was one of our occasional customers… A real nasty piece of work, by all accounts,' he added, conspiratorially.

Ian, it transpired, had come out of prison in June; and the rumour-mill was speculating about the size of his gambling debt.

'… It seemed that this may have tipped him over the edge.' Mr Arnold was loving the drama. 'His car was found parked up near the Martello Caravan Park and the last image of him was on *our* cameras — walking past the pier in the early hours of Sunday morning, heading along the walkway towards Frinton.

'There was no note, but everyone is saying it was suicide.'

Later that afternoon, the police finally arrived on the pier to make routine enquiries, and when he was questioned, *John* made sure he kept his answers as concise and as accurate as he could.

'God! Yes! I do recognise him…' *John* looked aghast when he was shown a photograph.

(*John* had already decided that he would acknowledge the fact that he was 'acquainted' with the victim, because anybody might have noticed them speaking in the arcade, or 'chatting' on the promenade).

'…He was a customer,' *John* explained. 'I didn't know his

name now [truth]… But he seemed like a nice enough guy [lie] … I bumped into him around town on a few occasions [truth]… And I spoke briefly with him down on the promenade a couple of times last week [truth] … Jesus! The second time must have been on Saturday evening [truth] … He said he had a date [lie]… And he headed off, up through the beach huts. Presumably, into town [truth].'

John was ready to account for his own movements late on Saturday night and into Sunday morning (of course, he would have been 'at home, in bed, officer!'). But *John* was never asked.

The young constable simply made a note of *John's* full name and address, then thanked him for his time — oblivious to the fact that he had just interviewed the murderer; perhaps oblivious to the fact a murder had been committed.

My ability to manipulate the situation made me feel powerful, but a little frustrated too, because once again, I was getting no credit for *my art*. The ultimate *catch-22*, where recognition will only ever come with arrest.

That night, I went to 'clean' the gun, but it turned out to be a starting pistol. Still, I scrubbed it thoroughly, and after gloving up, under the cloak of darkness, I tossed it out into the sea, allowing fate to decree whether or not it washed ashore.

I cannot tell you the coroner's verdict on Ian Stirling's death, but I can only assume it wasn't murder as I never read another word about it; and as *my friend's* untimely demise drifted from the public consciousness, life did as life always does — it carried on.

In the days and weeks after, Walton-on-the-Naze began the slow process of going into hibernation, and Mr Arnold 'regrettably' had to let *John* go from both jobs in arcade, but he did recommend *John* to a friend, and by mid-September, just after he had enrolled at the adult education college in Colchester, *John* was working again — cleaning at the Public Health Laboratory in Colchester, four hours, five-evenings-a-week.

The laboratory was within walking distance of the college, and the hours suited *John* fine, and although he was irritated by *the social's* sparing contribution to his rent, *John* reminded himself that it was a temporary state-of-affairs and that once he had his five GCSEs, life would get better.

John sat his exams in early December, and after another Christmas spent all alone, he spent January worrying that he might not get the grades he required. But he did — four *As* and a *B* — and with them came a future to look forward to.

At least, that was the hope.

Ten

Then this morning, I was walking along the pier when I was overcome by a sudden and very real sense of impending doom. I was near the end of the rickety walkway, when the feeling took hold, and I had to stop.

Leaning over the ornate, cast-iron barrier, I was staring at the sea below as it washed round me, hoping that the inexorable rushing of the waves would lift my mood as it sometimes does. But not today.

Perhaps it's the time of year, with the dark mornings and dark evenings, or maybe it's just because, in the depths of winter, Walton-on-the-Naze can be such a depressing place. But whatever the reason, as I looked down into the murky depths, I found myself contemplating what it would be like to take the ultimate *leap of faith*.

Over the past few years, other, more gruesome alternatives have routinely flashed through my mind: I have *seen* myself falling from a tall building, jumping in front of a speeding train, slitting my wrists and even setting myself on fire. By comparison, drowning seems more prosaic; more humane.

I recently watched a video on my phone: it was in the US, I think: a man in police custody. The officer was sitting the suspect down in a chair and reading him his rights. It appeared to be something minor. The man was middle-aged — a few years older than me, I guess — and once they'd filled out the paperwork, the officer asked him if he wanted a cup of tea. The man nodded and the officer disappeared out the door, closing it behind him. Then, cool as you like, the man pulls a gun from a leg-holster and blows his brains all over the whitewashed wall.

The officer was back through the door in an instant and understandably, he freaked. The suspect, however, never looked anything but calm: resigned to his fate, at one with himself, at peace. They do say, once you've *decided*, a certain serenity pervades; but to me it seemed so pointless.

Maybe there were unimaginable horrors which were about to be disclosed — this man might have been another Jeffrey Epstein or another Jimmy Saville — but even then, if I was in his shoes, if the worst of my crimes were about to be revealed, *fear of the other side* would hold me back.

Suffice to say then, this morning, I did not jump.

Instead, as day broke over the horizon, I stared out into the distance, gazing at the freight ships moving in and out of port, thinking about my life, asking myself how it had ended up here — *"in a seaside town that they forgot to close down"* — and as I continued to pick off bits of flaking paint from the rusted, metal railing, watching each fragment float down to the briny drink, that morbid part of me was again beginning to wonder what it might be like to join them.

Then suddenly, I was woken from my depressing reverie by a hand on my shoulder and a voice from behind uttering my name — *my real name* — and as the bile started to rise in my stomach, I realised my past had finally caught up with me.

'Frank Kelly,' he repeated, and having steadied myself against the rail, I turned to face my arresting officer.

But it wasn't the long arm of the law that had me in its grip.

No.

In many ways, it was worse.

'Frank Kelly,' he said for a third time.

But again, I didn't reply.

'Or would you rather I called you *John*?' Big D laughed, cynical as ever. 'I have your licence,' he continued.

Still, I said nothing; I simply wasn't able.

'I could use a man like you, Frank...' he said, meaningfully.

How the hell did he find out?

'Walton-on-the-Naze: it sounds so quintessentially British...' he persisted in his best English accent. 'And it probably was back in the days of the Empire. But I think you'd have to admit, if you stay in this depressing part of Little Britain for too much longer, then one day, your morning constitutional along the pier will end with a jump!'

'So?' I finally found my voice.

It struck me that I was about to be made another offer I probably could not refuse!

'So?' Big D mused aloud, waiting for me to bite. 'As I've told you before, *John*,' he raised an inquisitive eyebrow, 'I'm a man of my word. I have your new UK driving licence,' he grinned, tapping the top pocket of his tweed jacket, 'which means you can, if you so wish, crawl back under your stone and live out your days in the margins of society.

'Or...'

'*Or*?' I sounded far too eager.

'*Or* you could come back to Dublin with me. There's plenty of work there for *a man of your capability*. We could put you on the books as my chauffeur or something.'

He let it hang.

'To be honest,' he digressed, 'given the powers of modern science, I don't know how you've got away with it — killing the Carrolls, I mean. Did you kill Liam too? I'm guessing that's why your wife was shot.'

Big D paused for a moment, waiting for me to react, but once again, I was rendered mute. My silence undoubtedly confirmed my guilt, and Big D recommenced in a cheerier tone.

'Let me tell you, Frank, that there are plenty of people in Dublin who would like to shake your hand!'

'That's good to know,' I replied flatly, my words laced with more than a soupçon of sarcasm.

'Look Frank!' Big D smiled warmly, 'I can fix you up with a nice pad overlooking the Liffey, a fixed wage, and all the whores you can handle. Or you can stay here — as *John* — eking out a living on the scraps that this place has to offer, playing with yourself every night before you go to sleep and again in the morning when you wake up!' Big D gave me a little wink and a churlish grin. 'I know what lonely men are like!'

Then he produced John Doherty's licence from his jacket pocket, and his look turned serious.

'I reckon you're telling yourself that you won't be coming with me,' he teased, 'that you "want out". But, in my experience, men like you never get out... Perhaps you'll be the exception to prove the rule... But I doubt it.

'And, of course, you'll know where to find me *when* you come back to Dublin.'

'*If*!' I overruled.

'*When*!' he chortled. 'But let's not fall out over semantics!

'Anyhow. I'm not going to put any pressure on you. The decision will be yours and yours alone. And there's no rush … But just so you know: I'll be *leaving Dodge* this evening on the 20.44.

'Now, I'm going to get myself a coffee in that *beautiful-looking* café at the entrance to the pier.

'I'll wait for you there.'

I stayed where I was for a long time, assessing my options.

How, in God's name, had Big D worked out who I was? Maybe he'd examined the photographs I'd given him and compared them to the old picture of me in the paper? The how didn't really matter, though, I supposed, just the fact that he had recognised me for who I really am. And once Big D had connected me to the Carrolls, the other pieces of the murder jigsaw would have fallen into place.

If he'd not been a crook, Big D would have made a good detective!

I cannot deny I was tempted by what was on offer, but as I walked back down the pier I was decided — I would take *John's* licence and *crawl back under my stone!*

Big D was where he said he'd be, sitting in the café, waiting conspicuously at a table by the window, and having bought myself a coffee, I took a seat opposite and allowed him to regurgitate his spiel about there being work for *a man of my capability.*

He didn't stop there, though, and took great pleasure in telling me that, since he'd received the envelope containing my photographs and my new address, he'd googled *Walton-*

on-the-Naze, 2019 and *unexplained deaths.*

'... I got one good hit about a *death by misadventure* back in August. It happened right here, Frank — in the water below our feet. A local gangster... Were you living here then?'

I could think of nothing to say, and Big D was happy to let the accusation hang awkwardly in the air — his subtle way of letting me know that, if he had worked everything out, then somebody else could do the same.

'So?' Again, it was all I could say.

'So,' he sighed wearily. 'I guess you're what *the professionals* might term a psychopath: an evil man capable of doing evil deeds with no discernible effect on his conscience.

'Decent people would say that the key should be thrown away once you've been locked up. But I'm not decent. And, as you know, in my line of business, a man like you could be very useful.

'We'd make a good team, Frank.'

'I'd make a good puppet, you mean.'

'You're the sort of man who'd benefit from a benevolent puppet-master!' he chortled, gleefully.

'Huh!'

'You have a skill that I can put to good use,' he smiled darkly, 'and in return, I'll look after you! You will thrive in my world because you're the type of man who does not allow morality to get in the way of work.'

All of a sudden, Big D stood. He held out the licence, and I snatched it from his grasp.

'Thank you,' I sighed, wearily.

'You're at a crossroads, Frank,' he counselled. 'Take a few days. A few weeks. A few months even. But make sure you take the right road.'

With that, he left, and I haven't seen him again.

Epilogue
2021

I began writing my testimony that very afternoon, so that one day, even if I never get to see them again, and despite the terrible things that I have done, my children will, at least, know that I never killed their mother *and* that I avenged her murder.

My original intention was to lodge it with a solicitor, but fear of arrest continues to hold me back. I think, perhaps, a safety deposit box is a better option; I can then lodge the key with a solicitor along with instructions for opening it; but for the time-being, it stays with me.

Shortly after Big D's visit, Coronavirus called and the world went into lockdown. But while everybody else seemed to go stir-crazy, *John* coped manfully — self-isolation was nothing new to him.

When restrictions were lifted for the first time, last summer, *John* landed a job at a supermarket in Clacton where he made a couple of friends — Tom and Gerry (seriously!) — and when he bumped into Annie, a divorcee who had been in his English class at college, he began to see a future, a real future, for himself.

With the pandemic, the relationship progressed at a gentle pace, but at Easter, as things began to open up for a second time, *John* and Annie started spending much more time together.

John was actually thinking about buying a ring, but then Annie dropped the bombshell.

'You're just too needy, *John*,' she had said.

Last month, *John's* contract with ASDA was not renewed, and although he has been scratching around for work in the weeks since, in truth, his heart is no longer in it.

Then, yesterday, bad became worse, because I saw Annie with another man — her 'ex' (I recognised him from a photo that I once found at the bottom of her knicker drawer) — and I've spent the last twenty-four hours thinking about what I could do to them.

I would never get away with that one, though.

So, this morning, I phoned Big D — I'd always held onto the plane ticket — and I asked if there was still a 'situation vacant'.

'There certainly is!' he laughed mirthfully. 'I told you that *John* would not be able to spend the rest of *his* days in Walton-on-the-Naze!'

Well, what is there for *John* here?

What is there for anybody here?

Of course, *John* could have moved back to London.

But…

There's always a *but*.

Once I'd hung up the phone, I tidied the flat — left it spotless; always had it spotless — before packing the few belongings I would be taking with me into my small suitcase. Anything that could be re-sold went to a local charity shop; everything else went in the bin.

On his way back from Oxfam, *John* called into the estate agent — he told Karl he'd been offered a job he couldn't turn down — and although *John* did lose £140 of his deposit, fair play to Karl, he handed over £360 in cash when he came to collect the key.

I'm now at the station, waiting for the next train to Liverpool Street.

From there I'll catch the Stansted Express, and tonight, I'll doss down at the airport. I'm booked onto tomorrow morning's 06.30 Ryanair flight to Dublin — or rather *John* is — and only time will tell if it's a good call.

As Big D's *chauffeur*, I will have the money and the 'no strings' sex he promised, and although there are inherent risks that will come with my new position, I feel I will have a better life and a better standard of living than *John* could ever expect to have here in Walton-on-the-Naze.

It will come as no surprise for you to learn that, once I've settled in, I intend to take another shot at Flaherty — *yes, I still want him dead!* — but more than revenge, it is fear and hope that are driving my decision.

Fear — because Big D knows who I am.

So, one day, whether for his own amusement, or simply out of spite, he might choose to give me up to the police.

We both know that my freedom is forever in his gift.

And hope — because a man like Big D *knows people*.

And right now, he is the best hope I have of seeing my children again.

Actually, no!

Big D is my only hope.